The Last Texas Big Shot

By

Tom Talley
&
Louis Buck

Admiralty Enterprises I, L.L.C.
Cover Art Images:

Photo courtesy of National Nuclear Security
Administration / Nevada Site Office

Battleship *Texas*: Tom Talley Photograph

For information:
Admiralty Enterprises I, L.L.C.
PO Box 638, Millican, Texas.

ISBN-13: 978-1468127911

ISBN-10: 1468127918

1 2

Dedication

For our families, and yours.

Acknowledgements

The authors wish to express their gratitude to all the people who urged them on in this difficult undertaking. Our families, who had to put up with us when things didn't "flow", and our editors and proofreading friends when it "overflowed." We don't know how anyone could do this alone.

In particular, the authors wish to thank Sarah Stephens and Jim Panter for their invaluable editing, contributions and encouragement.

Table of Contents

Chapter 1: I Thought We Were On The Same Side

2:00 PM
Wednesday
November 16, 2011

Near the "Lone Star" offshore drilling Rig 1
Gulf of Mexico South of Galveston, Texas

Petit Jean II

Peter Olson took a sip of steaming coffee and enjoyed the rich chicory flavor. Nothing beats good coffee and good seas, and I'm lucky to have both, Olson told himself. He had been a seaman since he fled the family farm outside Brownsville—a barren piece of desert that barely provided the family a living—and shipped out on a freighter out of Galveston at seventeen. By thirty-three, he had earned his master's license and a captaincy on a container ship running between Osaka, Japan and Seattle. It had been a great life until a random inspection by the Coast Guard caught him liquored up while on duty, even though the ship was tied up at the dock at the time. With the memory of Joe Hazelwood, Captain of the *Exxon Valdez*, still fresh in everyone's mind, his indiscretion was not overlooked. The incident had cost him his job, his license, and his reputation. It took six years to get his license back and another six months before Matt Ralls, CEO of Rowland Drilling, took a chance on him and gave him the captaincy of the *Petit Jean II*.

The *Piss Jar II*, as the crew called her, wasn't a container ship, but it was Olson's command, and he knew he was lucky to have it. Money was good, hours were great, and his only responsibility was to get the supplies to the rigs on time twice a week. The only thing that gave Olson heartburn lately was the

1

idiot politicians in Washington and their determined efforts to wipe out the American Oil Industry.

When BP had the bad taste to blow a rig and spill millions of barrels of oil into the Gulf, the president, joined the halleluiah chorus demanding the destruction of the U.S. oil industry and banned all offshore drilling, thereby staying true to the old Washington DC adage, if reaction was good, then overreaction must be better. The ban on offshore drilling effectively destroyed the Gulf oil industry. The cost in jobs lost, bankrupting of small businesses, and lost income to the coastal states was unimaginable. Olson took another sip of coffee. How do these jackasses get elected, he wondered?

"Capt'n, we got company," said Matthew Parsons, the PJ II's helmsman. Parsons was a small man who sported a tobacco-stained white beard that framed a weathered, wind-burned face.

Olson unfolded his 6'2" frame from the command chair and stepped over to Parson's station. "What we got, Parsons?" he said.

"Contact's about twelve miles off starboard. Appears it's closing on us." Matt said as he pointed to the RADAR display on the console in front of him.

Olson picked up a pair of binoculars, walked to the starboard windows of the bridge and scanned in the direction Parsons indicated. "Looks like a Coast Guard cutter." Olson studied the vessel for a few seconds, and then said, "Probably out of Galveston on a drug interdiction run." Of course, all that information was on the enhanced RADAR display right in front of Parsons.

Olson turned to the first mate who was leaning on the rear bulkhead of the bridge cleaning his fingernails. "Allen, go get the men ready to offload the cargo. We should be docking with the *Star* in about fifteen minutes."

"Aye, Capt'n, I'm on it."

"And Allen." Olson added. "I want to be in and out in no more than ninety minutes."

"Should be able to handle that," Allen said. "Not carrying all that much today."

Olson put the cutter out of his mind and concentrated on docking the *PJ II* with the rig.

2

Cutter William J. Benson

Cmdr. Kelly Ackerman paced the bridge of the US Coast Guard Cutter *William J. Benson*. The *Benson* was a *Sentinel* class cutter fresh out of commissioning and was Ackerman's first command. She raised a pair of high-powered electronically stabilized binoculars and studied the supply boat as it slowed and maneuvered into docking position with the rig. "Dammit," she mumbled. "What in the hell am I supposed to do here?" Sweat collected under her arms and ran down her back.

"Helm," she said. "Bring us to course 165 degrees."

"Aye, aye, Captain. Heading 155 degrees."

Ackerman turned on the young seaman at helm. "Get the shit out of your ears, Begley. I said course 165," she snapped. "If you can't listen, then, by god, I'll get someone up here who can."

"Aye, Aye, Captain," a chastened Begley said. "Turning to course 165 degrees."

Jason Ritter, Executive officer of the *Benson*, noted the shrillness in the captain's voice and shook his head. This should have been his command. He'd earned it. But command in its infinite wisdom decided the first *Sentinel* class needed a woman captain, and word had it that Ackerman was selected to kill two birds: she was a woman, and she needed a sea command to earn her fourth stripe, and if she had her way, another promotion to admiral. Her mentor pulled strings and Ritter earned the consolation prize and XO. Must've been a good lay, Ritter thought.

"Captain, if I may," Ritter said. "That course is going to bring us pretty close to the rig."

"You have a problem with that, XO?"

Ritter felt his jaw clench. He gave himself a few seconds to get control, and, keeping his voice as even as possible, said, "As a matter of fact I do have a problem with your order. This course is practically an intercept course to the rig. We could create significant problems—"

"Leave the problems to me. This is my boat and I'll make the decisions," she said and turned away from the red-faced Ritter. She turned back. "If you don't like my decision, you may

3

return to your quarters" Her eyes narrowed. "Am I making myself clear?"

"Perfectly."

"Sound general quarters, XO," she said.

Ritter frowned. What in the devil is she doing now? "Are you sure you want to go to general quarters, Captain?"

She spun around, fists clinched at her side. "Does everyone on this bridge have hearing problems?" She glared at Ritter while the rest of the bridge crew suddenly focused on their duty stations.

"Resupply operations on the rig." She pointed at the workboat in the distance. "We have direction under Special Order 147 to disrupt and shutdown any and all operations related to drilling in the Gulf." She paused. "Or have you forgotten that order?"

Ritter shook his head, picked up the ship-wide intercom, and hit the klaxon. "General quarters, General quarters. All hands report to your battle stations. This is not a drill, this is not a drill." He replaced the microphone on its hook, turned, and left the bridge.

Captain Ackerman stared after Ritter for a couple of seconds, mentally noting what she would say in his fitness report about leaving the bridge during General Quarters…then she remembered that she had given him the option of leaving the bridge…that was sure to come up in the hearing. She didn't like Ritter. He was in her way. Instead of helping her with this command, he seemed determined to undermine her by raising issues constantly with all of her plans. Sure, he always came to her cabin to discuss the plans for the week and the day…all the routine stuff. Then the discussions would start about what he would have done. Well, she had asked him to let her know what he was thinking, so he could have interpreted that as trying to be helpful. But, some of his suggestions had been in direct conflict with what she felt should be done, and they got to the point of being almost disrespectful.

She turned to the talker and was about to have radio issue a warning to the supply boat when she heard the thump thump thump of the starboard stern 50 mount and out of the corner of

4

her eye she saw the 50 caliber tracers hitting the work boat and the rig. That's not right...why would Ritter do that?

When general quarters sounded, Seaman Herman Watters inhaled the last of his first crack pipe of the day. He had just gotten comfortable in his secret place in the bilges. It was difficult to find privacy on a 154-foot boat among 23 crewmen, but he'd managed to find such a spot and spent at least two hours a day with his pipe in the solitude of the bilges, and now this alarm crap. Watters considered ignoring the call, but decided the potential consequences were too severe.

With difficulty, Watters pulled himself up and staggered toward his duty station on the number four M2HB fifty-caliber machine gun position. His vision was blurry, and the bright sunlight hurt his eyes. He slipped on a pair of dark sunglasses in hopes his pain-in-the-ass loader, Bodine, would not notice his pupils. The prick would report him in a heartbeat.

Billy Bob Bodine, the loader, was already in position when Watters stumbled into the gun emplacement. He noted that Watters appeared more uncoordinated than usual. Jackass has been in the bilges again, he thought. Shit, that's all I need. "Watters, dumb shit, you okay?" Bodine asked as he slammed a canister of fifty –caliber rounds into the gun.

"Snap out of it Watters," Bodine said. "This ain't no drill."

With difficulty, Watters chambered the first round and tried to locate his target. The sun glared off the water and tears filled his eyes. He was both blind and confused. Watters tried to organize his thoughts, but the noise and confusion around him was too much. He shut down and awaited instructions.

"You piece of crap. You been in the bilges again, haven't you?"

Bodine was now truly screwed. He knew something had to be done about Watters. He looked around for the Chief who he knew was somewhere on deck checking the gun crews, but Bodine had no luck. Now Bodine faced a dilemma, leave his station and report Watters or stay and risk lord knew what if this thing really was an actual call to action. But when Watters slumped forward onto the gun, Bodine realized he had no choice but to leave his station and risk the wrath of the Chief. Watters was in no condition to be on a loaded gun.

"I'm gonna go find the chief," Bodine said. "You got no business on the fifty in your condition." No response, and Bodine hurried off to locate the Chief of the Boat.

There. Watters saw a target. It was blurry and indistinct, but he could make out a structure with a boat docked beside it. Drug runners. And, we caught 'em taking on their dope. Thumbs glided loosely over the fifty's trigger. "Just give the word, Captain," he mumbled. "I'll shoot the shit out of them." He didn't recognize the irony of the situation.

When Bodine and the Chief got to Watters's gun position, Watters was focused on the rig. The Chief watched for a few minutes then turned to Bodine. "You screwin' with me, Bodine?"

Bodine fidgeted under the Chief's glare. "No. Chief," he stammered. "Swear to God, Watters was actin' out of sorts." Bodine paused then said. "On second thought, he was not just out of sorts. Watters was acting weird."

"Acting weird. What's that even mean?" the Chief said. "You don't think the SOB will be able to shoot straight—"

Watters only heard the chief say "shoot" and he responded. Fifty caliber rounds hurled toward the *PJ II* and the *Lone Star* drilling rig.

The first 50-caliber rounds took out the starboard side bridge windows of the *PJ II* and sent glass flying throughout the confined space of the small bridge. Parsons went down clutching at a large piece of glass buried in his upper arm. Olson dropped to the deck, but not before 50-caliber shrapnel ricocheted off the bulkhead and shattered his coffee cup, slicing his palm and leaving a large flap of skin hanging loose. Olson didn't feel the cut or the hot coffee that splashed on his neck and down the front of his shirt. He pulled himself off the deck and noted blood flowing down his arm. He pulled a rag from his pocket and wrapped his bleeding hand tightly, then crawled to where Parsons lay moaning and clutching his arm. There didn't seem to be any more rounds headed their way.

A quick examination assured Olson that Parsons' wound was superficial, and he turned his attention to the rig in time to see an orange flame and smoke billow up from the under deck of the rig fifty feet above his boat. Olson watched as two flaming workers fell into the sea followed by several others jumping to the relative safety of the water.

Olson turned to a crewman who just came onto the bridge. "Get out there and start getting those workers out of the water." Olson paused and glanced toward the two burn victims floating in the water. "There's two floaters off the port bow. Get them out of the water and do the best you can to make 'em comfortable until we can get medical out here." If they're still breathing, he thought. "And make it fast so we can get out of here in case the safeties fail and this rig goes up like BP's."

Olson stepped behind the helm and reduced the speed of the boat as it approached the men in the water. He turned to Parsons who was pulling himself off the floor. "Get on the radio and send out a SOS. Tell 'em what happened and that we need med evac ASAP."

"What about the cutter? It's minutes away, and they must—"

Olson turned on Parsons. "To hell with that Bobby…Who the hell do you think fired on us?"

"But—"

"Forget it, I'll do it myself." Olson punched the buttons on the intercom to select all radios, HF company, VHF marine, VHF marine emergency, and UHF satcomm.

"MayDay, MayDay, MayDay, this is the work boat Petit Jean II. We have been fired upon by a Coast Guard vessel. We have wounded on board our ship, and there are wounded in the water near the rig 'Lone Star'. The rig 'Lone Star' is on fire. We need medical assistance. The rig is working on the fire and will come up on frequency when they can."

Olson deftly maneuvered the work boat as he watched the injured men being pulled from the water. What the hell had just happened? Why would the Coast Guard fire on us?

Cmdr. Ackerman hoped the bridge crew didn't notice her shaking hands as she lifted the binoculars to her eyes and watched the activity on the rig. The fire had toned down a bit.

7

She noted no further explosions or oil fires on the rig. Safeties must have worked, she thought. Thank God for that, and for the fact that no other guns joined in, though Ackerman didn't think that would help. A picture flashed through her mind of standing in front of a board of inquiry trying to explain. "Oh, yes, Admiral. Only one gun opened fire on the oil rig." The board would get a kick out of that.

"Helm, bring us on a course to intercept the supply boat," Ackerman said, and turned back to the rig. "Comm, contact the boat and offer our help." She paused and then said, "Get the doc on standby to handle casualties."

Ackerman heard the hatch slam open and turned to face the Chief, his face red from the exertion of running to the bridge, the XO right behind. "What in the hell happened out there?" she said.

The Chief wiped sweat from his face. "The gunner, Seaman Watters, on emplacement four, opened fire on the supply boat and rig."

Ackerman held the Chief's gaze until his eyes dropped. "And why did he do that, Chief?"

The Chief cleared his throat. "We think he was on drugs. His loader came to me with suspicions, and I was about to replace him when he opened fire."

"I assume he's in the brig," she said and thought, just like I'll be before this is over.

"He's in custody and on his way to the brig as we speak, Captain."

"Fine." She turned to the XO who had remained quiet throughout the exchange. "Secure general quarters and get the crew ready to assist with the injured."

Ackerman watched the supply boat recover men from the water. A couple looked to be in bad shape. Shit's in the wind now and I'm dead center in the path. Knowing her career was in serious jeopardy, Ackerman was already working to find a way to shift blame and avoid most of the political fallout that was sure to come. Aboard the *Petit Jean II*, Olson stopped just short of the crane hook dangling with a loading pallet over the side from the *Lone Star* rig and waited for the *Benson* to rendezvous. The radio crackled to life and a female voice announced…"Under special order 147 of the US code you are ordered to halt all support of drilling operations on the drilling rig Lone Star."

Olson grabbed the VHF mike and shouted into it "I am aware of special order 147" he blasted. "They finished drilling here last month you idiot…there is no drilling activity on this rig…and, by the way, what the hell are you doing telling me this now … after our men are dead and our equipment is burning? … what is this shoot first and ask questions later crap?"

The radio came back immediately, "We will provide assistance to you in your recovery efforts. We have medical staff aboard and offer that assistance to anyone who needs it. We are contacting Coast Guard Galveston to provide helicopter med evac for those who are injured."

"I don't think so!…no wait…let me rephrase that…The Captain of the *Petit Jean II* thanks the Captain of the Coast Guard Vessel close aboard that just fired on him for the offer of assistance, however if you come one yard closer to my ship or the rig I will see that your Captain is shot by a firing squad if it's the last thing I ever do. You've done enough damage for today…just stay the hell out of the way."

"Petit Jean, this is Air Gulf Global 127, we just came off rig 48 and are in route to you for evac…we can be there in 15 minutes. We can haul 14 people if we can drop some off at the rig."

"127…thank you…just try not to get shot by that idiot on the cutter to the North of the rig…I'm picking up the swimmers now and should have everybody up to the helipad when you get there."

"127 roger that … out."

"Lone Star…from PJ, we'll come alongside the hook you have down on the east side here so we can load the swimmers on it…hoist them to the helipad for pick up in 15 minutes."

"Lone Star…roger, you need anything Peter" asked the rig boss.

"Naugh…we have a couple of flesh wounds and I'm going to send them up to you with the swimmers. Take care of them would you please, John?"

"You got it, send them aboard."

9

He walked out onto the flying bridge as the crane lifted the injured men off his deck and stared at the bridge of the cutter 300 yards away…knowing that the captain's glasses would be on him…he raised his hand and rendered the only salute that came to mind. "There's gonna be some real shit over this." he mumbled.

Chapter 2: Getting Some Answers

5:00 PM
Wednesday
November 16, 2011

Texas Capital Building

It was the usual practice for Governor of the State of Texas, William "Bill" Clayton to meet with Lt. Governor of the State of Texas David Dalby in the Governor's conference room just after the sun dipped over the yardarm, or in the vernacular of the day, "…it's 5 O'clock somewhere." Sunshine laws notwithstanding, today, they would cover the list of legislative issues that he could consider for the next session of the legislature, decide who would be appointed as the new Public Utility Commissioner and decompress with their favorite refreshments. The two men had known each other for nearly twenty years, going back to the days David had worked in the legislature as a committee staffer during the Governor's tenure as state representative from his home town of San Angelo. The fact that both were Aggies (graduates of Texas A&M University) made the friendship all that much easier to maintain over the years.

"David, when we get this legislature back into session in January, how well do you think the speaker will be able to control the hotheads who want Texas to secede over this gun control issue the President is pursuing? We've already had the special session and sent a message to Washington, but I keep hearing people talk about secession like it was just a normal thing to do. We both know that absent some calamitous event not more than the most extreme five percent would consider such a thing."

"Bill, when the speaker wants to control things he can get pretty heavy handed and he'll have a serious 'come to Jesus'

11

meeting with anyone who gets too far out of line. We have way too many things that need to be done to get sidetracked by a few clowns who want their 15 minutes of fame on FOX News."

The governor laughed, took another sip from his Jack Daniels (neat), and nodded. David's Wild Turkey sat untouched near his right hand. Their choice in brown liquor was one of the few things of substance on which they differed. With a rapid three knocks the governor's long-time assistant Virginia walked in and turned on the television.

"Governors, you really need to see this," she said. The news story about the incident in the Gulf was already rolling and they were starting the interview with the longtime CEO of Rowland Drilling, Matt Ralls, a big financial backer of both of the two state officials.

"While we are still trying to gather all of the facts, what we know so far is that a supply boat making its final approach to our *Lone Star* rig in the Gulf of Mexico, about 50 miles east of Galveston, took fire from a U.S. Coast Guard cutter earlier this afternoon. While the *Petit Jean II* was not severely damaged, our *Lone Star* drilling rig took several rounds of heavy machine gun fire from the cutter. One or more rounds struck the riser of the well that was completed last month. The gas in the riser ignited and created a major fire under the main platform. Fortunately, the main wellhead controls were able to shut off the flow of gas and extinguish the fire within approximately five minutes. Two of our Rowland employees on the rig were seriously injured and there were also some injuries on the *Petit Jean II*. All the injured were airlifted to UT Medical Branch in San Antonio."

The camera swung back to the Situation Room and Blaze Wolfrum. "Mr. Ralls, why did the cutter fire on the supply boat or the rig?"

"Mr. Wolfrum, you will have to ask the dumbass on the cutter that started this. The *Jean II* was making a routine supply run to a completed well with some personnel changes when they took fire. We can only assume that it had something to do with the newly instituted ban on offshore drilling that the administration in Washington instituted last week. But so far, we have not gotten anything resembling a coherent explanation from the Coast Guard."

"Can you tell us if the rig suffered any serious damage from the bullets or the resulting fire?"

"We'll have to take the rig off-line and survey the damage before we can know for sure, but it doesn't take long for a fire that hot, trapped under a platform to do major structural damage. If it hadn't been for the outstanding performance of our rig boss Jack Johnson and the rest of the crew, this could have been a major disaster and a lot of lives could have been lost."

"Thank you Mr. Ralls. We are trying to contact the Coast Guard right now and get a response from them." Blaze signed off and moved on to the next story with the parting comment, "We can only wonder what was going on with the supply boat or the rig that would have caused the Coast Guard cutter to take such drastic action."

Neither the Governor nor the Lt. Governor said a word for a few seconds as they took in the seriousness of the news. Virginia broke the silence with an exasperated "Well if that doesn't beat anything I ever heard."

"Virginia, thanks for cluing us in on this mess. Please get Matt on the line for me." She padded quietly to the door, closing it on her way out, leaving the two men to ponder their response to this latest political bombshell. The Governor then drained the last of the Jack Daniels from his tumbler and turned to David. "When the legislature is gaveled into session the first thing we will hear from the far right is another cry for secession after this incredible screw-up! We will need to keep this under control and avoid a confrontation with the inexperienced knee-jerk liberals in charge of the White House right now."

"Governor, we need to get the senior legislative group here ASAP and get a plan together to stop all out revolt when the gavel comes down."

"Good idea! Why don't you make a few calls and ask Annie down at the Driskill to reserve the Governor's Boardroom tomorrow at 6:00 PM so we can try to control this insanity. Make sure Lance is there, he is the one democrat I truly trust. He reminds me a lot of his father. You know, Gonzalo never did adopt that kid. Except for that one mark on his record, Gonzalo could well have been sitting in my chair right now. His son is a different matter. I like that kid a lot."

David nodded and drained his drink in two big gulps, then made his way to the door. He turned and asked, "Who are you going to call first in Washington to try and figure out how this mess got started? I suspect you will be hearing from our senior senator any moment now." the Governor's phone rang and David let himself out to go make his calls.

David walked down the hall to his office and as he entered his long-time assistant, Linda was getting ready to leave. He asked her if she had heard about the breaking news on the incident in the Gulf. "Yes, I was talking with Virginia when she saw it come on the screen. I watched it on the internet until they finished interviewing Mr. Ralls. If there was ever a reason for the people of this state to get their dander up, this is it. Imagine, being attacked by your own government!"

He asked her if she could please call Annie at the Driskill and reserve the Governor's Boardroom for tomorrow at 6:00 PM before she left for her weekly dinner with her mother. Her husband was a Trooper Lt. in the Texas Department of Public Safety and appreciated a night at home alone to watch his beloved San Antonio Spurs without having to share time with Linda and listening to the great events of state that had transpired that day. She reached for the phone and he turned and walked into his office to make a few calls of his own.

The first call went to the Speaker of the Texas House of Representatives. Greg was a speaker in the great tradition of Texas. Although a Republican, he had many friends in both parties and he wielded considerable influence because he could be trusted to keep his word, and more importantly to keep a confidence. He had heard of the happenings offshore and his enthusiasm for a sit-down with the Governor and Lt. Governor was complete. "Lt. Governor Dalby, we are really going to have our hands full with this pile of manure. With a couple of months to go before we go back into session in January, the newspapers and talking heads will have this thing making the massacre at Goliad looking like an afternoon tea." Without giving Dalby a chance to speak, he quickly added, "We need to include someone

14

from the other side we can trust, but I'll let you and the governor make the call there."

"Greg, the Governor and I talked very briefly about this a few minutes ago and we thought Lance Santos would be a good choice. We trust him and he is a good thinker. What do you think?"

"Lance is the very person I had in mind as well. I will get a couple of the other leaders in the house and you can get a couple of Senators so everyone is connected. We should be able to control this thing without some of the young Tea Party folks getting too far off the reservation. I'll give Linda a call with the names tomorrow morning and I'll see you at the Driskill tomorrow evening."

The Lt. Governor then punched the speed dial to get the three senators he had in mind to attend tomorrow's social gathering.

Governor Clayton was waiting for the senior U.S. Senator to come on the line, all the while looking out the window at the darkening sky. He heard a click of the senator coming on and then the melodious tones of a long time Washington trained orator filled his earphone.

"Good afternoon, Governor. I would ask to what I owe the honor of a call from you, but I suspect I already know."

"Senator, I hope you are going to tell me who screwed the pooch today down in the Gulf."

"Governor, if there was ever a time for clear thinking and plain talk this is certainly it. Unfortunately, the only official word I have gotten so far is the sanitized horseshit that passes for open and honest communication in Washington. The Coast Guard is still assessing the situation, as they so calmly put it. The White House won't take my call and I don't expect the communications office there to come up with anything resembling the truth, if they can find it that is. "

"So what am I supposed to tell the press who will be beating down the door this evening or first thing in the morning about why our government in Washington decided it was open season on Texans in the Gulf?" Taking a breath, he continued. "And what do I tell the new breed of political activists who are already using the "S" word down here when they hold a rally on the steps of the capitol?"

Bob Runyon was in his third term as a U. S. Senator and although he and the governor were both Republicans, they were not particularly close since the senator spent most of his time in Washington or on the speaking circuit supporting other Republican candidates around the country. He did share a deep love for his home state and was a true fiscal conservative who had a reputation for being able to get the other party to compromise on their aggressive plans to rebuild the country according to their master plan. He chose his words carefully, "Governor, I appreciate that the people of Texas will take this a lot more seriously than the crowd here in Washington. That doesn't change the political reality that the spin up here will be that it was a minor incident and that it was surely caused by some over-reaction on the part of the supply boat captain or someone on the rig. That said, you are going to have your hands full!"

"Bob, you know full well that all that kind of response will get me is a bigger and angrier group of folks on the capitol steps. I talked with Matt Ralls a few minutes ago and he and the Rowland folks have no idea what precipitated this mess. The well was completed and all of the papers were filed before this ban was imposed on new drilling in the Gulf, and I stress the word, new."

"Bill, you have my word that I will stay on the Coasties until I get a truthful answer. The same goes for the White House, although I'm not sure they have a clue about anything that actually goes on in the real world outside Washington. They are so self-absorbed in their own importance that this probably won't register on their teleprompter unless a poll comes out telling them to tell the people why it was our fault." The senator was very much a political animal and understood the difficult hand the governor had been dealt. What he also knew was that this would give him some new chips to play with in the senate.

"Senator, I need some facts before I have to face the press tomorrow; I can put them off tonight but we are not in a position to back down and tell the administration that we know it was a mistake and we don't take offense. If they don't fess up to what went on out there today then there is going to be hell to pay down here." Feeling the urge to get off the line and do some fact finding on his own he concluded, "I would appreciate a call if you get the Coast Guard to tell you anything approaching the truth."

"Yes, well … Goodnight Governor."

Having made several more calls to other close associates in Washington without getting any additional information he asked Virginia, who had been patiently waiting at her desk, if she would please get the White House on the line. While he didn't expect to get the President, he did think he would get someone on the line who could give him some kind of an answer. Virginia buzzed his personal line and told him the White House operator was trying to get the President's office. "Thanks Virginia. You go on home and try to enjoy what is left of the evening."

She dropped off the line while he waited for someone to take his call. A few moments later, an assistant to the Press Secretary answered. "What can I do for you this evening Governor?"

While the Governor didn't really expect the President to take his call personally at this hour, he did expect someone a bit higher up the food chain than a 20-something staffer to be on the line. "Young man, would you please connect me to someone who can answer some questions about the incident in the Gulf of Mexico this morning?"

"Sir, I have been instructed to take all calls about the incident. What I can tell you is that the United States Coast Guard is taking this incident very seriously and will have a statement after they have gathered all of the facts. The President has instructed the Press Secretary to avoid making any speculative comments about how this incident may have been precipitated by someone on the rig or the supply boat until we have all the facts."

"Listen carefully, I am the Governor of the State of Texas and I have been unable to get anyone in the entire District of Columbia to give me a straight answer. I have already talked with the CEO of Rowland drilling, a man I trust implicitly. He assures me that the supply boat was on a routine supply run and the rig had filed all of the completion reports for that well over a month ago, so this can't have anything to do with the politics of your new ban on all new drilling in the Gulf of Mexico."

After a pause and no response from the other end of the line, he added, "I expect you to pass my request to speak with someone in authority along as fast as you can young man. If I don't get some straight answers pronto there is going to be hell to pay." While he regretted getting irritated with a young staff person who had no authority to do anything, the Governor was even more upset that he had been pushed that far down the information food chain. He added with a twinge of conscience, "I know you are just doing your job, son, but the administration needs to understand that this isn't going to just fade away overnight."

"I will be sure to pass your message along Governor."

With the discouraging call completed, the Governor thought he might as well head back to the newly refurbished mansion, catch up on his reading, and maybe even catch a little television with his wife after dinner before turning in for the evening.

The Next Morning

Both the Governor and the Lt. Governor were in their offices early the next morning. They had agreed that the Governor would handle all press inquiries that came in about the events of the preceding day and that David would handle the anything that bubbled up from the legislature. David had gotten three senators, two Republicans and one Democrat, and the Speaker had arranged for two representatives, including Lance Santos, to attend the evening's informal discussion at the Driskill. There was still a stack of routine administrative work to be done and the Governor would be handling the Rowland affair.

The Governor didn't have to wait long for the email from Virginia that a reporter wanted to talk with him about the "War in the Gulf" as it had been portrayed in the *Houston Post* that morning. He considered calling him back but thought better of it. It would be much more efficient to have a press conference if he could get some facts to indicate that he was on top of the situation. He pondered making another call to Washington, but he was unsure of whom else to call beyond the people he had already tried and he certainly didn't want to look desperate. He called Virginia and asked her to come into his office. As she entered, he waited for her to sit down with her note pad before he began laying out the schedule he wanted to follow the rest of the day and then find a convenient time for a press conference within a day or two. His schedule would be subject to sudden change for whatever time it took to get this sorry mess behind them.

Driskill Hotel, Governor's Boardroom

The Governor and Lt. Governor arrived within moments of each other and left their respective vehicles with the valet, which meant they would be sitting right out front when they were ready to leave. At this time of the year, it was already past sunset and the wind was blowing steadily from the northwest; having the cars close would be a bonus after the meeting. The Driskill had been in the business of catering to the needs of Texas governors and other state dignitaries for over a century. They walked in together and headed straight for the boardroom where the other members were awaiting their arrival. The House Speaker greeted them as they entered the room, then they proceeded to shake hands and pass their greetings to the others in the room. The Governor waved the waiter over and told him to get his guests whatever they wanted to drink and bring in a large tray of appetizers, including a double order of the *Stuffed Medjool Dates* he was so fond of; the smoked Spanish Chorizo gave them a nice bite.

As they sat down the Speaker once again spoke first, out of habit, since he enjoyed holding court in the house chamber, "Governor Clayton and Lt. Governor Dalby, thank you for getting us together. We have all gotten questions about this most recent and regrettable incident in the Gulf."

The female Republican senator from Victoria, who was in her second term, interjected, "Have you gotten any substantive information from the feds as to what in the hell happened yesterday? Like the representative from Galveston, my phone has been ringing off the hook with constituents, mostly in the

19

drilling business wanting to know if there is a danger of any additional attacks."

The Governor spoke before anyone else could jump in, "The Lt. Governor and I have been gathering every bit of information possible since this happened yesterday. I spoke with Matt Ralls, the CEO of Rowland Drilling, whom most of you know. He assures me that there was nothing out of the ordinary going on when then Coast Guard opened fire as their workboat was making their final approach to the *Lone Star* yesterday. All of the well completion papers had been properly filed and noticed by the right agencies. I did get a note from Matt late this afternoon that both of the men airlifted to the UT Medical Branch in San Antonio are going to make it, although one of them is still in serious condition. This was not a "new rig" subject to the latest order from the Federal Government. Our senior U.S. Senator hasn't been able to get any more information out of the White House than I have. Evidently the Coast Guard won't release a statement until they complete their internal investigation." He quickly added, "I haven't gotten so much as an apology of behalf of the injured men yet. The *Jean II* was inspected when it pulled into port by a couple of FBI special agents from the Houston office when they docked late yesterday; of course, they didn't find anything out of the ordinary. David, do you have anything you want to add?"

"No Governor, while the media is going nuts over this incredible mistake, the lid seems to be on in Washington and in all of the federal offices in Texas."

As one waiter brought in their drinks and another wheeled in a cart with a couple of trays of appetizers, the governor continued. "I have scheduled a press conference tomorrow at 11:00 AM in the Governor's office and would like for all of you to attend if you can work it into your schedules. This is not about partisan politics; it is about the rights of the people of this state to be safe from an unwarranted assault by forces of the United States Government. At the same time, I want us to be careful not to give the Tea Party or the secessionists anything more to get riled up about. Let's get a plate and let this young man put down our drinks before we continue." The Governor was trying to make this as relaxed and informal as possible, but the faces of the others in the room made him think that that would be a tall order.

Once they had all made a plate from the serving cart and reconvened at the table, the Speaker asked the three senators present if they had anything to say, deferring to the senior legislative body as protocol required. Having already asked her question the first time the senator from Victoria only asked that she get an answer to her original question. Next, the senator from Austin, the lone democrat of the three senators and one of the few ardent supporters of the current administration even among the democrats, nodded. After a most pregnant pause, he asked, "I think we should be very cautious before we go jumping to the conclusion that the Coast Guard is at fault and that there wasn't a good reason they fired a few warning shots, errant though they may have been. Although the Governor's good friend at Rowland says there was 'nothing unusual' about the supply boat's cargo or the status of the rig, we should wait until we get independent verification before we jump to the conclusion that it was the Coast Guard that was solely to blame for this unfortunate situation. If the Governor doesn't object, I will call a few of my contacts in the administration and see what I can find out."

The Lt. Governor glanced at the Governor and was inwardly pleased to see that he had managed to conceal his irritation at the intended barb. The senator had been the head of the Democrat President's campaign committee in Texas and had made public his aspirations for a significant appointment in Washington, which he did not get. He was an ACLU director and career public defender who made it a point to disagree with the governor at every opportunity. The governor responded, "That is good advice senator, no one needs to go off half-cocked and make a bad situation even worse. Please do call your friends and see what you can find out; perhaps they will talk to a democrat because they damn sure won't talk to a republican." He smiled and nodded to the third senator, a long serving and very conservative man from North Dallas.

"Governor, unlike my fellow senator from Austin, who thinks Washington is the land of milk and honey and only pure wisdom comes from the administration's lips, I am more than a little outraged that we have two fellow Texans laid up in the hospital and a rig is badly damaged as the result of a direct attack by the forces of the federal government."

Before he could say anything else the Lt. Governor interjected, "Robert, the Governor made it clear we aren't here to argue politics. We need to decide how to proceed as calmly and as united as possible."

The senator from Dallas apologized half-heartedly to his fellow senator from Austin and continued. "The administration has made it clear in the past two years that they don't like offshore drilling or the use of any carbon-based fuels. If they keep heading down this road, they will destroy the economy in this state and eventually the nation. We have got to make a firm stand and assert our rights as people of Texas! You just told us that the two special agents inspected the *Jean II* when it pulled back into Galveston and everything was in order. What else do we need to know?"

Although he liked the senator from Dallas, the Governor knew he was one of the few senators who had met with some of the most conservative members of his party and started planning to make secession an issue at the first opportunity. It was also one of the reasons he wanted him in the room so he would have an opportunity to gauge his level of fervor.

He nodded to Lance Santos, who quickly opined, "It is readily apparent just within a group as small as this that we have a range of opinions on how best to proceed. Having the senator from Austin check with his friends certainly can't hurt, although they may tend to gloss over this in Washington as not an overly serious matter. The main thing is to get an honest response from the Coast Guard on why they took such a precipitous step and then to ensure it never happens again, whatever the cause. As the Governor has already indicated, this isn't a party fight in Texas; it is a matter between a state and a federal government."

Smiling inwardly, the Governor thanked everyone for their open and frank comments before continuing, "You have been generous to give up your time this evening to meet with David and me to get a better idea of how to proceed in a unified way to address a potentially serious threat to the relationship between this state and the federal government. Texas has a

22

greater gap in the monies it sends to Washington and the benefits it receives than any other state. Now our citizens have been attacked and our energy economy is being threatened. We must find a solution that will restore the goodwill between us. I hope you will work with the Lt. Governor and me to achieve that end. I would ask that you not share the contents of this meeting with the press, since they are already looking to create a firestorm out of this situation. If you hear anything from Washington before tomorrow morning's press conference, I would appreciate it if you would share that with me personally. If you want to stay and converse among yourselves feel free to do so. The tab is mine tonight."

The Governor and Lt. Governor rose to leave, nodded to those seated and the table, and told the headwaiter to get them whatever they wanted.

As they were walking out, with surprisingly no one else in the lobby the Governor stopped and said quietly to his Lt. Governor, "David, you mentioned your wife had started to do some legal research on the question of secession. I would like her to get us something serious as soon as she can. I want to be able to refute the arguments of the more extreme elements of our party who are itching to once again make Texas an independent republic. I will need all of the ammo I can get once this starts to become a public discussion in the coming weeks."

"Not a problem Bill, she has been working on it for several weeks in her spare time. I'll talk with her tonight and see what she can get for us. The press conference tomorrow may give one of the right wing media an opening for that sort of question."

The two men walked out the lobby door and their cars were waiting out front. The headwaiter had called to let the valets know they were on their way down. It was simply the way things were done at the Driskill; know your clients and treat them the way they expect to be treated. It kept people coming back again and again.

They wouldn't be getting in their cars right away however, because just outside the lobby doors, there was a podium, with lights and microphones and a gaggle of the press crowding around to get a clear shot of the Governor. There wasn't going to be a press conference tomorrow, it was going to be tonight…now.

Governor Bill Clayton was never one to pass up an opportunity to be seen or heard in public, so he moved to the microphones. Just beside the herd of press photographers stood Matt Ralls, arms folded across his considerable chest and a scowl on his face that made it clear to the Governor that the answers he gave in the next few minutes had better be the right ones or there would be hell to pay, not to mention no more political contributions.

"Why did the Coast Guard fire on the Lone Star Rig, Governor?"

"We haven't been able to get any information from the Coast Guard as to what prompted them to shoot at either the work boat or the rig. It was an absolutely inexcusable act" he said looking Matt Ralls squarely in the eyes, "and I'm sure that we will get to the bottom of it." Ralls didn't blink and his expression didn't change.

"Have you talked to the Coast Guard?"

"No, I have asked our United States Senator to help us get a response from the Coast Guard. As yet, he has not been successful in getting an explanation."

"Has anyone from the federal government contacted you about this and what did they say?"

"We have had no contact with any federal officials yet."

"When the legislature gathers in January, how do you think they are going to deal with this incident?"

Bill, looked around at David Dalby who shook his head urging the Governor silently not to stir the pot on secession. The question was a plant from the Dallas bunch and they wanted the Governor to go on record now.

"I'm sure the legislature will want to know what happened to this Texas based business and why the federal government feels it has the right to attempt to destroy private property without explaining itself or following the law." Ralls nodded. "I will urge Lt. Governor Dalby to make the relationship between the government and the people of Texas and the government of the United States a primary topic of consideration for the legislative session." Ralls uncrossed his arms.

"what does that mean in the way of legislative action?"

"It means that the legislature will consider measures that will protect Texans and Texas businesses from the intrusion of Federal interference where it doesn't belong." Ralls smiled.

"Does that include voting on secession?"

There it was…

No one was ready to answer that question, and no one should have to at this point. The Governor stammered on; "The legislature will discuss what the legislature wants to discuss."

"But sir, will you encourage them to bring up the topic of secession?" The question hung in the air like smog over Los Angeles, but the Governor and Lt. Governor were already headed to their cars and didn't seem to hear it. They both slowed to shake hands with Matt Ralls. It was a firm and heart felt handshake with a pat on the shoulder to boot.

The drive back to the apartment was nice. The winding hilly streets of Austin always made David feel very lucky that he got to spend so much time in this wonderful scenic place. David pulled out his cell phone and called his wife. They hadn't spoken in two days and he wanted to get home for the weekend.

When the news carried excerpts of the press conference, the Director of the Federal Bureau of Investigation was summoned to a late night meeting with the President of the United States. Along with the head of the justice department, they had a discussion about the definition of sedition that lasted well into the next morning. The FBI director left the meeting with some specific instructions regarding any future utterances of the Governor of Texas on the subject of secession.

Chapter 3: Pushing and Shoving

3:15 PM
Friday
November 17, 2011

Texas Capital Building

Lt. Governor David Dalby sat in his office looking out across 15th Street, north towards the University of Texas Tower in the distance. It was Friday the 17th and it had been a very long week for everyone in the Governor's office. As he leaned back in his chair, he thought of the progression of events that had brought the state to this tipping point. It wasn't just the shooting in the Gulf, the tension between the federal government and the State of Texas had begun to really escalate almost a year ago now following Secretary of State Holly Barton's announcement about the gun control treaty the preceding October 9th. She came out publically and stated that the United States would reverse its long-standing policy and launch talks on an international treaty to regulate the sale of firearms, all firearms, whether for military or personal use. It had not taken more than a few hours for the NRA and others to begin commenting publicly on the unexpected policy shift. The current federal administration had responded to the first inquiries by stating categorically, "No U. S. citizen would be impacted by the signing of a treaty that is intended to finally regulate international arms sales to terrorist elements and rogue states such as Iran and North Korea". Even the Russians and Chinese had finally agreed to come to the table as the leaders of those states had become even more strident in their statements that they would not rein in their desires for regional influence, including the development and manufacturing of nuclear weapons.

Not much more news had been forthcoming for the first half of 2010; the story had faded from the public's notice as the continuing economic malaise and focus on the wars in Iraq, and Afghanistan had once again regained their place at the top of the news broadcasts. The evening news generally lead with a story on BP's problems in the Gulf of Mexico and the promises of the President's team to "take charge" of the situation. Still it did give the democrats some traction and visibility. It wasn't until July 7th that the gun control treaty talks started to draw some heightened attention.

The treaty preparatory meetings the State Department had suggested would take several years to negotiate had proceeded at a pace that no one could reasonably have imagined. Holly, as Secretary of State, with the expressed approval of the President, had conceded many of the toughest bargaining positions at the very outset, giving the European countries, some of whom viewed America as the source of all the world's problems, a considerable advantage. This was despite the fact that the EU's sales of arms on the world market collectively exceeded that of the U. S.

It was finally dawning on many Americans, particularly those in the Red States, that the White House was seriously considering a plan to subject them to gun control through the terms of an international treaty, effectively sidestepping the need to debate the measure in the Congress.

It wasn't until August 20th at a campaign stop in New York for the democratic candidate for governor, that the fat fell into the fire when the president uttered the most inflammatory statement of his still young administration's life. Following his speech at a local college football stadium before the game, the president walked with the gubernatorial candidate in what they thought was a private location where he could share a confidence with his friend and political ally. They neglected to notice that an ABC sports sound man carrying a football field type parabolic microphone had following them down the tunnel between the parking lot and the speaker's platform. Since the game hadn't started yet, the sound man decided to point the mike at the two politicians as they strolled down the tunnel some 30 yards away. What he heard, and what was recorded back in the trailer outside was…the presidents voice saying; "You and I agree that we need to get the guns off the streets, no matter how we have to do it. I have spoken with Holly and we believe that this treaty will ultimately allow the federal government to ban the sale of firearms and ammunition to civilians. This will, with time, also enable us to confiscate the guns that are already out there."

The ABC Evening News, with Jerry Hollander now on the anchor desk, had broken the story as a mere statement of the obvious. Since the DC law banning weapons had been overturned by the Supreme Court two years earlier, the liberal democrats in the Congress had been looking for a vehicle to get the NRA out of the way, and this looked like just the ticket. What could possibly be better? All they had to do was approve a treaty that our allies supported, and voila, the guns would be illegal.

The manure was pouring into the ventilator shaft at a terrific rate by the following Saturday morning. The President was quick to state that the comment was not to be taken literally, but that he was merely expressing his disgust with the most recent spate of gun related deaths in DC, New York and Detroit as people struggled with tough economic times.

No one in Texas was buying that spin, especially the Texas legislature. Under Texas law, the legislature only meets in odd-numbered years for 140 calendar days, but the governor has the authority to call a special session lasting up to thirty days as often as he desires. William "Bill" Clayton, Governor of Texas, had done it three consecutive times in his first administration. On August 31st the governor, responding to calls from both sides of the aisle, had called a special session to begin on September 7th. Although there was a 77 to 73 split in the House of Representatives and 19 to 12 favoring the Republicans, there was no one in Texas who believed that more than one or two of the most liberal members of either house would let the federal government confiscate the guns of the people of Texas.

The stated intention of the special session was to send a message to the president that his comments had touched a raw nerve and he needed to get back to the business of working on other domestic priorities and pull out of the treaty talks. Texas was not going to allow its residents to be deprived of their constitutional right to bear arms by some form of diplomatic end-run. The special session had ended with a joint resolution that amounted to a restatement of the 2ⁿᵈ amendment of the U. S. Constitution but with a little more oomph.

Now the oil-drilling ban, and the shooting in the Gulf, It was going to be very hard to keep a lid on emotions in the state. David had noticed that the "S" word was cropping up again in more of his conversations with legislators and staffers alike.

He shoved the papers on his desk into the top left hand drawer and grabbed his coat on the way out the door. This was one week he was glad to see come to an end. The flight back to Houston would give him a few minutes to decompress before he entered the "real world" again. He was looking forward to getting home for the holidays.

Chapter 4: Home for a break

7:00 PM
Friday
November 18, 2011

Houston, Texas

As he had done so many times in the past, David walked out the doors in front of the Hobby Airport baggage claim and waited for Patricia to pick him up for a relaxing weekend at home. He was looking forward to some time with her and the kids, and strangely he was also looking forward to fitting in time to have the discussion of her research on the topic of secession. He spotted her car as it rounded the outside of the pick-up lane. As was usually the case, Southwest had delivered another on-time arrival and Patricia was her usual punctual self. He opened the car door, got in and leaned over to give her a quick kiss on the cheek as she maneuvered the car out of the passenger-loading lane to exit the terminal area. "It is great to see you after a long week in the political meat grinder," he said.

She looked over at him and smiled, "I hope I get more than a peck on the cheek after a whole week without you."

"Of that you may be sure my little vixen," grinning broadly. "Where are we going to eat tonight on our way home?'

"It will surprise you to no end that Davey and Erica are having dinner with us tonight, since they both plan on being out tomorrow night and they don't get to spend much time with you. We'll go out tomorrow night." The news about tomorrow night's dinner party could wait until later.

On the drive to the house, they caught up on the events of the week and didn't get into anything too difficult. It was time for both of them to relax and not let the routine stresses of their weeks slough off onto the other. A nice peaceful weekend would be a true blessing.

Between the small talk and a surprising lack of traffic for a Friday evening, the trip to the house passed almost in an instant. Patricia parked in the circular drive and they entered the house to the sound of loud music coming from the den, where Davey had his latest favorite country song blasting away at what seemed like something north of 120 decibels. David walked over and turned it down to a much more survivable level. Erica's scream of delight came from the kitchen, "Whoever turned that hillbilly racket down, thank you!" Davey stuck his head in from the patio where he was tending to the grill. Fortunately, he saw his parents before he finished his "What the ..." question to his sister.

David grinned at his son and smiled, "It's nice to see you too Davey."

"Sorry about that Dad; I was out here getting the grill ready for the steaks Mom picked up yesterday. I am going to cook them all medium rare except for the one I have to burn for Erica; are you sure she is really a Texan?"

"I heard that!" came from the kitchen where Erica was making the salad. In spite of their constant verbal sparring, they actually got along about as well as two teen-aged siblings ever could. "At least I have better taste in music you big redneck."

As Patricia walked past David on her way to the kitchen she whispered, "I knew a quiet dinner at home with civilized conversation would be just perfect!"

David just shook his head and followed her to the kitchen where he hugged both of his kids and excused himself to wash up for dinner. Carrying his small carry-on bag with him he grabbed a beer from the refrigerator and headed for the bedroom to make himself more comfortable. A "quiet" night at home with the family was just what the doctor ordered.

About ten minutes and one beer later David walked back into the kitchen and was pleased to see that everything was in good shape for dinner. He hadn't had lunch again because of the back-to-back meetings and he was really hungry. "How long before the chef and the rest of the kitchen staff get the dinner on the table?" It really was a treat to spend the evening at home after a tough week of meetings and questions about the events in the Gulf and the subsequent press conference. He needed an update on Davey's college choices and to see if Erica had managed to make it through another semester with decent grades.

As he opened the fridge to get another beer, Patricia walked in from setting the table and told him to put it back because they were going to have a bottle of wine with dinner. That was certainly agreeable with him; the dinners during the week while he was in Austin were either with too many people at a meeting or in his apartment, where he seldom indulged in a drink, much less a nice glass of wine.

The door to the patio opened and the aroma of just cooked steaks caused him to turn around in time to see Davey carrying a tray of beef that would feed a small town. They all proceeded to the dining room and sat down to a real Texas home cooked steak dinner. Patricia poured a glass of wine for David and herself.

"I found this Argentinean Malbec at Richard's this week and he gave it high praise. What do you think?"

After taking a taste and savoring the full-bodied dry red, he replied, "As usual, Richard has hit the mark again." He and Patricia enjoyed finding quality reds without the pretentiousness of the much more expensive Napa wines that many of their neighbors talked about when they got together. Her palate was generally more refined than his was, but he was willing to live with that. He did admit to himself that a good bone-in rib eye steak with all the fixings and a glass of wine was about as good as he could imagine a dinner being. The conversation then turned to the children's activities and school events.

"Dad, although my guidance counselor seems determined to get me to go to the Ivy League, Yale in particular, I don't really think that is what I want to do. Maybe somewhere a little closer to home, perhaps Rice, would suit me better. What do you think?"

"What about Texas A&M?" he couldn't help himself as he grinned at Patricia. Her look of mock horror was exactly what he was trying for. Their Aggie – Longhorn rivalry was the source of great enjoyment to the whole family.

Patricia immediately jumped in, "We'll have none of that David; just because you went there doesn't mean Davey has to; he needs to make his own choice."

32

"And you would feel the same way if I had suggested that degree mill over in Austin?"

They continued the good-humored banter until Erica interjected, "Enough about where Davey gets to go to college next year, as if anybody really cares. We need to talk about something really important, like what kind of car I am getting so I don't have to depend on the big nerd to get me where I need to be on time."

"Just what did you have in mind my dear, perhaps a SLK-350 or something similar?" David asked tongue in cheek.

She was used to her father's sarcastic sense of humor and played along, "Yes daddy dearest, I want the light blue one to match my eyes. After all, if Davey goes to A&M or Texas we will have plenty of money to put to a good use."

"Your father and I will discuss this request and get back to you. But if the Benz isn't available in the right color will a used VW Beetle suffice?" Patricia couldn't help laughing as she said it; after all, her first car had been just that.

They finished dinner with everyone in a good mood and ended with a cup of mixed berries and a couple of ginger snaps, David's favorite cookies. Life was good indeed.

In the Morning

In keeping with the normal weekend routine, David was up first the following morning and, putting on his standard Saturday morning comfortable outfit. He quietly closed the bedroom door and headed for the kitchen to make the coffee and then read the paper in the quiet before the family got up, and for the two teenagers that meant somewhere after 10:00 AM, at the earliest. He had just poured his first cup of coffee when Patricia hugged him from behind; "What are you doing up so early?" he asked.

"Well, you told me on the phone the other night I needed to put the secession research on the front burner. I thought it might be better to try to talk about the research I have done on the question before our two sleeping angels arose and the day goes to hell in a hand basket. In addition, I didn't tell you last night, but we are due at a dinner party down the street at the

33

Phillip's tonight with two other couples. They have been trying to get us there for months now and we won't have another chance for who knows how long after this weekend."

This was not the way he wanted to start his morning, but he resisted the urge to tell her he really didn't want to waste the evening at a dinner party when he could spend the evening home with her. "Thanks for not spoiling last night anyway; I'll try to be sociable in spite of the fact you know I don't care for these dinner parties. I guess it just goes with the territory when you hold public office and have to put up with people telling you how to run the state right, as if they had any idea themselves. Please tell me I don't have to get dressed up."

"No tie, just country club casual, which means you have to put on a sport coat or blazer; as long as it isn't that god-awful maroon thing." she said sweetly.

She went into the kitchen to get a cup of coffee and then into the study to get her research. She had actually enjoyed the chance to do the research, although she didn't particularly care for the idea of Texas, or any other state for that matter, seceding from the union. Nevertheless, the intellectual challenge was enjoyable and the topic was more complicated than she had imagined at the outset. This would be an entertaining conversation with her husband, even if nothing else came of it.

Settling into the overstuffed chair across from David's recliner, she handed him a single page of the Texas Constitution and launched into the findings of her research. "Are you ready to get started?"

THE TEXAS CONSTITUTION
ARTICLE 1. BILL OF RIGHTS

That the general, great and essential principles of liberty and free government may be recognized and established, we declare:

Sec. 1. FREEDOM AND SOVEREIGNTY OF STATE. Texas is a free and independent State, subject only to the Constitution of the United States, and the maintenance of our free institutions and the perpetuity of the Union depend upon the preservation of the right of local self-government, unimpaired to all the States.

Sec. 2. INHERENT POLITICAL POWER; REPUBLICAN FORM OF GOVERNMENT. All political power is inherent in the people, and all free governments are founded on their authority, and instituted for their benefit. The faith of the people of Texas stands pledged to the preservation of a republican form of government, and, subject to this limitation only, they have at all times the inalienable right to alter, reform or abolish their government in such manner as they may think expedient.

"Fire away, my coffee cup is full and my mind is clear."

"The concept of the 'Right of Secession' has been a fundamental principle of law since the Glorious Revolution in 1688 – 1689 in England when the crown was claimed by William and Mary after a peaceful and lawful transition. It was understood that under extraordinary circumstances a people have the right to establish a new government or, in this case, to secede from a union without an armed conflict or the protestations of those in power in the government. The obvious counter to this is of course the desire of those in power to maintain their hold on power and thwart the efforts of those wishing to secede or establish a new government." Patricia then added with a flourish, "A story has made its way around the internet that apparently, in 2006 Supreme Court Justice Scalia responded to a screenwriter's request for an opinion on the constitutionality of succession in which he said there was no right to secede. Justice Scalia replied to the man:

"I am afraid I cannot be of much help with your problem, principally because I cannot imagine that such a question could ever reach the Supreme Court. To begin with, the answer is clear. If there was any constitutional issue resolved by the Civil War, it is that there is no right to secede. Hence, in the Pledge of Allegiance, "one Nation, indivisible" was inserted specifically to address that question. Secondly, I find it difficult to envision who the parties to this lawsuit might be. Is the State suing the United States for a declaratory judgment? But the United States cannot be sued without its consent, and it has not consented to this sort of suit. I am sure that poetic license can overcome all that -- but you do not need legal advice for that. Good luck with your screenplay."

David interjected, "Based on what you just said, assuming it is factual; any right to secession that existed legally was ended by sheer force of arms because one side decided the other could not enforce its rights. Is that what Justice Scalia's alleged statement says?"

"The simple answer is yes. However, the same cannot be inferred for the rest of the civilized world; but I will get to that later. The fundamental question is whether the U.S.

Constitution itself provides for the right of the states to secede in a legal and peaceful manner. As John Graham points out in detail in his exhaustive study of the question, the preamble to the Constitution was originally adopted on August 7, 1787 with the words, "We the people of the states of New Hampshire, Massachusetts, etc." Each of the states was enumerated to make it clear that these were independent, free and sovereign states, and not peoples of a single nation. This form was adopted unanimously and then sent to the drafting committee on style whose only task was to put the provisions adopted by the convention into more elegant language. When the committee on style presented its report on September 12, 1787, it substituted 'United States' for the list of the individual states, but did so with the meaning of that term expressed in the Treaty of Paris. What that means is that the original intent of the framers of the constitution, in unanimity, agreed that the states were individually agreeing to the Constitution and not collectively as one body."

Taking a sip of her coffee, Patricia continued, "James Madison in the 39th Federalist Paper stated '…that this assent and ratification is to be given by the people, not as individuals composing the entire nation, but as composing the distinct and independent states to which they respectively belong. It is to be the assent and ratification of the several States, derived from the supreme authority in each State, the authority of the people themselves.' The legislative power to secede was transferred to the people in convention, making it more difficult to secede and hence making a more perfect union."

"Other founding fathers, such as Alexander Hamilton, John Marshall and Nathanial Graham, conceded the right of the states to secede as a necessary solution to any future federal government that might be persuaded to exercise powers that would strip liberty from the people who gave them power. Those that have the authority to grant power also have the authority to rescind the same power, but not for trivial or transitory differences, hence the requirement for the individual states to convene a convention lawfully and peacefully. All of the legal research aside, the reality is that as soon as a state convenes a convention it is likely that the federal government will immediately seek to deny its legitimacy. The real problem will come in that when the state pursues redress in the courts, the case will immediately be kicked up to the U.S. Supreme Court as the ultimate constitutional arbiter. There is almost no possibility that the court as it is composed today would take long to side with the executive branch on the issue."

David nodded his understanding of the conundrum facing the state initiating a convention; it would be legal and constitutional, but it would be deemed unconstitutional by the court. The U.S. Supreme Court is currently composed of nine justices representing only three law schools; namely Harvard (6), Yale (2) and Princeton (1) and coming from only the states of New York (4), New Jersey (2), California (2) and Georgia. The all-Ivy League court was certainly not a balanced court from the perspective that it represented all of the people or was open to other interpretations that might diminish their supremacy. He voiced that thought to Patricia and she nodded in agreement. "I can see from the file that you have compiled a considerable amount of research on this subject, but in the end it will come down to who has the biggest arsenal, won't it?"

Patricia nodded, "Yes it would, but there is still another argument that could be used to change the focus of the constitutional discussion. Texas came into the union as a republic, a sovereign nation, unlike any other state. Following the Civil War, the southern states were then required to draft new state constitutions, and Texas' constitution is considered to be a model document, serving as a limiting document from the perspective of the government."

David was beginning to get the thrust of this line of reasoning, "I think I see where you are going with this, but fill in the gaps."

Patricia smiled. "You may not be a constitutional lawyer but you have never been short of common sense. The Texas Declaration of Independence in 1836 states that when a government has ceased to protect the lives, liberty and property of the people, from whom its legitimate powers are derived, it is the inherent and inalienable right of the people to, abolish such government, and create another in its stead, " she said in an abbreviated quotation.

She continued; "It states specifically in Sections 1 and 2 of the state constitution simply that '1. Texas is a free and independent State, subject only to the Constitution of the United States; and the maintenance of our free institutions and the perpetuity of the Union depend upon the preservation of the right of local self-government unimpaired to all the States.' And 2. 'All political power is inherent in the people and all free governments are founded on their authority, and instituted for their benefit. The faith of the people of Texas stands pledged to the preservation of a republican form of government, and, subject to this limitation only, they have at all times the inalienable right to alter, reform or abolish their government in such manner as they may think expedient.'"

She continued almost as if summing up before a jury; "This constitution remains to this day as the law of the land, one that was accepted by the government of the United States. It is hard to argue that the people of Texas do not have the rights agreed to by the federal government."

"Doesn't that still leave us with the conundrum that Justice Scalia laid out, namely that if the federal government wants to invade the state to prevent us from exercising these rights that they can do so, just as they did one hundred and fifty years ago?"

Once again, Patricia nodded, "In theory, that would be true, but I still can't imagine what circumstance would bring such an event to come to pass. The legal entanglements, federal properties within the state, such as Fort Hood, NASA, all of the air force bases, and let's not forget the U.S. Coast Guard stations that we have heard so much about recently, would be very difficult to untangle."

Patricia then continued for another half hour about the legal issues that would have to be resolved. David had originally thought, only as an academic exercise, that breaking away in a peaceful manner would be extraordinarily difficult. He was now realizing how greatly he had underestimated the magnitude of the effort that would be necessary to make a peaceful secession a reality. Surely, this would be enough for anyone to consider such action only after every other viable option was eliminated. "So what it boils down to is that it would be a legal nightmare that could take years to conclude even if it were possible to secede in a peaceful manner."

With a smile on her face, Patricia added, "As the Lieutenant Governor, I expect you to throw the legal work to my firm because it will make us wealthy beyond our wildest dreams if only we got a small fraction of the billing hours it would take to untie this knot. We could even afford that blue Benz for Erica. Seriously, I don't want to believe for a minute that this could really happen. I will send you my formal analysis after I clean up a few items. It is probably a little over a hundred pages, so I will leave it to you to give it to the Governor and/ or the attorney general. "

David looked down at his watch; over two hours had flown by and they hadn't had breakfast yet. Since it was already 10:00, he suggested they get the kids up and go out for brunch since they had to go the neighborhood soiree that evening. It had been too long since they had been to The Epicure. He asked Patricia if she thought that would be OK and she agreed since Gray Street wasn't too far and she liked the pastries.

Later That Afternoon

The day had flown by after their brunch that morning. Between the "honey dos" and the emails and phone calls, he was ready to relax for a few minutes before he had to get ready for the evening festivities. He took a shower and put on a pair of shorts and a frayed A&M sweatshirt with the sleeves cut off. He knew that would irritate Patricia, especially if someone were just to drop in for a visit. He walked out to the den and asked Patricia if she wanted a drink with him, to which she quickly responded in the affirmative. He poured a couple of fingers of Wild Turkey over an old fashioned glass filled with ice and made her a weak vodka tonic; the dinner party would most certainly include drinks and wine with dinner so they would keep it short.

He handed her the drink as they sat back in their easy chairs and made some small talk.

Finally, as innocently as possible, he asked the question he had been wanting to for a good part of the afternoon. "You mentioned that we were going to the Phillips' home, but you never mentioned who else would be there."

"Jeanne mentioned that the Burke's would be there as well as another couple, whose name I can't recall; they are old friends of Jeanne and Ken. I'm sure they won't be too boorish for someone who dresses as formally as you do." The dig about his "casual attire" had finally surfaced, but it was said with her disarming smile and a small giggle.

"That should make for a pleasant evening if we can avoid talking about politics," rolling his eyes to the ceiling. "Our friends know that what goes on at these get togethers is off the record, so I trust they have clued in their friends. I don't want an offhand joke to be reported in the *Chronicle* out of context as if it were in response to a serious question. There are any number of people who want to create a stir over the things that have been going on between Texas and the Feds lately. The last thing I need is to be a part of creating a bigger problem than we already have. "

"I'm sure these are nice people or they wouldn't have been asked to join us. Let's finish our drinks and get dressed so we won't be late." As if he was the reason they were ever late anywhere, but he knew better than to throw that branding iron on the fire.

They decided to walk the short distance to the Phillips' home, a very pleasant evening indeed for this time of year in Houston. They rounded the corner and headed up the walk to the very large plantation style red brick with white columns and breathtaking gardens. The banking business must be doing a lot better than it was a couple of years earlier; but then the TARP money had turned things around for the banks pretty quickly, even if it didn't filter down to the small businesses that were still on starvation diets for credit. That would be a good topic of conversation, one that was sure to hold the Coast Guard questions at bay for a while.

He rang the doorbell and Jeanne, who had seen them coming up the walk through the dining room windows, greeted them both with a hug and a kiss on the cheek. She looked the picture of the wife of a successful Texas banker, perfectly tanned and dressed. "The Burke's are already here and the Breedings will be here shortly. Head on back to the den and Ken will get you something to drink. I have to go make sure Consuela doesn't need any help in the kitchen." Consuela had worked for Ken and Jeanne for as long as they had known the Phillips; she was the glue that held their social schedule together.

They walked down the spacious hall and turned into the den, taking in the view of the expansive manicured back yard complete with pool and cabana. Ken walked over and gave Patricia a bear hug and a kiss on the cheek. At six-foot-four and nearly two hundred and fifty pounds, he was an imposing figure. Gripping David's hand in a death grip he asked "what can I get you two to drink? The lady goes first since I know you are having your usual Turkey and ice."

David nodded as Patricia told him she would have a weak vodka tonic, and as Ken headed to the bar, they stepped across the Persian rug to greet the Breedings, whom they had also known since they moved into River Oaks nearly ten years earlier. "Hello Mike, it's been too long since we have seen you. This flying back and forth to Austin every week doesn't give me much time for seeing old friends here in Houston."

They exchanged greetings as Patricia and Sue started to catch up about what their respective kids were doing and what else was going on in their lives. Mike had been in the oil business since he graduated with a master's degree in chemical engineering from Rice about the same time as David was getting his degree at Texas A&M. Sue, like Patricia, was an attorney with a small law firm in the city. She had a family practice with the occasional divorce case thrown in to keep things interesting. The conversation was light and breezy as the six of them chatted until the doorbell rang to announce the arrival of the final couple.

Moments later Jeanne ushered the Burke's into the den; David immediately recognized the face of the man entering the room but couldn't recall where he had seen it before. Jeanne began the introductions. "Let me introduce Jack and Toni Burke

42

to y'all. This is Mike and Sue Breeding; Mike is in the oil business, and Sue is a lawyer. You probably recognize our Lt. Governor David Dalby and his wife Patricia, another lawyer."

They all shook hands and said hello and Ken took their drink orders as they settled in for a few appetizers that Consuela had brought in right behind the final couple of the evening. David was hoping that no one had noticed his reaction when Jeanne had introduced the Burkes. Jack was a name David knew only from the news, as he was the latest federal judge to weigh in on the federal administration's health reforms. He was a republican appointed by George W. to the Texas Southern District Court in Houston, a conservative but somewhat unpredictable when it came to social issues. He had broken with many conservative judges and sided with the national healthcare program as being constitutional. That had not made him overly popular in Texas, but since he had not had to rule from the bench, and the appeals court had sided with the 26 state attorneys general and overruled the circuit court finding that there were indeed constitutional issues with aspects of the law, no one really made an issue of it. He glanced at Patricia, hoping that she recognized him as well. She glanced at him almost simultaneously and nodded knowingly. This could prove to be an interesting dinner indeed.

Fortunately, none of the conversation before dinner was related to anything to do with politics or the incident in the Gulf. Maybe Jeanne and Ken had explained the ground rules after all. Small talk and a discussion of the pros and cons of the Aggies going to the SEC and what might lay ahead for the Longhorns as they started the first year of their ESPN $300 million contract carried them to the call for dinner. They headed for the dining room and the southwestern dinner Consuela had fixed, although Jeanne would surely tell everyone about all of the special touches she had added like a dash of this or that to add some zest.

Ken poured each of them a glass of a very expensive California cabernet and offered a toast once they were seated. "Raise your glasses to the great state of Texas, our Lt. Governor in particular, to our nation and to good friends and families. God bless America!"

The food was delicious, and they were effusive in their praise of the tapas, guacamole, spicy rice with red peppers and poblanos stuffed with shredded beef Consuela served. Everything was indeed a treat to the palate. After they had taken enough of the edge off their hunger, the conversation resumed. Jack had not spoken directly to David other than during the introductions in the den, so David was a little surprised when he heard Jack's question. "When Ken made his toast, David, he mentioned both Texas and the United States of America. How would that play with some of the folks in the legislature who are beating the secession drum after all of the events of the last few months?"

In an effort to make light of the question he responded "Some of our legislators like to get a rise out of the people on the other side of the aisle by saying things they know will rile them up a bit, but I don't know anyone who really wants that to happen, or expects that it really could." He smiled and laughed; he certainly wasn't going to share Patricia's research with a federal judge at a dinner party!

The judge wasn't going to go quietly into the night, sensing there was more than that to the story after hearing second hand stories about conversations that had been heard in Austin and elsewhere. "I'm sure you and the Governor don't share that view, but I understand a couple of the Dallas area Republican State Senators are serious about seceding. After all of the events of the last few months, what with the Coast Guard shooting at the drilling rig, the offshore drilling ban, and then the EPA effectively regulating coal burning plants out of existence, some of your folks must be pretty riled up, as you say."

"Certainly people are getting upset in these difficult economic times, but that is to be expected when jobs are being lost to heavy-handed regulators who pursue their own agendas. For example, the Dodd-Frank bill is a back breaker for small community banks, those that are actually working with small businesses to grow employment and work for economic growth. That piece of legislation is so complicated and has so many unwritten regulations associated with it they can't even estimate the ultimate impact except that some estimate that the cost of compliance could literally put them out of business. But since

44

I'm not a constitutional lawyer like you I would prefer to hear your point of view."

"Of course, you know I can't opine on any issues that might come before me, but suffice it to say that the commerce clause provides a very large opening for the federal government to act when necessary to do what is right for all Americans, not just for those in a single state or group of states. Secession is virtually a legal impossibility; after all none other than our own Justice Scalia has said the court wouldn't countenance taking up such an action, and it would never even get a hearing."

David felt Patricia's elbow, knowing she wanted this to end now and she certainly didn't want to get involved in this discussion. But such was not to be, as Jack turned the question to the two lawyers in the house, namely Patricia and Sue. Ken tried to intercede and change the course of the conversation, but Jack would have none of that. "We are just having a little fun here Ken. No one is going on the record, and the news channels have been spouting this question for a couple of weeks now."

"What would you two members of the Texas Bar think about the legality of Texas or any other state trying to peacefully secede from the United States?"

Sue responded first, wanting to get out of the line of fire as quickly as possible; "I practice family law and the only thing I would have any experience in remotely related would be a divorce case. Even there the court has the final say unless the two parties have already agreed to all of the relevant terms and children are not involved. As you have already said, if the U.S. Supreme Court won't hear the case then a peaceful secession would be a legal dead end. I doubt anybody believes Texas would even think for a second about going to war with the U.S. Army!"

Jack nodded with a smile on his face, "The voice of reason should indeed hold the day. What about you Patricia?"

Patricia wasn't going to get caught up in this banter on a topic she knew would soon be on the Governor's desk. "I think Sue has summed it up pretty well. As a corporate lawyer, I seldom get to work on such purely academic questions. I haven't even done a divorce case so Sue is one up on me."

"Then I guess it is settled, Texas won't be seceding from the union." Jack was obviously pleased with himself. While he may have been playing a word game at David's expense, he had no idea how strongly David was reacting to the whole thing. It gave David an insight into how the idea would play out in the event the smoke was on the water. There would be few if any avenues open to Texas to do this the easy way.

Once again, trying to change the subject, Ken asked Mike about the impact of the oil drilling ban on the industry in Houston. Mike had been quiet until now, studying the faces of those whom Jack was quizzing. He had seen the flinch in David's face as well as that in Patricia's when Jack so high handedly rubbed David's nose in the political mess, as it were. "Quite frankly Ken, the administration couldn't do much that would be more devastating to the state than what they have already done. The rig count, on land and in the Gulf has steadily dropped since the President issued his order on drilling in the Gulf. Combined with EPA's consideration of a ban on drilling on shore while they evaluate the risk to ground water, the rig owners are heading for places that are friendlier to the industry. Once they leave they will be hard to get back until they are convinced that they won't get jerked around again. This is an administration and a President that doesn't have an energy policy, other than they want to focus on 'green'…" Mike used his fingers for quotation marks; "…as if the President even knows what that means, other than being a word on a teleprompter."

Jack was a little taken aback by Mike's direct comments in response to Ken's question. He pressed on before Ken could say anything. "You do have to agree that the government had to step in after the BP incident. It has to act to ensure the planet we leave for our children and grandchildren isn't so contaminated that they don't have the same future we had."

Mike was not surprised by the remark, as it was what he always heard from the liberal climate change lobby. They didn't see the world the way it was, but saw it with the eyes of someone who sees only what they want to see, without the constraint of reality. "It is always easy to imagine a better world; all of us want that, but wishing and hoping is not a strategy to get us there. The 'green' technologies, wind and solar principally, are still not close to being cost competitive with the oil, gas, coal and even nuclear industries. They are showing progress, and even if we had the capacity to switch to them tomorrow, the cost of heating and cooling our homes and running our businesses would increase so dramatically that the last recession would be a tea party by comparison to the one that would accompany the doubling and even tripling of energy costs. Furthermore, the transportation fuels would increase in price dramatically. We are caught up in a war in the Middle East, at least in my opinion, because the extremists there would love nothing more than to topple their governments and shut off the West from access to their oil."

Ken finally broke in "Mike makes a lot of good points Jack; the companies we bank in the oil and gas business, along with the related service industry, are all concerned about the direction our government is moving and the extent of interference in how business is done. Many of these companies are making significant investments in renewable resources, but as Mike has said already, they just are not ready to take over for the carbon-based fuels yet. We will get there but it will take a lot of years to perfect the technologies and deploy them on a scale sufficient to reduce significantly the existing energy infrastructure. It is also troubling that at the same time they want to move away from carbon they refuse to do anything substantive to move ahead on a nuclear strategy. They say they will support the industry with the new generation of reactors but it will take ten years or more to get a plant sited and that alone costs the companies hundreds of millions; that is quite a bet on a very uncertain outcome. The anti-nuke crowd, most of the same people fighting carbon fuels, will keep any proposed site tied up in court for ever."

Jack finally sensed that he had stepped into a hole much deeper than he imagined. "All very interesting and informative; I see Consuela trying to signal that dessert is ready. I really didn't mean to stir the pot too much."

The conversation resumed a much more neighborly tone and they relaxed and enjoyed the rest of dinner and dessert. It was already after 9:30 PM and with the obligatory after dinner drinks out on the veranda, the night would stretch out a while longer.

Chapter 5: On is Off, Off is On

10:00 AM
Monday
November 21, 2011

Remote Missile test site,
East Coast of N. Korea

Jung Po Guan, carefully connected the remote test cable to the guidance system of the missile. He could test all the control functions of the missile through the cable from the test panel he held on his lap. Looking closely over his shoulder was Sang Kyu Gim, his North Korean minder. Since this was the final set of tests before the missile was to be launched in front of the customers, Jung Po knew that the changes had to be made now, or not at all. They had to be made without Gim spotting them or else.

With the test switch on the missile in the "On" position, the missile took it's instructions from the test set in his lap. With the test switch in the "Off" position, the guidance was internal, so it flew as it was programmed to fly. The signals that passed from the test box on Jung's lap to the missile passed through the coaxial cable almost like cable TV signals.

Jung ran all the automated diagnostics so that Gim, Sang Kyu would be able to watch and see that everything was working as the Chinese Government had promised, or at least as the Chinese Army had promised. This missile was destined to be the final demonstration test for the sale of two of these missiles to a cash-paying customer, thus beginning a financial relationship between North Korea and one of the wealthy oil countries of the Middle East. The success of this demonstration was imperative if North Korea had any hope of getting out from under the thumb of China; which is exactly why Jung loosened the test switch bezel and twisted the "On Off" nameplate 180 degrees with his left hand as he was closing the test case with his right, distracting Gim. Now that the bezel was backwards, when the test-switch on the missile was placed in the position labled "Off", it would actually be "on". The missile would be looking for guidance signals to come in through the test port instead of from the on board guidance computer.

As a final touch, Jung removed the test cable from the test port on the missile. Usually, he would replace the open test port socket with a small cover, but this time he put a device that looked like a cover, but that was a little longer. In fact, it was a small microwave receiver/transmitter that looked almost like a lipstick case with a test port connector on the end. Now, test signals would be fed to the missile via microwave radio receiver/transmitter he had just installed. He flipped the test button to the new "Off" position, which was actually "on", allowing remote radio control to program the missile. He leaned back out of the way so that Sang could see his final motions clearly as the completed the checklist.

"Missile guidance test switch to 'Off'" Sang read from the test booklet.

Jung pointed to the switch that was now in the position marked as "off". "Missile guidance test switch to 'Off'." He repeated.

Sang looked over his shoulder and seeing the switch in the position now labeled "Off" he recited; "missile guidance test switch in 'Off' position, verified." and then placed a check in the box on the check list for that item.

Sang read the next item on the list. "Missile guidance cable attachment cap in place?"

Jung pointed to the extended cap he had placed on the cable port. He covered the antenna with his pointed finger so that Sang would only be able to see the metal retaining ring that looked exactly like the one on the cap they had removed and replaced hundreds of times.

"Missile guidance cable attachment cap in place." Jung recited, hoping that the slight quiver in his voice due to stress

50

was not enough to be heard over the hissing and humming of the support equipment that was operating only yards away.

Sang looked over Jung's shoulder again, observed the locking ring of the cap was in place on the cable attachment to which Jung was pointing. "Missile guidance cable attachment cap in place, verified" he said and checked the item off the list.

Here comes another tricky part, Jung thought to himself as he concentrated on slowing his breathing and stopping his hands from shaking.

"Replace the Missile guidance electronics bay access cover." Recited Sang.

Jung took the replacement access cover from his tool pouch where they had put the old cover when they started working on the missile half an hour ago. The one he took out however was made of painted fiberglass and carbon fiber instead of aluminum like the original. The fiberglass one would pass the radio signals from the control van parked on the hill about three miles away to the receiver that Jung had just installed. If Jung put the regular aluminum cover back on, no radio signals would get through to the guidance system and it would show a fault on the launch panel inside the blockhouse. Someone would investigate, and find his treachery. Jung remembered how hard it had been to get the nonmetallic paint to stick to the carbon fiber and still look like aluminum. He tightened the screws carefully so that the fragile holes in the cover would not crack, tipping off Sang to the fact that the plate was not aluminum.

"The Missile guidance electronics bay access cover is replaced." Jung mumbled putting his screwdriver back in the tool pouch.

"Missile guidance electronics bay access cover is replaced, verified." Sang Kyu Gim recited, placing the last check on the checklist. "Nice work, Jung. Perhaps this is the last time you will have to do this for us."

Jung smiled and nodded to the North Korean soldier he had put up with for this last two years during the development of this program. Jung had started working on missiles and guidance systems right out of school in the United States. As a graduate student at Cal Tech, he, with his green card, had been able to work for some of the professors who were doing cutting edge

51

research on the subtleties of missile guidance in a complex multi sensor environment. He had actually published papers in the Institute of Electrical and Electronics Engineers journals on the subject. When he returned home, the Chinese Army had immediately placed him in charge of a group of engineers working on the next generation of guidance for medium range missiles. Within a year of the announcement of the sale of some of these missiles to North Korea, he had been approached by a member of the Chinese Intelligence ministry and interviewed at length. They had made it quite clear that the Army may be highly motivated to aid their North Korean brothers, but the Chinese government was just as determined to keep North Korea poor and dependent.

When the North Koreans announced that they had sold several missiles to a Middle Eastern country and were going to be able to raise a substantial amount of cash, another team of specialists had arrived from China to support the demonstration tests, only that team was assigned to make sure that the sale did not happen by sabotaging the tests. Jung was assigned to that technical support team. They had worked out the detailed plan so that the flight would look normal, and the crash would not be blamed on the Chinese at all, but on the North Korean controllers. Now that the test switch was allowing the remote control of the missile, the stage was set.

With the checklist complete, Jung climbed down the ladder to follow Sang to the launch control center. The small trailer parked on a hill about 3 miles from the launch pad turned its antenna toward the missile test stand as the technicians inside began to upload the new flight test plan that would assure the destruction of the missile in a rather spectacular way. It looked like the plan to cause the missile test to fail might work.

There would be hell to pay between North Korea and China, and some face saving would have to be done, but in the meantime, North Korea would remain as it was, dependent on its neighbor to the North.

Chapter 6: OOPS

9:00 AM
Wednesday
Dec 7, 2011

The Loop, Washington D.C.

Brad Elkhart despised the FBI. They were officious, bloated, stodgy, inefficient, and hogged all the glory. He had to work with them quite a bit because of his position in the CIA. He lost contacts to them when they came into the United States where the FBI insisted that they had sole jurisdiction; even though the strings attached to many of these imports reached deep into his business as a foreign intelligence oversight manager. Brad had worked his way up within the agency after his short stint in the Air Force missile command at SAC under General Lemay. Quickly tiring of the rote life in the bunkers, the snow in Minot and the standardization teams, he had moved to testing and range management where he enjoyed the solitude of working as the only senior Air Force person overseeing the work of contractors and other NATO personnel. He soon developed a reputation as a "can do" kind of guy who didn't give much of a crap about formality, and was perfectly willing to jump tall test plans in a single bound if results were needed quickly. Everyone was relieved when he took the assignment to go to East Pakistan to help watch the Russian and Chinese missile tests from the CIA installations there. Over the following years he had just never "gone home" as they say, but migrated from post to post within the CIA coming up through the technology ranks but also becoming adept at developing assets that were also technical in nature.

Prior to the fall of the Shah of Iran in the late 70's, he had been working with members of Iran's technical university in the communications area to assist them in developing courses and labs. The CIA was gathering signals intelligence from the Russian Radars and missile guidance systems that had been used by Egypt in the recent war with Israel. Some of his associates worked very closely with the Iranian military and secret police, so he and his technical group quickly became targets of the new government when the Shah fell. One of the people he helped relocate at that time had been a good friend and Brad had gotten him out of Iran just before things completely came apart. Hamied El Jamallie had watched the students slaughter his wife as he grabbed his son, Haliel into his arms and bolted out the door of their small home in Tehran. Not knowing what to do, he had called Brad, his only contact with the outside world, and begged him for help. Brad had driven them from Tehran to Karaj, a small town east of Tehran, where they had been put into minibuses and hustled out of the country to Turkey. Hamied and Brad had immediately set up shop in the South East corner of Turkey where they could watch the electronic operations of Iran, Iraq and Syria from the high mountains there. Hamied's son had turned out to be a good student, and Hamied had doted on him. Every spare minute that Haliel was not doing homework, his father was teaching him Morse code and training him to read electronics diagrams. Brad had even gotten a Radio Shack TRS model 3 computer for Hamied to give his son, Haliel for Christmas of 1980. He had included some games, spreadsheet and text editing software. By the summer of 1981, Haliel had the computer hooked up to a short wave radio and was using it to decode weather forecast faxes from satellites. Haliel was clearly gifted at bit diddling, even for a 10 year old. Through Brad, his Dad got copies of Byte magazine for the boy, and as the world of digital communications began to become more complex, Hamied found himself asking his son more and more technical questions that involved the work that he and Brad were doing. Brad had no problem getting the boy assigned to the group, cleared and set up for training. By 1987, when Brad left for Washington, Haliel was ready for college.

54

It was one of Brad's last official acts to get the company to clear the way for Haliel to attend Cal Tech on a full scholarship. It was the least he could do for his friend Hamied, and besides, the kid might be useful sometime in the future. Haliel would be an ideal technical specialist, but might prove to be a technical agent attractor for the other side. Brad figured that he would have to nudge Haliel in that direction first. Haliel would be the hook, but he would have to look like really good bait first.

Over the next 10 years, Brad had been manipulating Haliel's environment. He had some of Haliel's friends hassled by the FBI. Brad had talked to his Dad and left the impression that Haliel was drifting toward a more radical Islamic view of the world. His Dad had reacted as one might expect, which had driven a wedge between the father and son, further isolating Haliel. Brad had assets who traveled in and out of the country for various reasons and who he involved in pushing Haliel further to the Islamist wing of things. He wanted the boy to be fully qualified as an extremist. Brad knew that Haliel would be great technical "bait". He figured that the other side wouldn't pass up the opportunity to try to use Haliel, and since Haliel was "fully wired", any activities they might recruit Haliel for, Brad would know about within minutes, or so he thought. The pain in the ass part had been that since one end of all these conversations and relationships were taking place in the US, he had to deal with the FBI at some level to stay "in the game." He didn't need them, but it was the PC thing to do these days.

After 9/11, Haliel had faced a significant amount of personal alienation from his fellow workers at Lawrence Livermore Nation Lab. He had been there three years and was doing a good job. He had been promoted twice, but he was now almost completely isolated from his work and home community and left with only his connections to the few other Arab people in the area and his mosque. Brad and the hijackers had done their job well. After a couple of years, Haliel had gotten word through a fellow member of the mosque that there was a method of passing word of mouth messages to those who were resisting the US takeover of all the oil and politics in the middle east. At first Haliel had not been interested at all, but finally one Friday after prayer, he had told his friend that he would like to help in some small way if he could.

Well it had to happen sometime. Brad was going to meet with his counterpart at the FBI to talk about "The kid." These meetings had happened before, but this summons to the meeting place in the burbs outside the loop had been rather abrupt, and not the usual "thought I would bring you up to date" kind of meeting invite he usually got from Robert Munson.

Brad parked in the coffee shop lot and spotted Bob through the window as he entered. He made his way over to the table, shook Bob's hand in the usual "I have no weapon in my hand" gesture between warring opponents. Bob started out with the bombshell.

"As I'm sure you know, we monitor the contacts of any Top Secret cleared individuals at our national laboratories. Haliel has hit our radar again, mainly because he has gone quiet."

"Gone quiet?" Brad hoped that Munson hadn't seen his real reaction to the news.

"Yes, no contact that we can track with any of his previous sources."

"What does that mean to you?"

"Well, usually it means that the subject has decided to do something different than he is already doing, and he severs relations with his existing communications network to begin using another one."

"How long has this been going on?"

"For the last few months."

"Crap!"

Chapter 7: Bert and Ernie do the Texas Two Step

10:25 AM
Wednesday
March 14, 2012

Houston, Texas

Bert backed the truck up to the loading dock. Ernie jumped out of the passenger seat, took the steps on the loading dock up to the raised floor of the warehouse, opened the rollup door of the warehouse that was directly behind the truck. He entered the warehouse and mounted the forklift that was parked just behind the door and turned the key. The little York 4 cylinder started immediately, puffing a little smoke out the back. Bert pulled on the lower control lever to tilt the lifting bar to vertical making the forks level with the floor then pushed the top lever forward until he heard the bottom of the steel on the forks hit the floor. Then he tickled the upper lever back just a little and the forks rose from the floor about 1", perfectly level, as the York began to move forward along the rows of materials stacked in the warehouse. He came to a row containing wooden crates that were sitting on pallets. The stack was four pallets high.

Bert knew the little forklift would not reach the top pallet. He also knew that lifting two pallets at the same time was about all the little lift would do. He pulled back the top control lever and watched as the forks rose to the same height as the third pallet. He edged in closer, carefully inserting the forks into the holes in the pallet. He squeezed the top lever back, raising the forks up until they took the weight of both the third and fourth pallets. The back end of the forklift began to rise off the floor as the forks lifted the pallets off the stack. This was a sure and certain indication that the pallets weighed more than the counterweights on the back of the forklift, and that if something wasn't done soon, the load would rock forward, hitting the top of the stack where they had just sat so patiently. Ernie pulled back on the bottom control lever just a hair and the lifting bar rotated ever so slightly back toward the forklift, pulling the forks and the heavy load back. The rear end of the forklift settled to the floor as though it was landing by hot air balloon, barely touching the ground and ready to leave again at any moment. With the pallet about 1" above the second crate on the stack, and the forklift precariously balanced, Ernie shifted into reverse and carefully let out the clutch. The forklift rocked forward slightly, almost tipping the load over forward, but then it settled back again and began to slowly move backward. When the pallet had cleared the stack it had been sitting on, Ernie pushed the top control lever forward, lowering the two pallets and their heavy loads steadily to the floor. When the pallets reached the floor, Ernie landed them like a 10,000 hour pilot would land a 747, smoothly, with finesse. Ernie let the forks drop to the center of the opening of the pallet, tilted them forward enough to make them flat again and then backed out from under the two pallet stack, raised the forks to the height of the second pallet and lifted it quickly off the top.

The floor of the truck was even with the dock floor, so Ernie drove the forklift with the pallet into the back of the truck and lowered it carefully over the rear axle. He moved it just a bit forward to balance the weight of the pallet between the front and rear wheels of the truck. He lowered the load to the floor of the truck, expertly nosed down the forks to make them level so they wouldn't scrape on the pallet or the floor as he made a clean get away out the back door of the truck and back into the warehouse. Bert pulled the loading door down on the truck. Ernie returned the pallet that remained in the middle of the warehouse floor to the top of the stack, and backed the forklift to the place where it had been parked. He turned off the engine, vaulted from the seat to the floor of the warehouse and headed for the open rollup door. He closed the door from the outside, walked down the steps and returned to the cab of the truck, just as Bert climbed in on the other side.

58

Without a word, Bert slipped the idling truck into gear and pulled away from the loading ramp, turning into the perimeter road of the warehouse district. At the gate, he waved at the rent-a-cop, who didn't even look up from his newspaper. Bert brought the truck to a complete stop at the cross street just outside the gate. Turning right would take him, the truck and Ernie to Houston, but turning left was their usual path, along refinery row, into the monument entrance, around the parking lot of the tower, into the drive headed for the *Texas*.

Bert entered the parking lot and pulled the truck to a stop about 30 feet short of the visitors ramp leading to the deck of the *Texas*, which put the tailgate just about under the construction crane that they had been using for months now. Both men bailed out of the truck and headed to the rear.

Ernie stepped onto the motorized tailgate while Bert raised the lift handle, bringing the tailgate out from under the back of the truck, and began raising it up to where it was level with the floor of the truck. Ernie stepped aboard the rising platform and rode it up to the deck of the truck. Ernie flipped the truck door locking handle guard out of the way, moved the rear door handle into the unlocked position, grabbed the lift handle and threw the roll up door open. He stepped into the cargo bay of the truck, moved carefully around the pallet that held a large crate, to the front of the truck bed where he found the portable hydraulic lift. He expertly fit the lift arms into the holes of the pallet set the pump control to "lift", and moved the handle up and down 9 times. The pallet, with its cargo, rose an inch off the floor of the truck. Bert pulled on the crate while Ernie pushed on the pallet jack as they grunted to move the load to the tailgate. Bert stepped to the side just as the pallet cleared the rear door of the truck and came to rest smoothly on the tailgate. Bert pushed down on the tailgate-lowering handle with his foot as Ernie stepped around the box to stand on the other side of the gate as it lowered to the pavement. Once down, the tailgate with its load of two men, a pallet with a crate on it made a scratching sound as it landed on the sand-covered asphalt parking lot. The two men struggled to move the pallet jack and its heavy cargo partially off the tailgate. As soon as the pallet jack rollers hit the hot pavement of the parking lot they began to sink, making it

59

impossible to move it any further off the tailgate. This was far enough, though, because they just had to get the crate clear of the truck so that the crane could pick it up. Ernie folded the handle back up on the pallet jack as Bert raised the tailgate a couple of inches, walked to the front of the truck, climbed aboard and moved the truck forward a few feet. As he moved the truck forward, the pallet jack slipped nicely off the tailgate onto the parking lot surface. Bert got out of the truck and walked around back again just in time to see Ernie pull the pallet jack onto the tailgate, leaving just the pallet with the crate on it sitting by itself in the parking lot.

The hook from the crane hung motionless just above the crate as Ernie tossed Bert the two ropes from the bed of the truck. Bert threw one end of each rope through each of the two holes in the pallet, while Ernie grabbed the ends from the other side as they came through, pulled them through the pallet holes and up to the top of the crate where they met the other ends of the rope being raised by Bert. They slipped the metal rings in the ends of the ropes over the crane hook. They draped the ropes around the side of the crate as the crane began the lift to be sure that the box didn't fall over during the lift. The pallet and crate rose gracefully from the ground and swung slowly over water and then over the rail of the ship, lowering onto some location that was not visible to them from the ground. In a moment or two, the hook of the crane returned, with the ropes dangling to where Bert Johnson and Ernesto Alarcon were standing. Ernie removed the ropes from the hook, threw them in the back of the truck while Bert raised the tailgate, pulled the pallet jack up to the front of the cargo compartment and then returned to the tailgate to lower it, pull down the door and lock it and then stow the tailgate for travel.

Bert reached the cab just after Ernie, started the truck, and they both enjoyed the cool air that came blasting out of the dash board vents as the truck pulled out of the parking lot and headed for the maintenance building at the memorial site.

On board the ship, the docent and his two volunteers used an A frame hoist and lowered the crate down an access hatch into the ship. The entire operation had taken 25 minutes start to finish.

They were getting good at it now.

Chapter 8: Happy Holidaze

Thursday
December 29, 2011

The Texas Capital Building, Austin
The Dalby Office

The Christmas holidays had been relatively quiet for the Dalby family. Davey had gotten his early admission letter from Rice along with a scholarship offer for half of his tuition and Erica had actually gotten relatively good grades for the semester, so they were spared the angst of talking about what she needed to do to get into a desirable college. Perhaps her desire for a car this coming spring was a catalyst for acting more responsibly, whatever it was, the family was able to spend quality time together. Patricia had been in a good mood after the Governor and State Attorney General had lavished such effusive praise on her for the legal analysis she had provided them. Now David was headed back to Austin for the special session of the legislature the governor had called to deal with a myriad of state fiscal matters and the more pressing problems with immigration, offshore drilling and other politically charged issues.

Under the Texas Constitution, the Lt. Governor's role is actually more important in the legislative process than the Governor's. He is responsible for setting the legislative calendar and overseeing the state budget process. The Governor could call the legislature in to special session to consider only the issues he set for the agenda, but it was left to the Lt. Governor to do the necessary logrolling in the pits. He had met with Governor Clayton to lay out the agenda and get his input, but both of them understood that David would manage the agenda as the situation required once the session opened. The pressure on both of them was intense to get the oil & gas exploration business back to something approaching full employment.

Oil prices were down as the result of a soft world economy, but $80 per barrel was still enough to entice the big oil companies to invest in the Gulf if they could break the ideological logjam in the federal administration. The real trick would be to convince rig owners and operators to take the risk that the administration in Washington would not arbitrarily shut them down again without warning. In the last two years, the only sustained drilling had been in deep formations on land and the success rate had been excellent, in spite of the eastern environmental lobby's call to cease ALL drilling due to their concerns about the impact on ground water thousands of feet above. The federal government had asserted its right to dictate to the states how and when they could drill. The house and senate in Texas were set to pass a bill declaring that all activities associated with oil and gas production would henceforth be subject only to the laws of the State of Texas.

The incident in the Gulf the previous Thanksgiving was still "under investigation" and had seemingly faded from the public view, but for the occasional question from a reporter with nothing else to do.

The leaders of the house and senate also had made it clear that the unresolved question of the federal government entering into a treaty, that by extension would restrict the right of all citizens to bear arms, was something that their constituents were demanding be addressed in this session. As was typical for the administration, statements that laid out absolutely none of the details in a sea of pandering generalities had been the order of the day since the story had broken the previous summer. The resolution passed by the legislature the previous session had received no comment whatsoever from Washington, almost as if it wasn't worthy of comment. Maybe passing a law was the only thing that would get their attention.

On the more pragmatic agenda was the question of how to deal with an increasingly dysfunctional federal immigration policy. It was more a campaign sound bite than a policy. None of the rhetoric was of much use in actually securing the border against the drug cartels and protecting citizens, legal residents or

63

not, from the violence that spewed from their internal battles on both sides of the border. Against the backdrop of a federal ATF plan gone incredibly wrong that had provided high-powered arms and other munitions to the cartels, immigration was potentially the most emotional issue in the state. Once again, federal bureaucrats, with no experience or knowledge of the actual situation had managed to do more harm by accident than the states could have done deliberately.

Texas was using every means possible to deal humanely with the reality of an open border with Mexico, while being challenged by the ideologues in Washington, in particular those from states with no foreign borders who provided sound bites to any news agency that would listen that they had a solution to the problem. Additionally, there were the more mundane budget and internal regulatory issues that required attention, such as consolidating the Public Utility Commission of Texas and the Railroad Commission under a single agency with a more appropriate name.

One of the Railroad Commissioners had testified before the Congress in the fall in strong opposition of the sulfur dioxide regulation that the EPA had amended without an opportunity for the state to comment. The restated regulations meant there was a six-month window to reduce emissions 47 percent, when the state had achieved a 33 percent reduction in the previous 10 years. Anybody with any common sense knew that each successive reduction is more difficult and more expensive that preceding reduction. In essence, the EPA was telling Texas not to burn coal, and oil was probably next. "It seems to most Texans that the EPA has singled out the citizens of the state of Texas by adopting an unscientific, politically-motivated rule scheme that is designed to kill jobs and jeopardize the operation of our electric grid," concluded the commissioner. The EPA had not even bothered to respond other than to assert its right to regulate as it decided was appropriate. Obviously, the economy and jobs in Texas and the other oil producing states were not even a consideration for the northeastern liberals who dominated the EPA staff. The legislative session would be a real barnburner for sure!

Although he had done so numerous times in the past, standing in front of the senate chamber, David was unusually awed by the majesty of the scene before him. Although there were only thirty-one senators, each with their own spacious desk, the historic chamber was truly a magnificent arena in which to do political battle. In his own mind, he knew that this would be the most important session of the legislature the state had seen in over one hundred years. The gallery surrounding the room was nearly filled to capacity with press and state officials, all anticipating an eventful opening session and days to follow. The Governor had already welcomed the senate and house back into session the previous day, so it was up to him to get the business of the state accomplished.

The senate sergeant at arms called loudly from the back of the chamber that the senate should come to order and David pounded the oversized gavel several times to call the session into order. "This session of the legislature is called to order. I ask that the senators take their places so that we may begin this session, one that will challenge all of us to work together in the best interests of the citizens of this great state. We have those items that have been determined by the Governor to be the agenda for this special session." The session would begin with committee reports on each of the enumerated items and then begin the task of making sense out of the stack of legislative proposals made by alliances within the house and senate. They were off and running.

After the usual spate of administrative details and special recognition of various senators and their special guests, the chamber began its slate of activities late on the first day of the session. First was taking on the issue of jobs, more specifically jobs in oil and gas production taken away by the administration's ill-conceived plan to bypass the U.S. Congress and simply use regulatory agencies to implement its far-left agenda. Even the Democrats in Washington had been caught off guard by the brazen nature of the assault on legal due process; however, they were so dysfunctional that they couldn't get the U.S. Senate to do anything to address the problem. The committee in the Texas House was dominated by independent oil companies, or at least their money and the legislation they presented had been the focal point of their efforts behind the scenes for nearly a year. The legislation, entitled "Regulating State Natural Resource Production" had already been vetted by nearly every member of the senate and a nearly identical house version was being introduced that same day. In short, the proposed legislation drew a line around the state and stated unequivocally that all production of natural resources within the state lines and extending 200 miles into the Gulf of Mexico would be governed by the rules established and promulgated by the soon to be consolidated PUCT and Texas Railroad Commission. The new agency would be known as the Texas Natural Resources and Energy Regulatory Commission. The new commissioners would be selected by the Governor, with one-half coming from each of the existing agencies.

The Lt. Governor was prepared for a lengthy debate and the proffering of multiple amendments on this legislation, but the only one submitted was by a senator from Austin that required the new agency to have a more robust Office of Consumer Protection to protect utility consumers from abuses by regulated companies. After a little spirited back and forth debate containing the favorite "...Senator, I can't understand it for ya', all I can do is explain it to ya'..." phrase, the Senate accepted the amendment without more than a cursory objection by one of the senators submitting the legislation who argued that the legislation as presented was sure to do that very thing. Nevertheless, the Senate moved rapidly to pass the bill and send it to conference where it would be unified with the house version. Five days in session and the biggest issue was almost a done deal; nothing was going to slow the confrontation with the administration in Washington!

While the energy bill was rapidly winding its way through the committee process, the chamber took up the issue of the right of the citizens of Texas to bear arms, regardless of any treaty the administration might enter into with a foreign country or countries. In Texas, the ownership of guns for hunting, sport or personal protection was considered an almost sacred right, one not to be infringed upon in any way. Nearly every elected official in Texas, at one time or another had been photographed with a rifle or shotgun out hunting for use in their campaign materials. The rumor mill in the nation's capital had the administration very close to reaching an agreement to bring the gun ban treaty to the signing table. This issue was almost as important to Texans as the jobs that were being destroyed by the same administration. The house had already drafted a bill to codify the resolution passed the previous fall and sent to Washington. The Texas delegation in Washington had been stonewalled by the liberal democrats in the senate and the Speaker of the House had not been interested in spending any political capital on the issue thus far. The bill passed in the Texas house was essentially a restatement of the second amendment language *(A well regulated Militia, being necessary to the security of a free State, the right of the people to keep and bear Arms, shall not be infringed.)*. There was additional clarifying language thrown in to make it crystal clear that Texans would not be registering their personal firearms with the federal government under any circumstances. As David watched the progress of the debate in Austin, he was certain that the U.S. attorney general would quickly move to have the law overturned in court, just as it had attempted to do the prior year with immigration legislation passed in various states, arguing that the federal responsibility could not be unilaterally taken over by any state.

None of these issues were actually being ignored in Washington; in fact, the administration was paying close attention to them and building its files on the leaders of the debates, as well as developing its own plan to crush these expressions of states' rights in the federal courts. The U. S. Attorney General and the Assistant Secretary of State assigned to shepherd the international treaty to control the sale of firearms had been reviewing every state's laws on firearms to ensure their grand plan to disarm all American citizens would not be thwarted in any way. It might take into the president's second term, but they would have their way. They would argue the Commerce Clause gave them all of the authority they needed to regulate personal arms out of existence after they got the treaty signed. How to get it through an increasingly less liberal congress was a plan to be dealt with later when they had beaten back the efforts of states to oppose their plan. If they were successful, they knew that this issue would spark outrage in many parts of the country; where they were dead wrong was in assuming that the people's outrage would quickly die out.

The Governor called David into his office on Friday morning at the end of the session's second week, wanting to get the Lt. Governor's view of the progress of the special session. The Governor was already aware of the rapid progress on the energy bill and so he asked David to skip on to the rest of the agenda. "Governor, the Second Amendment legislation is almost finished in committee and will come to a vote in both houses next week, probably on Tuesday. The thing that has me concerned is that our junior senator in Washington called me to pass along the news that the Treaty was indeed going to be signed next week. Our bill will be seen as a direct attack on the administration and open up a serious conflict; I just want you to be ready when the shit hits the fan. As soon as you sign the bill, which will pass with only a couple of the usual opponents, the Feds will try to have it invalidated."

He rose from his chair, walked to the window, and looked out before resuming his report. "The immigration bill we both want passed. It provides a mechanism for documented workers to cross the border for confirmed jobs. It's running into a little opposition from the Dallas delegation, they want to add sanctions and fines for employers hiring undocumented workers. If they don't get that they won't support it. Fortunately, the Democrats don't like their proposal and will vote with us on this one, so I do expect it will pass by a comfortable margin, but it is the toughest one to nail down right now. The administration has been relatively successful in overturning statutes in other states that are in conflict with federal immigration policy, but I don't see that this will be a major issue for them, we are not trying to seal the border, only to have firm control over who enters from the south. The President in Mexico City is supportive as long as we don't let this evolve into an excuse to seal the border. He has indicated he will support us as long as we do what we have promised in this regard. That alone should make the Washington crowd happy for a change."

"The PUC commissioners are grousing about the bill to consolidate them with the Railroad Commission, but they'll get over it. Two of the three didn't want to be reappointed anyway, so it just hastens their departure. The EPA has already instructed its local field agents to accelerate their inspections at the East Texas coal plants. Even mixing the Powder River Basin low-sulfur coal with our own lignite won't get those plants in compliance with the heightened regulations, and the boilers are not built to handle the higher BTU coal without mixing it. Even if they could the plants would all require new scrubbers and the cost would have a catastrophic impact on utility rates. Before long only wind and solar will meet the requirements as they keep getting tighter. We both know that is naive and won't work. When the FERC tried to talk some sense into them, the EPA administrator told them to go to hell. When the FERC commissioner used the term 'capacity factor' the EPA administrator had no idea what he was talking about."

The Governor leaned back and stared at the ceiling for a few seconds. "It sounds as if everything we are working on for the good of Texas is opposed by one part of the administration or another. They really don't want Texas or its people to prosper do they?" After a pause he added "I wonder if they don't believe deep down, that every decision is better made in Washington than in the individual states or by individual citizens."

David knew where the Governor was headed, the talk of seceding had once again risen to a palpable level because way too many legislators had come to the Governor's conclusion on their own. Even one of the Austin liberals had opined in the Austin American Statesman that if the EPA acted in such a way as to drive electric rates up or tried to shut down non-compliant plants that the EPA inspectors should be run out of the state. "Governor, the short version is that I expect that we will have all of the legislation passed by the end of the session and be ready for the Texas Independence Day celebration at Washington-on-the Brazos. You might even want to announce the signing of the bills and declare our energy independence at the same time. I have been able to persuade some of the Dallas delegation to refrain from adding any secession language to any of the pending issues, as much as they would like to."

The Governor rose and David turned to face him. "David, how did we come to this point? It seems as if the federal government is actually trying to make the lives of our people worse; it isn't supposed to be like that. Everything they do makes it harder for us to compete with the rest of the world. I just wish I knew how this was going to play out. I suspect some people will get hurt before this is all over." He didn't know just how right he was.

David had been speaking with the head of the Texas Bankers Association and the two of them had met with the President of the Federal Reserve Bank of Texas a few days earlier. They had discussed the unthinkable, namely how to keep the Texas economy moving if there were a period of instability with the United States, even for a brief period. The three of them had settled on the cautionary strategy of increasing the amount of U.S. currency held by the banks in Texas, but doing so in a way that wouldn't ring any alarms in Washington. Fortunately, the Texas economy was still stronger than those in the majority of the other states were and they could make a good case for the additional currency if questioned. They were counting on the Treasury being too focused on Europe and the political debate in Washington to pay any serious attention to currency and bank reserves in the near term. There was simply no plausible way to create a new currency quickly enough if there were a breakdown in relations with the rest of the country. The market would not be prepared to trade a new currency due to the huge uncertainty as to the exchange rates and ability of Texas to withstand the virtually instant challenge to any announcement of secession. They had already put that contingency plan into action. The Governor didn't really need to get involved just yet; he could honestly deny any knowledge or involvement if it became an issue. Another factor was that the U.S. dollar would still be the currency of transactions with Mexico and other countries.

David returned to his chair, all of the issues spinning in his head, but focused on keeping everything balanced. "Bill, we really need to define our plan for how we respond to the barrage of questions we will be receiving as these bills emerge from the legislature. Final passage can be delayed until shortly before the Texas Independence Day ceremonies at Washington-on-the-Brazos. That will give you the chance to defer them for a few days and then address them all at once on a big stage with strong support from the crowd. The one thing we cannot do is to let the word "secession" be brought into the conversation; the press or someone else may ask the question but that means you can dismiss that as merely evidence of people across the country being frustrated with the inability of the administration to connect with the real concerns of all Americans."

"David, I agree with you on that, but I am becoming more and more convinced that it is not a question of them not connecting, it is that they simply don't care what you and I or anyone else thinks. This president is convinced that he is smarter than all of the rest of the people in the country put together. Even the senate majority leader and the former speaker don't agree with major parts of his agenda, not that he cares. I am more worried about the future of this country than at any previous time in my life. If Texas were to succeed, it would only be because we have no other choice. They have fired on our citizens, destroyed our jobs, and are trying to ruin what is left of the state's economy. You know the last thing I would ever want to do is to be the Governor who let Texas leave the union, but I don't know if you can stop the movement any easier than you can stop a bullet half way down the barrel."

"My point Bill is that you shouldn't be the one to propose that Texas secede from the United States, nor should you side with those who might shout it from the crowd. Emotions are running high already and we need to keep this fuse away from the match. The President is already itching to make an example of us and we need to make sure we don't give him an excuse to do something stupid, if that's possible."

Chapter 9: The Shot Heard all round Texas

11:00 AM
Saturday
April 21, 2012

Washington-on-The Brazos State Park

San Jacinto day is a big deal in Texas. It celebrates the
date of Texas' independence from Mexico after Sam Houston led
the Texican forces against General Santa Ana and took a little
revenge for the Alamo. When the battle had been won near what
later became Houston, news was sent to those waiting anxiously
at the capital of the Republic of Texas, Washington-On-The-
Brazos. Therefore, on San Jacinto day 2012, to celebrate the
independence of Texas from Mexico, the end of the first 2012
special session of the Texas Legislature, Governor Bill Clayton
planned a day of speaking and celebrating around Texas.
Scheduled stops included the steps of the Capital Building in
Austin, the Washington-On-The-Brazos state park, San Jacinto
state park with lunch on the foredeck of the *Battleship Texas*, and
finally the Houston Yacht club to watch the "fireworks" out on
the Houston Ship Channel.
    A speech had been carefully crafted to avoid using the
exact word "secession". The speech was meant to let the people
know that they would have a say in the future relationship that
Texas had with the United States and how that relationship might
change. Copies of the speech had been given to the press the
previous day, and one copy wound up on the desk of the
President of the United States, who, after conferring with his
entire cabinet, ordered the FBI office in San Antonio to go to the
Washington-On-The-Brazos site and let the Governor know that
they were there. Further, if the Governor used the word
secession in his public utterances, he was to be arrested for

sedition. He was tired of the harassment he was getting over the gun control issue and was going to put a stop to it, one way or another.

"...and on this most important day in our state's history, when we celebrate our independence from Mexico, I promise you that I will bring the legislature into special session to consider whether Texas should be independent once again. I will ask you, the people of Texas if you want to be the Republic of Texas once again, or remain simply another one of the now enslaved states in this perverted United States we now find ourselves crippled by. We will once again draw a line in the sand, remembering the Alamo, and Goliad, and San Jacinto, those places where Texas bought her independence. We will bring it to a vote. I promise you that we will do it as soon as humanly possible. Texas will speak to the rest of the nation, and it will say 'farewell'."

The governor waved to the crowd that was giving him a thunderous ovation and walked to the edge of the stage. Descending the steps, he saw that his DPS Trooper escort was formed to help him get to the car. The Lieutenant Governor joined him as they descended the steps and fell into lockstep heading across the field toward the waiting motorcade.

"So much for following my advice about leading the way on secession, Governor." Jibed Lt. Gov. Dalby with a bit of a frown.

Governor Bill Clayton, simply smiled broadly waving to the crowd and said under his breath, "That's why they pay me the big bucks, David, to lead. Remember that sign on my desk, 'I must hurry, for I am their leader, and they have gone?'"

FBI Special agent Sheldon McDanials, and two associates were headed to the cars too. On McDanials left wrist he had one locked handcuff with the other end opened in his palm and not visible to the casual observer. As he reached the Governor's party, he placed his team between the Governor and his car, extended his right hand and smiled. The FBI badge hanging from his left jacket pocket had been all the permission he needed to get past the DPS Troopers in the caravan and the Ranger standing off to the side of the gaggle.

When his right hand met the Governor's right hand in a firm handshake, he smiled and said, "In the name of the President of the United States, I arrest you for the crime of sedition, inciting the forceful over throw of the United States Government." As he spoke the words, his left hand moved swiftly to place the open cuff contained in it onto the Governor's wrist. Officer Delbert Jefferson had been standing just behind the Governor's right shoulder, and when the word "arrest..." was spoken he reacted as the former defensive linebacker he had been many years before. His 6' 2" 295-pound frame launched itself at Special Agent McDaniels, blasted between the Governor and the Lt. Governor. His left hand grabbed both of the right hands that were still shaking in cordial greeting. The cuff that Special Agent McDaniels wanted to place on the wrist of the governor was blocked by the intruding hand of Trooper Jefferson. Delbert continued forward bringing his right hand over the top in an overhand pitching motion hitting Special Agent McDanials in the face with such force that the three of them, tied together by the officers iron grip, were propelled toward the cars.

Special Agent Donald Evers, standing just behind and to the left of Special Agent McDaniel's, saw the trooper launch himself at McDaniels, and reached across his own body to draw his 9mm Glock from its holster under his left arm. When the weapon came out, he pointed it at the head of the still advancing trooper and snapped off a shot. The report of the Glock was deafening to trooper Jefferson as the gun had practically been pointed at his right ear. But by the time Evers fired, the whole crowd had moved forward just enough for the bullet to graze the back of the troopers head, ultimately leaving him with little more than a burned bald spot and one hell of a head ache. What the bullet did after that will be recorded in history as the second shot heard 'round the world. It seems that all wars start with one of these...an errant bullet...an unexpected surge of violence...a fallen duke, or president, or in this case, a Governor. This bullet passed directly into the right cheek area of the Governor, through the right sinus cavity and below the mass of the brain until it reached the Modula Oblongata, which it proceeded to obliterate. The Governor was already dead by the time the three of them;

the now deceased former Governor, the wounded Trooper Jefferson and Special Agent McDaniels hit the ground.

Unfortunately, that shot was only the first in what came to be known as the beginning of the second war of independence for Texas. DPS troopers and the ranger had their weapons drawn by the time the group hit the ground. No one was sure what happened next, until the news footage was reviewed in detail. Apparently, the Troopers and Rangers held their weapons directed at the FBI agent who had fired the shot that killed the Governor. The agent who was behind McDanials right bent over to try to help McDanials get out from under Trooper Jefferson, who by this time was nearly unconscious. As the third agent saw that he would not be able to assist McDanials immediately, he stood up with his hand in his coat reaching for his weapon. He took two rounds in the face from the Trooper standing directly in front of him who had been to the Governor's left, as the Trooper swung to his right to address the agent who had just shot the Governor, the Ranger fired first, killing Agent Evers with three shots … two to the chest, and one in the right temple. The other agents, standing near the black suburban that had brought them from San Antonio, had their guns out and were running to the scene when they were engaged by two men from the crowd in plain clothes. The booming sound of the 45's used by these plain clothes men were decidedly more robust than the popping sound made by the 9 mm's used by the FBI agents. In the end, 5 FBI Agents, and One Governor lay dead on the field at Washington-On-The-Brazos. One DPS Trooper, Trooper Jefferson, lay wounded. And so it began.

The Lt. Governor, nicked in the left shoulder by one of the many shots fired in the melee, knocked clear of the scrum by Trooper Jefferson, was pulled out of the fray by DPS Trooper Dan Whitaker. Trooper Whitaker practically dragged the Lt. Gov. to a nearby golf cart that the grounds people had been using to run ice and supplies around the park grounds. The roads were clogged with parked cars, and there was no hope of a fast escape using any of the motorcade vehicles, so Trooper Whitaker took out across the fields in the cart headed for the front entrance to the park about a mile away. Some of the people who had heard the shooting were running along with the cart trying to escape the blaze of gunfire that had erupted near the speakers stand. Others were just standing in shock, looking at the scene in complete disbelief.

As Trooper Whitaker and his passenger neared the front entrance, he pulled the cart between two parked cars and headed out the entrance road. There, parked across the entrance road between the stone pillars that anchored the fence on either side of the road sat the other FBI black suburban. Trooper Whitaker veered off the road again and headed to the right, protecting the Lt. Governor with his body as the shots from the agents using the suburban for cover began to ring out. He got about 100 yards down the fence before the lucky bullet found him squarely between the shoulder blades. He slumped over the wheel of the cart with his foot planted firmly on the floor sending the cart down the slight incline into the creek bottom below. It came crashing to a stop, throwing Trooper Whitaker into the steering wheel and out the left side of the cart. He didn't notice. The Lt. Governor was plastered against the Plexiglas, and was then cushioned by the rush of water as the cart entered the creek and came to a halt. The Lt. Governor, half conscious, hearing the continuing shots being fired from the fast approaching agents, jumped clear of the wreck and headed up the other side of the creek bank into the yaupon thicket on the other side. Kneeling as he dove into the brush, he disappeared from view. All that was left for the trailing agents was the sound of crashing branches as the thicket swallowed him whole.

He couldn't remember how far he had run, all he knew was that he had to get to the road and away from … what … the feds, … the shooting … the war … all of the above or take your pick … he just had to get away. As he burst out of the brush, he slammed into the barbed wire fence with enough force to impale a few barbs into his already bleeding left arm and chest. Regaining his balance, he pulled the wires apart and rolled through, tearing his coat on the upper wire and his pants and leg on the lower one. He ran up the hill to Hwy 105 when he spotted an approaching truck pulling a trailer with a big green tractor on it. It was moving slowly due to the crowd of cars it had just passed at the entrance road to the state park. He could hear the agents crashing through the brush behind him as he grabbed for the door of the truck. He thought he could hang onto the truck, standing on the running boards if he had to, even if the door was locked. He yanked at the handle of the rear door of the crew cab one ton and it came open with a squeak. He dove in yelling "Go Go Go" to the stunned driver … as the agents, now clear of the fence line, began snapping off shots at him and the truck. The rancher inside the truck glanced over his shoulder and took in the situation in a split second as the sound of the big diesel engine came to full throat. Glass shattered up front somewhere, but the Lt. Governor couldn't tell where because he was firmly planted on the floorboard of the rear seat and intended to stay there for a while.

Chapter 10: Can I Hitch a Ride?

11:15 AM
Saturday
April 21, 2012

Hwy 105 near Washington-on-The-Brazos

"Go…Go…Go…" he yelled as he dove into the back seat of the one-ton diesel dually truck. Tim Watson, retired engineering professor and now gentleman rancher, instinctively pounded the accelerator to the floor. The back passenger door slammed shut and the sound of automatic weapons fire all seemed to happen about the same time. "What the hell is…"

"Shut up and drive if you don't want to get shot" came the not so reassuring voice from the floor of the back seat of the crew cab.

The speedometer climbed slowly. One of the drawbacks of having the tractor on the trailer tied to the back of the diesel truck was that nothing was going to happen very fast. But, there is always a flip side, maybe all that junk back there will stop a few of those incoming rounds, Tim thought as he hunched down in the driver's seat, foot still planted firmly on the accelerator.

The mirror on the right side of the truck exploded in a shower of glass shards. Something out there was obviously much closer than it should have been. Another round shattered the rear window and passed through Tim's right shoulder before exiting just above the inspection sticker on the windshield. The truck continued to accelerate and the gunfire seemed to drop further behind. At first there was a little burning, then stinging, then a wall of pain that took Tim's breath away. The force of the impact forced his upper body forward in the seatbelt and twisted him around to the left. His right hand slipped off the steering wheel, then his left, letting the big truck and trailer combination

78

start a slow swing into the oncoming traffic lane. Tim raised his head back up, reached for the wheel with his right hand, but it didn't work and he thought he heard someone yelling with pain and discovered that it was him. He tried with his left, swerving back into his lane. Too hard: the trailer began to sway with the top-heavy load but after a couple of cycles followed the accelerating truck as it headed east on Highway 105 toward Navasota. Tim moved his knee of his left leg up until it contacted the bottom of the leather-covered steering wheel. He knew that wouldn't work as a permanent solution, but would have to do for the moment. He jammed his left hand up to his right shoulder. It came away covered with blood.

"Head east…" said the voice in the floor of the back seat. "They'll have a car again in a minute, but head east. Can we make it to Navasota?" came the question from the head that had just peeked over the armrest from the floor of the back seat. The face was visible in the inside rear view mirror. It looked like the one Tim had seen earlier that morning on TV, only much dirtier and definitely much more scared shitless.

"Get up here and help me, the truck might make it to Navasota, but I'm not sure about me…" The guy in the back seat seemed to ignore Tim's plea until Tim took his left hand off the wounded shoulder and held it up in front of the passenger's face. "Come put pressure on this." Tim said gritting his teeth. The passenger looked around the back seat and found the red rag stuffed in the back of the driver's front seat pocket. He wadded it up in his right hand and deftly shoved it into the exit wound while pulling Tim's hand away. There is very little room between the front seats of the truck, and damn near none over the head rests, but somehow the passenger managed to slither through the openings to the front seat while keeping pressure on the profusely bleeding wound.

"You steer" said Tim.

"Got it" came the reply as the passenger moved his right hand to the wheel, slick with blood, while keeping his left firmly pressed against the rag.

"Are you OK?"

"Hell no, I'm not OK. I can't move my right arm, I'm getting drowsy, I can't see and they are shooting at you but

79

hitting me…" came the reply. "I don't think we can make it very far before they catch up with this rig." Tim replied, "Best chance would be to get off this road … and head back to my place." Realizing that in a split second, he had chosen sides in a situation that he had been watching dispassionately develop for weeks. Tim felt a bit sick to his stomach.

The announcement hadn't been much of a surprise since there had been hints about secession for months. When the actual event came, that was a different matter. It was unreal. Completely not real. Remote voices on the local radio station interrupting the country and western music Tim favored. Disconnected, as though the Earth had flown off its orbit or something. David, the guy in the floor of the back seat, had introduced the Governor on the podium at steps of the capital building this morning to announce that Texas might once again become a sovereign nation. "As Sam Houston and Stephen F. Austin achieved independence from Mexico from this headquarters at Washington-On-The-Brazos, Texas once again becomes a sovereign nation." The Governor had said so eloquently, and everyone had cheered and applauded. "Since Texas joined the United States by a joint resolution of Congress and the Texas Legislature, and no treaty binding Texas, a sovereign nation, to the United States was ever executed; Texans will choose whether or not to renounce that resolution and to effectively separate itself from the United States, as is its right to do." Tim had heard over the radio.

"Turn right here…" Tim said between gritted teeth.

With both of them steering, the truck and trailer pulled onto the gravel road and quickly disappeared from view of the highway as it made its winding way back to the ranch house and barn three miles from the turnoff. When it made the sharp turn off the gravel road into the gate at the home place, it swung wide to make sure the trailer didn't get hung up in the ditch. Pulling to the end of the drive, over the small rise in the drive, Tim braked the rig to a stop, reached over the steering wheel with his left arm and pulled the gear selector up into park. He turned off the ignition key and then reached around to flip open the seat belt. When the belt snapped across his body, it hit David's right arm, which was still putting pressure on Tim's right shoulder. The bleeding had stopped, but Tim's shirt, the rag and David's hand were all soaked with dark red drying blood. When the belt hit David's hand, another growl came out of Tim as the small blow sent waves of pain radiating from his shoulder down his right arm and into his chest.

"We need to get you to the hospital." The Lt. Governor said. Tim turned to look at him just as his eyes rolled slowly upward and the lids closed down over them as he slumped down in the driver's seat.

For the last few miles, David had been thinking about next steps. He knew that with the Governor dead, he was the senior elected official in the state. He knew that the FBI was searching for him and probably had a fix on his cell phone. He had taken it out of his pocket while he was lying on the floor of the truck and pulled the battery out to disable the GPS feature. He saw a small flashing green light in Tim's left front shirt pocket and reached across his now unconscious companion to retrieve the flashing cell phone. He dialed the number for the emergency communications center in Austin, hoping that a short conversation and quick reaction by his "folks" would pull him out of this situation before the feds could get to him.

"ECOM...Officer King" came the clipped answer on the other end of the line.

"This is Lt. Governor David Dalby. I need help."

"Stand by one..." came the reply...after a short pause..."This is Colonel Stewart McCracken, Governor...I have your coordinates from the phone you are on...are you all right?"

"I'm ok, but the fellow who saved me is in pretty bad shape. Come get us and send medical help as part of the deal. He has a gunshot to the right shoulder and has bled quite a bit, and I have a small flesh wound."

"A helicopter is on the way sir; we had one standing by for the Governor in Brenham. We picked him up about 10 minutes ago and he is headed to Austin. We will reroute that aircraft to you."

"Then the Governor is OK...? I saw him get shot in the head...and it looked very bad."

"No, sir, he is not ok. The Governor is dead. You are the Governor now, sir, or will be as soon as we can get you sworn in."

"Where are the FBI people who were shooting at us? Are they following us?"

"No, sir. All but three of them are dead, and two of those remaining are aboard the helicopter with the governor. We were taking them to the UT medical center in San Antonio, but that can wait."

"What about the other one?"

"Well sir, the Rangers are discussing the situation with him."

The sound of a Black Hawk in full go mode with its rotors ripping the air apart began to get louder. It was approaching from the southwest, the direction that the truck had come in on the gravel road. It blew past the truck just feet off the treetops, pulled up hard, rolled into a 90-degree bank to the right and headed for an open patch of ground between the ranch house and the front fence. The tail came down as the dark gray helicopter slowed and settled rapidly to the ground with its right side toward the truck about 100 feet away. The side door of the chopper burst open before the machine hit the ground, and two camo-uniformed individuals leapt to the ground at the same moment the wheels touched down. They ran toward the truck. David opened the passenger door as they approached and pointed his thumb across the top of the truck to motion them to the driver's side. They ran to the left side of the truck and opened the driver's side door, pulled Tim over on his left shoulder, and slid him gently out onto the stretcher the second med-tech had placed beside the truck. The first guy through the door grabbed the rag and kept pressure on the wound as they had moved him. None of that backboard and safety belt crap…these guys dumped Tim on the stretcher, lifted it and headed to the chopper at a trot. David dove out of the passenger door and headed to the chopper. He got there as they were loading Tim on the floor, stepped up into the aircraft, and took a seat facing forward against the rear firewall. The two FBI agents were sitting in seats facing him. Their white shirts were soaked with blood and their hands were tied together with duct tape. Pressure bandages were applied to their wounds and were held in place by the silver tape. Their mouths were taped over, and their eyes were glazed. One of them noticed the arrival of the new passengers, but the other one simply hung forward on his seat harness.

The Governor, the dead Governor, was strapped into the center rear seat. His head cavity was open and a portion of his brain was hanging over his left shoulder. It was clear that he had been moved from the stretcher to the seat when the crew got the call to pick up David and his wounded companion.

As the door went shut and the med-techs began to fasten their seat belts, the chopper leapt off the ground and tilted violently forward, rolled hard left and spun 90 degrees before settling into its maximum cruise attitude headed for Houston, some 90 miles away. The movement had been violent enough to cause David to have an immediate case of nausea. The more conscious of the two FBI agent's eyes got very big as he emptied his stomach onto his shirt. With the tape in place across his mouth, the contents of the stomach had to take a rather unusual route. He shook his head when the convulsion was over. David reached across the stretcher and held out his hand to the agent's face. The plea for relief from the agent's eyes was clear. David grabbed a small tab of the tape that was sticking up on the left cheek of the agent, paused to get a good grip, and then ripped the tape off one of the men who may have been shooting at him 30 minutes ago. As soon as the tape cleared his face, the agent turned his head to the right and retched again on the port side door of the helicopter. He spat a couple of times to clear his mouth, turned to the Lt. Governor, and looked him in the eye.

"Sir," he shouted above the roar of the twin turbos and the rotor blades, "you are under arrest for..." trapped by his seat harness, David's right hand would only reach the front of the agent's face, but the right cross nailed him square on the jaw, snapping his head around. The agent was unconscious before his head stopped moving. The med-tech seated in the seat beside David said "Nice one, sir. I didn't want to have to listen to those bastards all the way to Houston anyway."

"No problem, Glad to help out." The new Governor of Texas said as he settled down for the strangest ride of his life.

Chapter 11: Save The Governor

11:43 AM
Saturday
April 21, 2012

On the way to Austin

The helicopter veered to the right after 5 minutes of flight. David, the former Lt. Governor and soon to be sworn in as the Governor of Texas, noticed the change in course and pressed the talk button on his headset chord... "where are we headed?"

"We have to get you to Austin, sir." Came the reply from the copilot.

"The hell we do; we have to get these men to the hospital first."

"I'm sorry sir, the emergency center needs you there and we will take these men on to San Antonio...the medics say they are stable and you need to be in Austin."

Well, there it was.

Duty...priorities...sacrifices...tradeoffs...risk: all the things that weigh on your mind when deciding what to do. The new Governor was part of a system now...one that had just grown into the size of a nation instead of a state if things continued as they were.

The med-techs were pumping fluid into Tim now at what looked like a pretty good rate. He still wasn't conscious, but his color was returning from that absolute chalk white it had been when they pulled him out of the truck. The noise was deafening as the chopper thrashed its way to the ecomm center in Austin. The group in the back sat in silence. The med-techs looked after Tim, occasionally checking the two FBI agents and looking at the new Governor periodically to make sure he didn't need any attention. The deceased Governor, his left side covered in blood and brain matter, slumped in his restraints; his head...what remained of it...bobbed up and down and side to side with the motion of the helicopter. David couldn't take his eyes off of him. Gunned down as an outlaw in his own country, or was it gunned down by foreign elements in his own country?

Suddenly, David realized that this was going to be the exact question that would be asked of him when he stepped off the chopper in Austin. He also realized that his answer would be the basis for the future of the state, or the Nation of Texas and its relationship with the rest of the states...or with its neighboring foreign power. Did this constitute the beginning of a war between Texas and the United States or was it just an unfortunate accident due to a misunderstanding between federal and state authorities? It was what it was, but how it was perceived would be controlled to a large extent by what David said when he stepped off the chopper in Austin.

The helicopter leveled off, slowing and descending toward a group of buildings north of Austin's downtown area. As it neared the ground, the nose came up, and it slowed further until it gently touched down in the parking lot of the ecomm center. The door to the chopper was thrown open by one of the Texas Air Guard uniformed members, and the Lt. Governor stepped out. Two DPS officers reached out, one taking each arm just above the elbow, and moved him toward the building entrance. A group of DPS officers surrounded the party as they moved across the open ground, stooping a little until they were clear of the rotor blades of the helicopter. There was no press, there were no civilians in the area; it was all military and police. As the crowd cleared the rotors of the helicopter, its blades once again seemed to assume their angry attitude and blew dust off the parking lot as it rose into the air and headed south to San Antonio. Even with this longer trip, everyone would arrive at the University of Texas Health Science trauma center well within the critical hour, which wouldn't matter at all to Bill Clayton.

Through the entrance door, down the stairs, along the hallway, and into the ecomm center: The Governor was brought to the little glass conference room overlooking the working floor of the ecomm center that looked a little like NASA's Apollo control room. The conference room was already full, with men and women, each standing as the Governor entered. Some of their eyes got considerably larger at the sight of the blood on his coat, shirt and hands. The med-techs had swabbed at it while they were seeing if he needed any medical attention. When they had slapped on a bandage and determined that he was in passable shape, they moved on to the others who needed them more, leaving the Governor a blood smeared mess that now appeared in front of his new staff for the first time. He knew all of them of course; James (Jimmy) Jeffries, head of the Department of Public Safety; Fred Handy, head of the Texas Rangers; Bob Northcut, commander of the Texas National Guard; Belinda Sikes, the Governor's Legislative Aid; and Travis Detwiler, the Governor's staff assistant. The head of the Texas Homeland Security office and his deputies were all there as well.

Now came the moment.

David had to decide what the events of the morning were; accident; aggression; war; secession. What he said next would become the official position of Texas toward the meaning of the events of the day.

He took a deep breath. "Ladies and Gentlemen, we have lost our Governor. He was killed by an FBI agent who was attempting to arrest him following his speech at Washington-On-The-Brazos, where he promised to leave to the people of the state of Texas a choice about whether or not we should remain in the United States." He looked around the room. Every face was rigid. "I think that he had a really good idea." He scanned the room again…took another deep breath and said "But, I think the federal government has taken the decision out of our hands. By their acts, they have shown their unwillingness to allow us and our fellow citizens to express our opinions about this issue. Because he even brought up the subject of letting the people decide, he was being arrested." No one blinked. "I believe that we are now essentially at war with the United States of America, a war for our independence. A POLITICAL war. God knows we don't want a fighting war, so let me make it clear right now; there will be no attacks on federal property or personnel. We will act effectively against them, but not by exchanging bullets in the open battlefield…that is a war we cannot win and each of you knows it. As much as I would like to extract some pound of flesh for what has happened, we must move quickly to make sure this ends well. As always, we Texans didn't start this, but we will damn sure finish it." David looked at the people in the room and decided he didn't need to say anything else after that.

"Governor, will you stay here or do you want to work at the Governor's office?"

"I need to make some calls from here and then I will head up to the hill. Do we have good communication between here and the Governor's office?"

"Yes sir, top notch…audio, video conferencing…multiple channel, independent satellite for voice, video and data…we can do whatever you need from here or from there, whatever you need, sir." came from one of the ecomm troopers in the back of the room.

"Good, please return to your duties and I will meet with Belinda and Travis for a minute. Thank you all."

Chapter 12: All Dressed Up and Nowhere to Go

12:15 PM
Saturday
April 21, 2012

Battleship Texas, San Jacinto Monument

They didn't salute. But for 60 year old men this was as close to attention as they were going to get. Greg Brothers stepped off the gangplank and onto the battleship gray wooden deck of the *Texas* exchanging a nod with the group as he turned to his left to look over the towing arrangements that had been made that morning. *Texas* was going to get a bottom job. For years, the ship had been on display at the San Jacinto monument site at the north end of the Houston Ship Channel. During those years, her steel bottom had withered away like muscles on a retired boxer, the shape was still there but the strength was gone. It was all the parks and wildlife department boys could do to keep her from sinking at her moorings.   With the shutdown of the oil industry, there were thousands of offshore and shipyard workers out of work. And now, a miracle of sorts was going to occur.

It seemed that a group of people had been at dinner in Houston one night, and the topic of the gun treaty had fired up a heated debate. The group decided that they wanted to hear the biggest gun in *Texas* fire as a symbolic gesture…they wanted to hear the Battleship *Texas* fire her 14 inch guns "…as the last voice of freedom." They had finally gotten hold of the head of the Texas Parks and Wildlife commissioner at about 3:00 O'clock in the morning and convinced him that they were serious…(and still quite drunk.) They were undeterred when Jay Layton, the commissioner, told them that the Texas would probably sink if she fired her guns. They insisted that they had the ships and the shipyards that could raise her if that happened, so what was the problem. Jay explained that the state couldn't pay for such an undertaking, that they had tried and tried to get a budget item for the repair of the Texas, but none could get past the legislature. The men on the other end of the phone said, "Hell son, we'll pay for it…we just want to hear the old lady bark." The commissioner took the name of the person on the other end of the phone, promised to call the governor in the morning and then went back to sleep. In the morning, he called the governor just to keep his promise, because the name he had written down belonged to a rather substantial individual.

"What would this new bottom cost, Jay?"

"It's not just the bottom, sir, you have to put an experienced crew on board, you have to have air compressors and pumps installed on her deck to keep the bowels of the ship pressurized so that if you spring a plate or hole in the ship you can keep her afloat long enough to get her to the dry dock, tugs to drag her down the channel without running aground, and then all the way to the ship yard where the dry dock is."

"But what would it cost?"

"About $100 million dollars, Governor."

"Thank you, Jay." Was all the governor had said. He waited until afternoon to pick up the phone and called the significant name, and got through to him once his office staff realized that it really was the governor calling.

"Bob, this is the Governor, how do you want to pay that $100 million you promised Jay last night…I'll take a check."

"Well, hell governor, I'll have it wired to you, what's the account number…?" he said laughingly. "But, $100 mil is a bit steep just to hear a gun go off; I can do that by riding around with the police down here in Houston after midnight for nothing."

"It's not just the firing of the gun, Bob. The Texas is about to sink at her moorings and if we fire her guns, even once maybe, she could sink on the spot. Now I know you said you and your friends would pay for the recovery, but I'm sure you didn't have any idea how much that might come to."

90

"Yea, that is a bit more than we had in mind, but still, there must be some way we can work this out. I mean, with the gun ban thing going on, this is the biggest gun in Texas, and you're telling me we can't shoot it. That's just not right."

"Well, if you can figure out a way to keep her from sinking and get her to a shipyard, I'll find the crew and the shells and we'll do this on San Jacinto day next year. How about that?"

"You got'a deal Governor."

The governor had hung up the phone expecting never to hear from the group again, so he was taken completely by surprise when a week later he received a FedEx containing a bound proposal from a ship yard for the repair work, a tug company for the towing, and an off shore oil drilling company for the ship stabilization equipment and project management, all to be donated with the proviso that The *Texas* fire her forward facing guns and have the shells land out in the bay off the Houston Yacht club on San Jacinto Day 2012. That would be about 13 or 14 miles, which the proposal had pointed out was about the maximum range of the *Texas* in her current configuration. Since the Battleship *Texas* had a charitable donations trust set up as a 501-(c) (3), the cost of the overhaul would be donated and the expenses used as tax deductions for the companies involved. This would amount to having the federal government paying a significant portion of the expense of the overhaul. The governor smiled when he read that part.

So it was that Greg Brothers, a retired US Navy Admiral, and long suffering volunteer coordinator for all the tour guides, the work parties and aborted attempts to get legislation passed to care for the Texas, strode her deck with a righteous heart. He, with a small group in his wake, proceeded to tour the deck from stem to stern...actually, he headed stern first. The compressors and pumps were lashed to the deck with chains that were welded to tabs that were welded to the frame of the ship. They weren't going anywhere. Each of the air compressors was capable of filling the superdome with enough air to pump the roof up in about an hour...and there were 6 of them on the deck. The pumps could fill the dome with water in about an hour.

The tug was lying quietly aside the stern of the ship, tied to both the stern and the port side spring line position that was

91

amidships. All the display shells and tents had been removed from the battleship's decks and all her hatches were closed. They had pressurized the ship yesterday to insure that all the lower decks were closed up with the tar and canvas seals being applied to all the hatches. Actually, there had been some concern that over pressuring the hull from the inside might rupture it, but the test had gone well. She was pressure tight below in case anything happened.

The luncheon tables were spread out on the foredeck in three neat rows, with a podium at the bow. The TV cameras were arranged in front of the first turret and the scaffold for the press photographers. This provided the best shot of where the Governor was going to speak, with the barrels of the guns overhead, and the San Jacinto monument in the background.

The catering crew was standing ready and all was ready for the Governor and his party to arrive from Washington-on-The-Brazos. Word came instead.

Chapter 13: They Have What?

1:00 PM
Saturday
April 21, 2012

The White House

The computer screens in the White House secure situation room were filled with the scenes of the events at Washington-On-The-Brazos that had occurred only an hour before. The cabinet and joint chiefs were taking their seats when the President entered the room, and they all stood again. He motioned them to their seats and nodded toward his head of the Department of Justice.

"Mr. President, there are basically three options to handle this Texas situation as I see it. First, we can treat it as an administrative argument between federal and state jurisdictions and run it through the courts. Or, we can treat it as a criminal situation and go arrest those involved who have committed a crime, or we can treat it as a significant military situation, one that requires a significant response of federal forces, destruction of property, loss of life and potentially significant damage to important National US resources."

"They haven't closed any borders and they haven't taken anyone prisoner; all they have done is to announce that they are considering whether or not to become independent from the United States. The word secession was not used, and they relied on lots of history and legal arguments, but basically it boils down to their desire to leave the union…which we obviously can't permit."

"As you instructed, we sent a team of agents to the press announcement in Texas. Immediately after the announcement was made, our Senior Special Agent on the scene took control of the situation, identified himself as a Federal Bureau of

Investigation Special Agent in Charge and announced that the person on the stage who had made the announcement was a criminal, and then attempted to take him into custody. The subject ran from the agents and managed to elude them by jumping into a passing vehicle. Shots were fired. Several agents have been killed, and two others wounded. The crowd at the meeting overwhelmed the agents, disarmed them and took them to Austin. We received a call from the Head of the Texas Department of Public Safety, their state police, indicating that the bodies of the deceased agents and the unwounded agents would be turned over to our office in Austin within the hour..., which they were. One agent, who was shot, was flown by life flight helicopter to the University of Texas Health Science Center in San Antonio. He was treated in the emergency room there and is reported to be in stable condition. Our people in San Antonio are with him now and getting statements about the incident. It is not known how many civilians at the meeting were wounded."

"Who shot our agent?"

"Mr. President, it is not clear at this time who actually fired the shots that killed our agents. There was a rather large crowd as you saw, and we have not completed our review of the broadcast tape."

"Was it one of their police or military people?"

"Sir, as I said, we have not completed the review of the video tape and cannot definitively identify who the shooter or shooters may have been."

"When will we know?"

The Chairman of the Joint Chiefs interrupted, "Mr. President, we have a group of computer image forensics people working this as we speak. They will have completed an initial review of the tape identifying the potential shooter or shooters within the next hour. Then they will have to work on individual frames of the video doing facial recognition analysis in order to identify those individuals who might have been involved in the shooting by name. Mr. President, I might also point out that the bullets that killed our agents were removed from the bodies before they were returned to us."

"Mr. President, we need to get down there with some force sir, some overwhelming force. We have Air Force bases, a

94

large Army base and lots of reserve components in the state. Those locations can't be secured without a significant amount of force. We need to place clear fire perimeters around our facilities down there immediately. Some of our largest aircraft production and spare parts manufacturers and vendors are down there. If we don't secure all that stuff, the loss of it will affect our ability to fight anywhere in the world. Not to mention that a huge quantity of the domestic refining capacity is there with the pipelines and shipping ports, sir…this is a serious problem and we need to respond aggressively and with overwhelming force." Admiral Mark Meltrose sat bolt upright in his chair, much as he did as a plebe at the Naval Academy. He hadn't been able to break down the wall between the Commander in Chief and the uniformed services like he had hoped to. Now this Texas thing had popped and he could see lots of problems cropping up with the Afghanistan and Iraq area operations because of the distractions. He raised one hand from his lap, and placed it on the table, leaning forward slightly for emphasis. "And Mr. President, we can't let this go too far, because Texas will almost immediately become a nuclear power."

"What the hell do you mean by that, Admiral? Have you let them get their hands on one of our nuclear bombs or something?"

"No, Mr. President, they have their hands on approximately 250 of our bombs right now. The Pantex plant in North Texas is where all of the nuclear material and special devices are processed when they need to be reconditioned and tested. It is the only such facility in the United States. The facility is a Department of Energy facility with a small detachment of Nuclear Security forces. They will not be able to secure that facility against a force assisted by those who are already inside the place. There has been no report of any attack of any kind against the facility and we are in constant contact with the head of the security force there, but sir we need to get down there with some troops."

The president looked around the room. "We can't let this situation develop into one that is detrimental to the United States. It is clear that there must be decisive action taken by us to prevent this from escalating to a point where it becomes a distraction from our responsibilities to the people of the rest of our nation and the rest of the world. I will not allow this to become an important event by making it an important event. We will treat this … this … "

"misguided action, sir"…

"…misguided action by the leaders of one state to confound or reduce by any significant amount the resources we must spend on our primary goals. We will not dignify this misguided action on the part of several criminals in Texas by wasting precious resources destroying property down there that we will ultimately capture by the force of our considerable resources. I want you gentlemen to come up with a plan that will allow us to return the lawful order of political administration there as quickly as possible."

"Mr, President, if we consider that Texas has seceded, are they a foreign power, can we then use our military to aid us in returning them to … the Union…? If we don't acknowledge that they are a sovereign nation, separate from the United States, we are prohibited, by law, from using our military in any way. We can move forces around, we can secure federal facilities within the facilities themselves, but other action would be precluded. If they are not a foreign power, our intelligence agencies will not be able to operate legally within their borders. The FBI would retain jurisdiction, and not have the assistance of any other agencies used for international intelligence gathering."

"I will not grant them the status of being a foreign power. There are simply criminals within one of the political units of the United States who must be apprehended and brought to justice. That does sound like the FBI has the lead. On the other hand, there will be a need for assistance from the intelligence community that would be helpful to the FBI. Further, we need to clarify with the folks on the hill what emergency powers we might best propose to deal with this situation. To begin with, we have to send them a signal that they are embarking on a trail that will lead to the destruction of much of what they hope to achieve. How could we do that without risking a direct confrontation, something of a show of force?"

"Mr. President, we have lots of aircraft there, but if we burn much fuel with them we may find that it is difficult to replenish it, so flyby's and sonic booms over population centers might be what we could do, but not many of them. I wouldn't recommend getting any troops involved sir, as that offers too much potential for a repeat of what happened at the press conference. Perhaps we could send a ship to 'guard' the refineries near Houston, or Beaumont."

"Mr. Secretary, we can easily destroy any facility within the state in a matter of minutes from locations that are not within the state or even near it. I think we need to assemble a list of targets and get back together when we have had time to consider some of the risks involved in what we are about to do."

"Very well, gentlemen. We will reassemble in two hours. By then we should have the FBI report and a target list from the joint chiefs. Thank you very much."

The Director of the CIA shuffled the papers in front of him, wasting time as the rest of the group rose to leave the room. He locked eyes with the president for a moment and raised his eyebrows in a question, which the president answered with an inclination of his head. Both men headed down the hall to the oval office, and once inside the Director spoke first.

"Mr. President, I believe that we can solve this nuclear question quietly. I have been working on a situation involving the nuclear stockpile and maintenance facility at Pantex for some time."

"But that is within the US, how have you been working on it, which would be illegal wouldn't it?"

"Yes, Mr. President, but we have been working the other end of a situation internationally that involves personnel within the United States who have access to the Pantex facility. One of my top people is prepared to communicate through back personal channels with the Texas people at Pantex. He can let them know that if Texas will agree to the movement of the nuclear devices out of the state, we might be willing to grant some reciprocal favor, like not blowing them off the map."

"And, you say you have a man positioned to do that."

"Yes Sir, he is a classmate of the director of the facility, the civilian director, not the actual DOE head, who knows the Governor. We can safely communicate through him and not let anyone know that we are making a deal. It will look publicly like you suggested that having nuclear weapons within Texas was just too dangerous given the circumstances and that you had told the Governor that you were going to remove them, and that you had the Governor's word that there would be no interference in that plan."

"That sounds good, but we have to be sure that the Governor understands that this is only a temporary promise of non-intervention, that we reserve the right to move heavily against them in the future if things change."

"I'm sure we can make that clear to him sir, and that he will agree. After all, they don't want to become a smoking hole any more than we want to make them one."

"How fast can you set this up?"

"By this evening sir; I would expect that we could coordinate with the Air Force to get the weapons moved out starting tomorrow."

"That's fine, except I think we need to keep your activities separate from those of the Air Force. Send your message and call me when the Governor agrees. I'll let the Secretary of Defense know that he should plan on making the move."

"Thank you, Mr. President" said the CIA Director, rising as the President stood, signaling the end of the meeting. The Director felt completely frustrated. This had been an excellent opportunity to get control of a DoD and DoE operation, and now the President was going to leave it in the hands of the Defense Department. When would they ever learn?

Chapter 14: Not Now, Not This Way

2:00 PM
Thursday
April 21, 2012

CIA McLean, Virginia

As CIA Brad walked down the corridor to meet with the boss, he was almost in tears. His hands were trembling and his breathing restricted...he was furious. Everything had gone so well on the phone this morning when he had assured his boss, that he could get Texas to move the nuclear devices out of the state voluntarily. And now, as he was ready to pull the trigger on the biggest operation of his life...and they wanted to second guess him.

Not now...,not this way.

There is no way they are going to understand how I can pull this off he thought. They will lose confidence in the project and call it off; 30 years down the drain; hundreds of assets and thousands of communications. Never a clear mandate; Never a clear schedule; Until now. Now, I'm prepared to pull off the biggest coo ever, and they want me to explain it to them. They want me to give them warm fuzzy feelings about how I can blow in the horn here and push down this valve and the note will come out there. It's not like that. It's not like playing an instrument. It's not like conducting an orchestra. It's not like writing music. It's like life, friends, acquaintances, relatives, bosses, enemies, owners, politicians, all of them are playing at the same time. Like they are floating on a lake with waves and wind moving them around, first this way and then that. Then they decide to compare one wave to another and if it doesn't check out they reject it, or downgrade the next wave from that direction.

I helped get Hamied out of Iran during the last moments of the revolution just before the revolutionaries were going to kill him for working with the Shah. I set him up in Turkey where he could work and have a life and continue to help me. I got his son, Haliel into Cal Tech. I even managed to get Haliel a job at Livermore National Labs. And I managed to turn him into a radical, with help from several mullahs, half a dozen of his friends, his father, and some people in Iran. Over 20 years it took to cultivate his personal network. Over 10 years it took to manage his conversion to radicalism. The alienation of his father, the demotion of his friend, the deportation of his mullah in San Francisco, the messages back and forth from him to his friends in Turkey. It took the coincidental contact with my Iranian, working on his ego, working on his disenchantment with his father, and with us, fabricating the stories about the death of his mother at the hands of the Shah's men during his father escape to move him.

I cultivated my friendship with my old classmate who is a top guy at the nuclear storage and repair facility in Texas. I have him believing that he is a key player in keeping the US and Texas from going to a shooting war over this Gulf thing. So the Governor got shot...so what? So they want to vote on leaving the union. Good riddance. I made him important. I am setting up Texas. I am setting up Israel. I am setting up Iran. It's me! It's me! It's ALL ME!

Years, and years of making every message and influence support each other. One false step and the house of cards would have come down. And now, when I am ready to make a final move with this man, they want to examine THE PLAN. SHIT....there is no plan. There is innuendo, there are relationships, there are moments and places and things and opportunities...and this is one of them. I am now ready to have an Iranian born citizen of the United States, who has converted to radical Islam, install software in a nuclear device, have that device shipped by enemies of the United States; Texas, China, and North Korea, to Iran. And then the bomb will be flown over Tel Aviv, Israel and exploded. Texas will take the blame. Israel will cease to exist, and the Arabs will turn on each other as they always have. *I against my brother, my brother and I against the*

100

world. When Israel is out of the way, with all its ties to the US, we will no longer be a target of that part of the world and can deal with the aftermath in a sorrowful way...blaming Texas for their treachery, making them a pariah in the world of international relations. And what if I fail? The bomb goes off in Iran, and we can take the credit with the rest of the Arab world for eliminating the revolutionary threat...putting Texas out of the Oil Business before it ever gets started.

But how could they possibly understand that I am ready, all the players are ready, and the events will allow this feat of hocus pocus to take place. Is it risk free? No. Does it need to be done? Yes. Am I going to do it...? You bet your ass!

So what do I tell them?

Nothing!

Nothing!

That's what I'm going to tell them.

As the door swung open to his bosses office, Brad's heart jumped into his throat like he had just been caught doing the neighbors wife by her Navy Seal husband. It was the director of the CIA standing just inside the door.

"Come in Brad." His boss said coldly. "Let me bring you up to date."

The door shut behind him, and the full situation in Texas was explained to him. Then, he told them everything. It didn't take 30 minutes, it took about 5. There wasn't time for anything else. The President was about to level Texas, unleash the Air Force from San Antonio who would bomb the capital in Austin on the way out of the state. The tanks from Fort Hood would make tracks through Houston on the way to Fort Polk in Louisiana, leveling the entire city including the refineries along the way. Only Brad's half-told tale that had been passed up the line this morning about having a solid contact with someone at the Nuclear Weapons Maintenance facility in Amarillo, and his assurance that he could get his mole to steal a bomb, and that he could give it to the Arabs all the while gaining favor with China...China ... that was the big part of the deal. All we needed to do was to make the delivery with a Texas owned military aircraft so that if anything went wrong...the blame would not fall on Washington...that was the key. If we could get

China to just leave the U.S. alone for a while about all this debt, then the president could have some maneuvering room…this looked like the way out to everybody in the room. So, this long term plan of Brad's had just gone operational. After the 5-minute explanation, the director had called the president on the secure line and asked him for 1 hour to try to reason with the Governor of Texas while solving a security issue with China.

"We believe we can do it sir. We have the right people in place to be able to move a nuclear device safely out of the country for China while we are moving the rest of the devices out of Texas to New Mexico and Oklahoma. All this confusion down there gives us an opportunity that will not ever come again."

The one sided conversation wasn't too difficult to decode.
"Yes sir…we will."
"No, sir…we won't"
"One hour from now…I'll have the agreement of the acting Governor of Texas to move the nukes out or else."
"Thank you, sir." The director of the CIA hung up the phone. He turned and looked squarely into the eyes of CIA Brad and bored a whole clear through his head and into the next room…, he looked hard.

"Brad, get on the phone to your friend. Tell him the situation here…,as much as you need to…,have him get you on the phone with the Governor and then you explain the rain of ruin that is about to happen unless they agree for us to peaceably move the nukes out of the state. Further negotiation will follow, promise them anything you have to, but just get them to agree to give us the plane and stand down until we can work all this out."
"Yes sir."

Shit, I told them everything, Brad thought as he stumbled into the conference room to get to the secure phone. The group followed him out of the office and next door to the conference room.

He hit the speed dial for the white house operator. He wanted the call to come from the white house switchboard so there would be no doubt what his authority level was. The operator immediately grasped the situation, especially after she identified the Director of the CIA as one of the callers, and

102

within seconds he heard his old classmate's puzzled voice on the other end of the phone.

"Chuck, this is Brad, do you recognize my voice."

The long silence on the other end of the phone meant that Chuck was processing all the information that he had about the events of the day that was beginning to make the news, in the context of now being called by his former classmate, Air Force buddy, from a phone located on the white house switchboard.

"What the hell are you guys doing up there, Brad. I've got Texas Rangers and DPS troopers at the front gate and sitting in the front office. The guards didn't have orders to shoot them so they let them in to the administrative areas. The rest of the security detachment has been deployed to the bunkers with orders to fire on anyone or anything that attempts to get to the weapons."

"Hold your questions Chuck, and listen. This has to happen fast or things are going to get out of hand, more than they already are. I want you to get the Governor on the line and tell him who I am. I want you to tell him that I am the only thing standing between him and his state and the strategic missile command of the United States Air Force...,they are resetting the targeting on a few of their toys as we speak. We have about an hour to play 'let's make a deal' and I'm the only one who is going to call with an offer. Is that understood?"

"Got it...,how do I get the Governor on the phone?"

"Operator, what is the number for the emergency coordination center for the State of Texas."

Instantly a voice came on the line and recited the 10- digit number.

"Call him there, Brad, and then conference us up...secure or not...after you convince him he needs to talk to me.

The newly sworn in Governor received the call at his station in the emergency communication center just as he was handed a report from the DPS that they had blocked the front gate of the Federal Reserve building in Dallas. As he listened to the caller, whom he had never met, but who seemed quite sincere, the enormity of what was about to take place was beginning to overwhelm him. So far, a few people had been killed and some property had been damaged. But, an all-out

103

United States vs Texas war…,it was unthinkable. 1.2 million armed and licensed Texas hunters don't equal the US Army, Air Force, Navy, Marines and Coast Guard. The hunters may have better rifles, but thinking of them as a military force for doing anything else but defending their homes was ridiculous, especially without air support. And, duallys don't equal tanks. And, most of the Texas National Guard was deployed overseas.

"Who am I talking to?" said the Governor of Texas after several clicks at the other end of the phone.

"Sir, my name is Brad Elkhart. I am an employee of the CIA. I am sitting in a conference room at the CIA with several people including the Director of the CIA. "

"What do you want?"

"I want to stop a war, sir. And I think you do too."

"War between whom?"

"Governor, …" Brad felt the blood pressure rise and then get dialed down as he carefully spoke the next few words. "…If you and I cannot make an agreement within the next 45 minutes, the President of the United States is going to declare that Texas has attempted to secede from the union illegally, and that you have killed FBI agents who were lawfully attempting to arrest you and the Governor. He will announce that the United States will take the necessary military action to put down this irresponsible, dangerous, unlawful and insidious treachery with overwhelming force, starting with you, sir, since you seem to be the leader. The only thing keeping him from doing just that is the hope that you will let me convince you to let us help you. And we can do that by keeping the President from doing anything beyond what has already been done while we negotiate all this out…,all we ask is one small favor?"

"And what might that be?"

"We would like for you to remove your Rangers and DPS officers from the federal facility at Amarillo, the Pantex Plant where Mr. Hall is calling you from now. We want you to do this to take the threat of losing control of nuclear weapons of the United States off the table. If we can agree to do that, then the President will agree to put all other military action on hold while you and he work out the rest of your differences. Can we agree to do that?"

"We have no interest in becoming a nuclear power. But releasing our current presence at the Pantex site would certainly reduce our ability to negotiate with you or others about what we want."

"Governor, sir, please let me make this plain. If you and I cannot agree for you to allow us to remove the nuclear weapons, all the nuclear weapons from Texas, then there will be no further discussions about terms."

"I see."

"The problem is not so much with you, Governor, but with NATO and the other nuclear powers. If the United States were seen to lose control of any of its nuclear weapons, it would be seen by others as a situation that they would have to react to in some way. How they would react, particularly the Middle Eastern and former soviet bloc is unpredictable at best, and when you are dealing with nuclear weapons, unpredictable is undesirable."

"I see."

"Could we announce at least that you have placed your Rangers and DPS officers at the Pantex plant as a gesture toward recognizing the enormity of the situation that might occur should something unexpected happen to any of the nuclear devices there? We would feel much better if we could announce with you that we are both concerned about this and that we have at least agreed to take this move toward securing the nuclear facility together?"

"I would not be opposed to making an announcement from down here that you had requested our assistance in securing the facility and that we had agreed to help you to assure that there would be no incidents involving the nuclear weapons."

"That is completely acceptable to us."

"So that's it, that's all you want?"

"That is certainly a big first step, but what we want is to actually move the devices out of Texas so that they are no longer a problem for either of us."

"Where would you move them to?"

"We have facilities that can handle them, and I think it would be best if I were just to say that once they are out of Texas that would be the end of any concerns you might have about them. We would take complete responsibility for transporting them and securing them for travel."

"What do you mean securing them for travel?"

"Well, sir, the devices have lots of computers in them and they all need to be put in a secure mode of operation for the devices to be moved. Normally, this is done on a device by device basis as they are moved in and out of the facility, but inerting all of them at once will take a concerted effort on our part."

"How do you propose to move them, by road in trucks."

"No, we believe that the safest way to move them is to use C-130 type cargo aircraft. They can land and take off at the facility directly, which would not expose the devices to any impromptu action that neither of us would want."

"I can see that...,and if we agree for you to remove the nuclear weapons, preventing us from being 'the mouse that roared' so to speak, you would agree to forgive any further action based on the events of today."

"I have the authority to speak for the President on this issue. He specifically instructed me to make this agreement with you and I will do it. There is one other issue, however."

"And what is that?"

"We have calculated how many planes we will need to transport all the devices out by the end of the day tomorrow, and sir, we are one aircraft short. Would it be possible for you to loan us a crew and aircraft from the Texas Air Guard for this mission."

"Give me a minute..."

The Lt. Governor waved to the Texas Guard coordinator who trotted across the room.

"Yes sir."

"Do we have a C-130 available to us tomorrow?"

"We have a few at Bergstrom that are being overhauled and are due to be sent back to Iraq, but we could probably put one in the air tomorrow."

"Ok, get it ready, I'll get the info on where and when after this call."

"Yes sir." as he trotted back to his desk and grabbed the handset, while pressing the button for the Bergstrom alert hanger.

106

"We will probably be able to provide one tomorrow, is that the last of it?"

"Yes, Governor, I believe that is all we will need. I will have our flight planning personnel work through Mr. Hall at Pantex to pass the necessary information to you. I am going to hang up now, call the President, and tell him that we have made an agreement. I am going to tell him that you have joined us in protecting the weapons by providing Rangers and DPS personnel. I am going to tell him that you are going to help us move the devices out of the state by providing an aircraft from the Texas Air Guard. And, I am going to tell him that we have agreed that the actions of today, while tragic, should not get in the way for your working with him to bring about a peaceful solution to this difficult matter."

"So what happens next?"

"Let's move the nukes tomorrow and then work on it a day at a time after that. If we can slow the pace of events a bit, Governor, then there is time for conversation. "

"I agree with that. I will wait for the President to call me and confirm all that we have said."

"I think his actions will speak loud enough, sir. After the nukes are moved, I'm sure there will be an opportunity for you to have a direct conversation with him."

"Ok, then."

"Thank you Governor, thank you very much."

"Yes, ok."

Brad realized that he had been leaning over the speakerphone with his head in his hand for nearly 20 minutes. He stank of sweat. As he reached for the hang up button on the phone, he said into the phone, "Operator, you can tear all this down now, and thanks."

"You're welcome" came the crisp reply.

As he raised his head up from looking down at the table, he saw his boss for the first time since the call had started. His face was made of stone. No sign of approval or scorn, there was no way to tell. But the Director was smiling, from ear to ear.

He had forgotten all about Chuck. Oh, well, he would call him back in a minute when he could get a little privacy.

The Director went to his office and called the president. He told him that the plan to evacuate the weapons from Pantex was being implemented. He listened for a while as the president brought him up to speed on the meeting that he had just left with the joint chiefs and the FBI. "You told the Navy to do what, sir?"

Chapter 15: Haliel L. Jamallie

1:00 PM
Saturday
April 21, 2012

Lawrence Livermore National Laboratory
Livermore, California

      Haliel L. Jamallie was born in Iran in 1962. He attended college in the United States at Cal Tech, majoring in nuclear physics. He graduated cum laude and went to work for Lawrence Livermore National Laboratories after performing his internship at Oak Ridge. He decided early on that he liked bombs better than power plants so he specialized in them. Everything about them. Especially the software that ran them. Each bomb was like a small factory that produced one product...raw energy. But it was a complex process. All the ingredients had to be brought together at just the right time, in just the right order for the outcome to be predictable and significant. Haliel studied hard, held a teaching position at Cal Tech part time and was a Senior Member of the American Nuclear Society. His papers on software strategies for mitigating warhead sensor failures to assure safe weapon control were the foundation of the latest generation of systems now sitting in the silos of NATO. His team members at Livermore viewed him as a solid contributor to their work in the lab and a reliable partner in the management of these awesome weapons that were scattered around the world, ready to tear it apart at the command of the president.

      One of the most difficult problems in dealing with the bombs was that they were becoming so smart that testing them and calibrating them was becoming more difficult. They could be set to go off at any height above the ground, so the bomb had to know how high it was. There were pressure sensors and ground radio altimeters that had to be calibrated. The computer that read the height of the bomb had to read the data from the sensors and make sure each sensor was telling the truth by comparing all of them to see if they agreed. The computer got its instructions from the aircraft throughout the flight to the "final destination" and used those instructions to decide when to detonate the bomb. The internal bomb computer was several computers actually. One is never enough. They all had separate sensors, and separate instructions, and separate power supplies, and then they had to finally vote together for the bomb to go off. That's what happened in the plane, on the way to the "final destination." However, in order to test the software, what had to happen in the lab was much more difficult. Each sensor had to be fooled into thinking it was in the plane, exposed to cold air at high altitude, and that the radio altimeter (when it was clear of the bomb bay doors) was reading approximately the same altitude as the pressure sensors. Then they had to make all of the changes that had been brought about by adding GPS receivers with their capability to provide location, velocity and altitude readings. It was necessary to make that collage of sensors match in the lab to exercise the internal computers one by one, and then to exercise them as a group. Being the good engineers and scientists that they were, the team responsible for the testing of these awesome devices had written a set of programs that allowed them to simulate all the sensors with data injected directly into the bombs control computers. They could take the sensors out of the loop and tell the computers in the bomb that it was falling, set to explode at 5,000 feet above the ground even though the guts of the bomb, but not the nuclear warhead was sitting right in front of them on the test stand. This was handy, because it allowed them to change the software in the bombs very quickly and then test to see that the systems still worked correctly.

Usually this work was done by a contractor like Lockheed or Boeing, but the Livermore team always...ALWAYS...checked the changes in the software to make sure that the bombs would continue to do what they were intended to do. For the last 10 years, Haliel, or a member of his

110

team, had been called to the Pantex facility near Amarillo, Texas to verify that the software changes had been done properly.

When the call came from the Secretary of The Department of Energy, for the entire group to pack up and head to Pantex in order to help the Air Force move the entire complement of bombs out of Texas, it was a complete surprise. The instructions had been to bring the simulation software in the test laptops and prepare to inert the bombs for transport. There would be so many of the bombs that there wouldn't be time the normal amount of testing before a bomb was shipped. This time they just wanted the bombs to be put to sleep to be awakened at the other end of their trip.

"Thank you, Dr. Gibbons" Haliel said as he moved to the front of the room with his laptop. He plugged the projector video cable into the video out connector on the back of the laptop so that the others in the room could see what was on his screen. Nothing happened. Then he remembered that he had to enable the video out on the laptop by pressing Alt F8 on the keyboard. When he did that, the screen on the laptop went blank and the projector shimmered and stabilized with a picture of his computer's screen being shown on the conference room wall. He hit Alt F8 again and the laptop screen came back to life as well, showing the same thing that was being projected. That's what he wanted, so he could see what was on the screen behind him without having to turn around…this was going to be complicated enough for all the team to follow without any presentation hiccups.

Haliel demonstrated the software the team was going to use to make the nuclear devices "inert" while they were being moved. The team was going to introduce a new program into the bomb that would tell it to ignore all of its actual inputs and just sit quietly while it was being moved from place to place. These bombs had the warheads attached. It was far different from working on just the computers on the workbench. The alternative was to turn the electronics off, which had to be done even more carefully because turning them back on again required special handling to insure that at the other end of the trip the newly awakened bomb was once again working the way it was supposed to. If they just told it to sit quietly and ignore inputs, the electronics stayed "hot" and all of the maintenance and security software remained operational so that when it was time to activate the device at the other end, it took only minutes rather than hours to get the thing ready for use. In effect, the team was going to put 256 nuclear bombs to sleep rather than killing them and hoping for resurrection. This procedure had been used before on a case by case basis, but never this many times, with this many computers, and this many operators at the same time. Haliel wanted to make sure there were no mistakes.

Haliel had led the team in creating and testing the software. He had hired the external verification and validation contractor who reviewed the specifications, the software, the test plan and provide personnel to oversee the testing of the software to make sure it did what Haliel and the team wanted it to do. As Haliel went over the software operations that the team would have to perform tomorrow step-by-step, he couldn't help but grin slightly as he completed the presentation. He knew that the software he had in his laptop was just slightly different from the versions of the rest of the team. His version would allow him to set a special state in the simulation software in the bomb, to place it in manual detonate mode with a countdown timer set for 5 seconds activated when the software first started running. He was going to get the chance to put this deadly modification into one bomb going to each of the two new storage locations. Whoever was unlucky enough to plug in a maintenance computer and start the simulation software in one of his "special" bombs would have 5 seconds to hit the stop keys on their laptop or the bomb would detonate. Only he knew the stop key combination, and he wasn't going to tell anyone, and he wouldn't be around. He had already scheduled his vacation to begin immediately upon his return from Texas. He had gotten approval to spend time with his father, in Turkey. Haliel planned to drop off a copy of the software at his apartment in Istanbul and then fly on to Iran as he had been instructed in the last message handed to him at the mosque. He would visit with his father when this was all over.

"So, gentlemen, that's how the software is going to operate. Each of you will now take your laptops and install this new maintenance software version 2.1.1 in them from the DVD that is before you, and go to the lab to test it. Our test supervisor will be Mr. Douglas from ACRE, and each of you must complete the inerting process test and get it signed off by him before we lock up everything for the trip tonight. Once you complete the test, leave your laptop on the workbench until I come by and place it in the shipping box. The box will be sealed and placed aboard the C-130 that is going to collect us in the morning. We will not all travel on the same aircraft for obvious reasons. You will sleep here on the base and lab uniforms will be provided for you in the morning. Take nothing with you, just dress in the lab dungarees. Everything we need will be aboard the plane or at the work site. This way we don't have to do the usual searches, we can just get on the plane and go. Time is short for this one. We should be home by tomorrow night. The weapons will become the property of the Albuquerque and Ft Bliss personnel when they are unloaded from the planes. They will be responsible for setting up the weapons again once we have delivered them. "Are there any questions?"

There were none. Each team member took the DVD from the package in front of them and loaded the software in his computer. One by one, they filed out of the room headed for the lab. Haliel didn't have to go. His work laptop was already in the box ready to ship. He had tested the software several times, both versions, before Mr. Douglas had arrived on site, and then once again after the formal testing session was set up. He knew that with the click of a single key, he could insert either the inerting software that everyone else was going to be using, or the rigged version he had set to automatically detonate the weapon. Not even a trained observer would be able to tell the difference. All the screens looked the same, with one exception. In the rigged version, the next time someone plugged a maintenance laptop into the bomb he had rigged to detonate: the screen would turn red and begin a 5-second count down. He didn't have to do that. He just wanted to let them know that he had beaten them. He knew they would know by the size of the smoking hole he left in the new storage areas, both of them. He could hardly keep his mind on the packing he was so excited. There was no chance of getting any sleep. Tomorrow was going to be good, but not as good as three days after that.

Chapter 16: Just Off Red Fish Island

3:00 PM
Saturday
April 21, 2012

Channel Traffic Management Center

Roy Dellato, the harbormaster for the port of Galveston had a lot on his mind. Ever since the Governor's office had called and said that they wanted to fire the guns on the *Battleship Texas*, he had been up to his neck in problems. The date had been set and all the surrounding facilities on the Houston Ship Channel had been notified. Refineries, towing companies, cruise lines, and private boaters had to be aware of the noise levels they might experience from the big event. Not to mention that there would be 4 good size explosions on the flats near Red Fish Island as part of the celebration.

When they told him they wanted to use live rounds and have them land out in the flats just off the Houston Yacht Club, things had gotten completely out of hand. Roy had a special problem. Since Galveston sat on the Gulf of Mexico, at the entrance to the Houston Ship Channel, he had to manage all the ship traffic entering and leaving the area. Galveston was one of the busiest ports on the Gulf of Mexico, and the Houston Ship Channel gave access to refineries up and down its length, amounting to nearly 1/5th of the capacity in the United States. It is a critical and busy waterway.

After getting over the shock of all there was to do to get ready for the big day, he had gotten into the spirit of the thing after the Governor had actually called him personally to apologize for all the problems and explain why the firing of the big guns on the ship was important symbolically, particularly during the San Jacinto day celebration. The governor was going to make a speech at Washington-On-The-Brazos in the morning, fly to the monument for a luncheon with the donors who were footing the bill for the *Texas* restoration at noon, and then go to the yacht club to watch the show that was scheduled for about 3:00.

"Not a problem, Governor." Roy had told Bill Clayton. "We will have to stop traffic on the Channel for about an hour for the event, but there shouldn't be any adverse effect in the long term if we get the word out beforehand. All the shippers and tug companies will just plan around it and should be able to make up the traffic by sometime the next day."

When he hung up the speakerphone from that conversation, he turned to his chief pilot in charge of the team of pilots who shepherded the big ships into the port and up and down the ship channel, smiled, and said; "Right, Jeff?"

Jeff Spizer, Chief Houston Ship Canal Pilot, was a Galveston native who had retired from the Navy in 1991. His late teen-age years in the Navy were spent steering ships as helmsman on the bridge of some of the largest vessels in the world. He progressed from helmsman to Coxswain finally retiring as Chief Petty Officer when they decommissioned the ship he loved most, the battleship *USS New Jersey*. He had been called to a special re-commissioning billet on the "Big J" during the Viet Nam war when the higher ups decided that her 16-inch guns were the perfect tool for dismantling tunnels and gun emplacements along the Demilitarized Zone between North and South Vietnam. Her big guns could reach 25 miles across the zone and leave holes in the earth the size of basketball stadiums. It was his first chance to handle a ship of that size and he had never forgotten it. When she was decommissioned in 1991, he figured it was time he did the same.

After a few months, make that weeks, at home, he had done all the honey dos that his lovely but middle-aged red haired wife could think up. He had kissed all the 7 grandkids and figured out that his Navy retirement pay would not support him in the style that he would like to become accustomed. His favorite haunt in Galveston, had been the same type place he frequented his entire career, near the docks, filled with nautical people and selling good cold Shiner Bock in dark long neck bottles. The smell of the booths was a mix of spoiled sandwich meat, beer and rich leather.

One evening he met another "senior citizen" with a short haircut who turned out to be the Galveston Harbor Master, who also happened to be another retired Chief to boot. As the evening wore on, and stories passed between the bottles on the table, it became clear to Jeff that what he missed was pushing large ships around and what he didn't miss was being gone all the time. Roy Dellato, the harbor master offered Jeff the perfect solution when he said, "Why don't you get your ticket as a harbor pilot for Galveston and the Houston Ship Channel? You could con the largest ships in the world, the weather is usually nice and you get home the same day. I can set you up. With your experience, we would be lucky to have you around. Besides, when the Coast Guard and Navy guys come in and out of here, they like to know who they are dealing with and they would feel pretty good about seeing you come aboard. Jeff thought about that offer for about 10 seconds, decided right there and then to become a pilot, and had been doing it for nearly 20 years now.

That 20 years had flown by in a pretty routine manner with everyday emergencies, staffing problems, safety issues, schedule conflicts, homeland security oversight and now this, stopping all traffic on the Channel while a battleship fired live rounds just for display purposes. Only politicians could think that kind of crap up, he thought and wisely kept to himself, since his boss seemed fairly enthused with the idea.

The traffic had been cleared. The shutdown had been scheduled. The pilot boats were spread out up and down the 50-mile channel to make sure that no ships or boaters intruded on the scene, and then word had come of the shooting at Washington-On-The-Brazos.

It didn't take long for Roy and Jeff to figure out that their world was about to get much more chaotic when they scanned the automated ship tracking system they had recently installed in the masters dispatch center. The center was responsible for communicating with all the ships in and around the channel and approaching the channel from the Gulf. The addition of equipment that had been on aircraft for years, let the center have a good picture of each ship, its name, its location, based on GPS information, and its heading and speed. This was invaluable information and they had come to depend on it to keep the ever increasing amount of traffic in the area flowing. The system had originally operated by VHF radio that only let them have a view of the ships that were within radio range of the tower at Galveston. The recent upgrade to include data from the satellite-based system had given them a view of the entire world, but especially the Gulf of Mexico near their port. It was that satellite view that told them that there was big trouble afoot. Every Navy ship in the area had turned toward the mouth of the Channel at Galveston or toward the facilities at Beaumont, about 70 miles to the east along the coast. The ship nearest the ship channel was steaming at what appeared to be a very high speed, and then suddenly it had disappeared from the automatic tracking system database.

"She is headed for us, Jeff."

"Yep, and damned fast too."

"We need to know where she is. I know they can come barging in here any time they want, but we have lots of ships stacked up in the harbors and in the channel because of the thing today."

"I understand, but it doesn't look like they are interested in playing nice with anybody at this point. My guess is they have been ordered to take up station somewhere up here and 'control things'."

"Yes, and with their AIS off, we don't know what they are going to do. Would it be possible for you to get on board under these circumstances?"

"It's been a while since I was in, but the Captain is under orders and will carry those orders out if he has to level the whole channel to do it. The only way we can get in the game here is if we can give him some tool that he doesn't have, and that would be your knowledge of the channel."

"Right, but they have charts and sat updates and all that stuff. They can see all the same AIS stuff we have here and more from their fire control and net systems."

"Right."

Both men paused and mulled the situation over. Finally, Jeff turned to Roy and said, "We could good cop, bad cop 'em."

"How would that work?"

"You could move some shipping in to block the channel and I could fuss about it over the radio. If we work it right, it will look like you are attempting to shut them out of the channel and I have the loyalty of the tugs to keep it clear."

"Wouldn't he just blow the barges out of the way?"

"He might, but he couldn't depend on not leaving some rubble in the channel that might disable his ship. I don't think he would do that unless he had to. He might put some marines over the side and just move the blockage at gunpoint. It all depends on what his orders are."

"I see."

"In any case, if we give him an easy, safe, way out, he might take it. That's what I'm hoping anyway."

"Might work."

Jeff pointed to the screen where the symbol for the tug *Jonsey* sat waiting for the events of the day to clear so she could take her barge tow up from Galveston to the turning basin near Houston that evening.

"If Curley is on the *Jonsey*, he would play."

"Don't use the radio."

"Got him on speed dial." smiled Jeff. Curley had saved his bacon several times by pulling offending disabled ships and broken loose barges out of the channel in a hurry when Jeff had needed help, and Jeff had paid him back by pointing big tows his way.

On the phone, Jeff explained the deal to Curley, who immediately got ready to move his tow.

"All set. Let me get to a pilot boat so I can get out to the entrance before they get here and we will see how this plays out."

"Ok. Give me a yell when you spot them coming in, and I'll move Curley to block the channel, and you can fuss about it. Curley will listen to you but will not move the tow back until you are on the ship, right."

"Sounds like a plan."

119

Jeff hustled out the dispatch center door to the dock down the street where he signaled the pilot boat skipper, Bobby McFarland, to get ready to go with the traditional wind 'er up motion.

"Where are we headed, Jeff?"

"Down the channel and out, we are trying to head off a Navy ship of some sort that has gone dark on the AIS. They were coming pretty fast, but we should be able to see them before too long. When they went dark they were about 100 miles out, and they were at 35 knots then. I bet they are well above that now and so we should see them in less than two hours, and it will take us about an hour to get out to the mouth where we can spot 'em."

"Got it." Bobby shoved the throttles forward to creep away from the dock, looked around for small boats or light craft moored near their facility, and shoved the throttles on the twin Mercs nearly all the way forward. One thing about a pilot boat, they have to be able to move, because the customer is not usually very happy to wait. When they got out into the channel headed for the Gulf, Bobby turned to Jeff. "Heard any more about the Governor or what happened up there?."

"No, just that he is dead, and that a bunch of FBI guys went with him."

"That's some bad shit!"

"Yep."

"Is this part of this deal?"

"Probably, don't know yet. I have to get aboard and try to find out what I can."

"Are we still going to shoot the shots at 3:00?"

"I don't know. It doesn't look like it. This has turned into a whole new ball game. Are you still in touch with the *Texas* for coordination this afternoon?"

"Yes, I call them every once in a while to see if they have heard anything, but they are just standing around waiting to find out what is going to happen."

"That's ok. We don't need to do anything until I find out what's up with these guys anyway. Check in with them and … no wait … everything we say on the channel will be monitored on the incoming ships, so we can't discuss openly what we are

120

doing. I'm sure they will have been briefed on the little display that we were planning down here, but they may not know where or when it was to take place, so let's not discuss that on the air."

"Ok."

"When I get on board…that's thinking positively, and if we need to do the demo shots, I'll let you know by saying 'check the horizon for smoke.'"

"Got it."

"Ok."

After about an hour of traveling toward the Gulf and another half hour bobbing up and down waiting for a sight of the oncoming Navy ship, Jeff spotted the tops of her mast on the horizon.

Jeff picked up the radio. "Galveston Harbor and Houston Ship Channel, this is the pilot boat Percy, we need the channel clear for incoming military traffic."

Roy himself was on the Galveston radio channel and could be clearly heard. "*Jonsey, Jonsey*, move your tow across the mouth of the channel and hold your position there."

Curley responded from the tug *Jonsey*, "Ok, Roy, how long do I need to stay here?"

"'till I tell you to move."

"Ok."

"*Jonsey*, this is Chief Pilot Spizer, you will keep that channel clear or I will personally come up there and strip you of your paper."

"Mr. Spizer, I have been ordered by the Harbormaster to take up this position, and I have to comply."

"*Jonsey*, you are bound to comply with the instructions of a pilot when you are in the channel, not recommendations from a harbormaster when you are not in the harbor."

"I don't know, Mr. Spizer. Let me call my office and get this straightened out."

Jeff thought that had gone about right. Curley had referred to the harbor master as Roy, and him as Mr. Spizer. Curley called him Jeff all the time, but this change conveyed a certain amount of respect for authority that Jeff was going to need if he was to work his way aboard the Navy destroyer that was steaming down on him in the tiny pilot boat. Now he turned his attention to the incoming problem.

"Navy ship approaching Galveston, this is the chief pilot for Galveston and the Houston Ship Channel. I am stationed at the entrance to assist you in navigating these waters."

Nothing…

Nothing…

Nothing…, then.

"Thank you chief pilot, but we are well equipped to navigate ourselves." came the voice that was obviously not the talker, but one of the officers on the bridge. At least he had gotten their attention. He hoped that Curley was listening.

"Mr. Spizer, this is the *Jonsey*. Our office says that we are to follow your instructions, but you will have to tell us where to go and clear berthing for us, since the Harbormaster has ordered us out of Galveston."

Jeff liked it, this might work out after all.

"Hold your position and I'll come to you as quickly as I can." Jeff was sure that he could be seen from the bridge of the destroyer, and his AIS was on, so they would have no doubt about which boat he was. He turned to Bobby.

"Head for the *Jonsey*, one engine about half throttle."

"Right."

The pilot boat didn't even plane off as it moved slowly back toward Galveston. The destroyer, on the other hand, had come up over the horizon and was now abeam of the pilot boat and still making what looked to be about 30 knots. That was good, Jeff thought. At that speed, they would reach the mouth of the channel and just have to sit there until he arrived. It didn't look like they were in the mood to just sit and wait for him to show up, so maybe being in a hurry, he would choose to pick Jeff up. The captain was going to complete his mission, and it looked like he might need a little local help to do it. Jeff's intervention on his behalf had been noted, and so when the radio crackled aboard the Percy again, Jeff knew he was in.

"Percy, this is the destroyer *USS Ramser* close aboard your port side. Can you put a pilot aboard?"

"I will come aboard personally." Jeff replied, knowing that they had already looked him up on the internet, verified his credentials and looked over his service record.

"We will slow and lower a ladder over our starboard side 'amidships. Please come aboard as quickly as possible."

"Can do." Jeff said; imitating the Naval Academy jargon he had heard on so many ships that passed for insider slang among Annapolis graduates.

The rope ladder dropped from the side of the ship as Bobby maneuvered the pilot boat next to it. There was very little swell, so grabbing the ladder wasn't much trouble for someone who was experienced as Jeff. He was getting older, so the trip to the deck took a little longer than he would have liked, but not embarrassingly so. He would probably be faster than the out of shape techie that was sure to be stationed below fixing the sonar and radar equipment.

Jeff could feel the destroyer accelerate as he came through the rail and was led to the bridge by what he noticed was a chief and an armed escort. The ship looked ready for anything. Nice ship.

Jeff was brought to the Captain who looked him up and down like a new commanding officer doing his first inspection of a ship. He knew the drill. Speak when spoken to, so, Jeff waited. He did not extend his hand in greeting, and neither did the captain. This was going to be one of those "professional" relationships of an officer with someone he needed to help him get his job done who happened to be a former enlisted person, albeit a former chief.

"Pilot, what is the situation up there?"

"Well, sir, the Harbormaster has ordered a tug with a large tow to block your access to the channel."

"Can you get the tug to move his tow and clear the channel for me to proceed?"

"I don't know yet, sir." Time to trade a little information. So far it was all going one way. "How far up the channel do you need to go?"

"Let's just say I want to be able to maneuver over its entire length."

"That would be difficult, sir."

123

"And why is that?"

"Well sir, there was a special demonstration scheduled for today that caused us to shut down the channel for a while. There are ships anchored at all the mooring births along the channel, and some of them are even anchored in the channel making ready to proceed when the ceremony is over."

"How far up the channel can I precede without interference from the ships that are anchored in the channel?"

Jeff knew the answer. He knew the captain knew the answer. What he didn't know what how far the captain wanted to go up the channel.

"If we can get the mouth cleared, I would feel confident taking you abeam of Kehma, about half way up the channel."

"Is that just North of Red Fish Island were the demonstration was to be held?

"As a matter of fact, it is, sir."

"Then that is where I want to go."

"Well, let's see if we can't get the channel cleared and get you there."

Now that Jeff knew that the destroyer was going to sit on the demonstration site, obviously daring anyone to "shoot the big ones" he had a pretty good idea what should come next. He took the walky talky from its holster on his belt and made the radio call.

"Percy, this is pilot Spizer, please check the horizon for smoke so that we can be sure there is no traffic moving as we proceed."

"Will do." Bobby responded as he flipped open his cell phone and called the number he had been given for the Bridge of the Battleship *Texas*.

Destroyer USS Ramser

The cold gray bow of the Arley Burk class Aegis equipped destroyer *USS Ramser*, sliced through the water of the Gulf of Mexico and entered Galveston Bay headed for a place where it would be able to fire on half the oil refinery capacity in Texas, control its largest port and stop the transit of all of the shipping up and down the Houston ship channel. At 11:00 that morning the ship had steamed at a classified speed, well above the published 35 knot capability you might read about in the magazines, in order to be here, slowing only momentarily to pick up the Galveston Harbor pilot who helped clear away the obstacle placed in their way by the Galveston harbormaster. The pilot knew the waters of the ship channel like the back of his GPS connected laptop. Now, in the warming sun of a mid April Texas spring, the ship brought a full complement of death dealing equipment past the Galveston Bay Lighted Whistle Buoy GB as it slowed to a speed more appropriate for the narrow channel it was charging up.

"Just off Red Fish Island should be an optimal spot sir. That puts all of the refineries from Galveston to the southwest part of Houston within range of the 5-inch gun, sir. Texas City, Bay City, all the complexes and the port of Galveston as well." Lt JG Elvin Johnson pointed to the spot on the chart where he hoped the captain of the *USS Ramser*, an Arley Burk class Aegis Destroyer would choose to park for the night.

"How about maneuvering room in there, EJ? It looks tight."

"Yes, sir, the Houston Ship Channel carries a lot of deep water traffic, but there are no real good places to maneuver short of the turning basin up near Houston. The channel would be large enough for us to pivot with the help of a tug, but we aren't likely to find a friendly one of those around."

"Very well, set up the approach courses and let's get in there. I want to be in there at anchor by 15:00 local, so we can shut this thing down before the close of business today. Shut-'er down by sundown...I like that..."

"Yes, sir. By sundown sir." and EJ smiling at the bit of cowboy movie humor of the captain. He went back to the computer and began working out the approach course from the Gulf of Mexico, through the Galveston Bay entrance up to Red Fish Island even though he knew the pilot knew those courses by heart. The junior officers of the watch looked over his shoulder like buzzards ready to snack at the first sign of weakness. Ensigns Chance Goodenough and Constance Keith usually ran the courses, but this would be the first time the ship had been in such close quarters since it launched from the Bath Iron Works and traveled down the St. Lawrence River. That passage was tighter than this one and the bottom had been rock; this would be muddy bottom and lots of room by comparison. The only real difference that mattered in this case was not knowing how friendly the folks on the water with them would be. Connie would man the starboard range finder while Chánce would handle port. As they slipped past navigation buoys and landmarks that EJ called out, they would take azimuth readings. The depth sounder would provide a constant stream of data about the depth of the water under various parts of the ship. All this information was compiled into a situational awareness display alongside the radarscope. Pretty simple really, as long as everything went according to plan and the plan didn't have any fatal flaws.

EJ looked and pointed up to Chance and Connie who had designated to three locations on the chart, indicating silently that those were the places where the outside range finders would be used. The ensigns nodded and moved to their stations for the entrance passage.

"Recommend all engines ahead slow, course three one one degrees, sir," said Jeffrey Spizer, the Galveston Pilot who had boarded the destroyer to help her through the channel.

The captain glanced over his left shoulder. EJ nodded.

"Very well, ahead slow, course three one one."

"All ahead slow, course three one one, aye sir," answered the helmsman as he moved the wheel slightly to the right and moved the engine telegraph to ahead slow. The destroyer almost immediately slowed from its thirty knots to a speed more appropriate for tight quarters.

GB entrance channel light Buoy 7 slid by to port, then GP 12 to starboard as the ship headed west into the channel, passing Pelican Island and the Sea Wolf Park at the mouth of the Port of Galveston. Leaving them to her port side, she slid up the channel coming to a northerly course past Texas City where the string of refineries started.

She moved up the channel with the ease of an athlete moving lightly along a path where ditch diggers usually slogged. The 5" gun on her foredeck trained forward almost as if saluting the passing buoys, ships and the traffic on the bridge she was

126

passing under. Able to throw a 70-pound shell nearly 14 miles, the ship could easily sit in the middle of Galveston Bay and reach the entire refinery district and the Port of Galveston itself. It would control the Houston Ship Channel, which is exactly what the president had told the captain he wanted. Not only did the president want to control the channel and all its oil refinery rich resources, he wanted to be seen to be in control it. Having his ship stand offshore in the middle of the Gulf, lobbing in cruise missiles would not make the point he wanted to make. Blocking the channel and spraying the refinery district with fire from the auto loading 5- incher would. Not to mention shutting down the little "my gun is bigger than your gun" demonstration the Texans had cooked up in protest over the new treaty. This was to be a pushing and shoving match over the 2nd amendment, and he wanted to win. The president was very sensitive to that one. He told the captain that he was confident that the presence of the *Ramser* would put a stop to the demonstration the Texans were planning. He neglected to brief the captain on one small detail.

The noise, the smoke, the sight of the ship blocking the passage of the other ships, that's what he wanted. In fact, with the ship standing off Kemah, she would be visible from the largest recreational center in the South Texas Area. Being able to station this ship here, only hours after the despicable actions of those thoughtless and witless Texans was the best part of it all. Right in their face: Close enough to see the Johnson Space Center from the ship's bridge, that is what he had personally told the Captain of the *USS Ramser* to do… "get in their face".

She slid quietly to a stop just North of Red Fish island before she reached the narrowest part of the channel near the salt mines. Dropping anchor here, she could swing without concern for running aground, but just barely. Her 28-foot draft made the channel rather tight, no matter how she went at it.

As the weather began to clear, she trained her 5" gun to 276 degrees, elevated it for a shot of about 9 miles and fired her "hello" over Kemah into the shallow water of Nassau bay. The shell rose to its maximum height and then plummeted into the shallow water of the bay, entering the water almost vertically, impacting the bottom of the bay almost immediately after breaking the surface of the shallow water and exploding with enough force to be heard throughout the entire South Houston region. She had not intended to hit anyone or anything of value, and in that she had succeeded.

San Jacinto Monument

At the San Jacinto monument complex, BJ and Ernie left their shop and got into the truck that they had been using to move their boxes of shells and powder for the past few weeks. They headed for the park to make sure that all the gates were closed and any visitors who might have gotten in earlier were escorted out. As they rounded the corner headed to the parking lot at the entrance to the Battleship *Texas* exhibit, they noticed that tug *Mr. David* had pulled stern of the big ship to port, pointing her guns just to the right of the San Jacinto Monument, just about 11 degrees to the right they would later be told. She was free from her stern starboard side mooring piling and her direction was now being controlled by the tug. The forward mooring was still in place but had been slackened sufficiently to let the great ship pivot around it as needed to point her guns where she wanted to, and right now, she wanted them trained at Red Fish Island.

She was slightly down by the stern now, having been flooded down some in the rear compartments to elevate the guns for added range. The spire of the monument was the same shape as the Washington monument in D.C., but like everything in Texas, it was just a little taller. As they parked the truck, and ran up the gangplank, Greg Brothers waved his handy walky-talky at them from the flying bridge, indicating that they should hurry every chance they got. BJ went first, and ducked into the hatch just below where Greg was standing. Once they got inside, they scrambled up to the bridge, arriving just as the *Texas* answered the 5" shell fired at Kemah from the *Ramser* with a pair of 14" shells the likes of which had devastated the bunkers on the hilltops overlooking Normandy on D.Day. It seemed that the President wasn't the only one who would be sending messages with guns today. This one said roughly … "bring your lunch…!"

The sound of the 14-inch guns set off car alarms in parking lots several miles from the San Jacinto monument.

Several of the systems in the refineries across the channel from where the Texas was parked shut down because the blast front shook process control sensors and sent confused signals to the control computers, causing them to basically throw up their little electronic hands and say "I give." The sound in the number 1 turret was a muffled roar. Actually, it was probably the quietest place on the ship, or in S. Houston for that matter. Tons of steel surrounded the sweating men who had just fired what they thought was a celebration salute. As the deck stopped ringing, they left the turret and moved to the second forward-facing turret. The order of the day was to fire four rounds, two from turret one, and two from turret two. The first salute had gone off without a hitch, as far as they knew. Actually, the pressure waves that traveled through the ship and met with the incompressible water at the stern of the ship had shredded the hull like stepping on a dried wasp's nest. Water was beginning to flow into the after bilge spaces at an accelerating rate. Since the ship had been lowered by the stern by flooding the aft torpedo panels and some of the stern compartments, there was already a little water on the deck toward the aft of the ship. It would be minutes before any increase in the tilt angle was noticeable, so the guns of turret number 2, elevated as they were, remained pointed at the spot just North of Red Fish Island where the Destroyer *USS Ramser* sat, contemplating her next move.

Jeff Spizer was standing on the bridge of the *Ramser*, reminiscing of his days aboard the *New Jersey* when at approximately 3:00 pm local time, the sound of the *Ramser's* phalanx anti-aircraft system spraying bullets to the north and the launching of radar jamming foil canisters from the foredeck of the *Ramser* stunned him back into the present. The 14-inch shells from the *Texas* shrieked toward them. He had heard hundreds of 16-inch rounds leave the *New Jersey* when he was in her, and gone ashore with a spotter crew only once to observe shot fall when some incoming 16-inch shells had passed overhead near their position overlooking the DMZ. He recognized the sound immediately. He suddenly realized that he was sweating profusely, the stinky sulfur filled sweat of fear and heightened awareness, not the nice spring induced sweat of the active 62-year-old just standing on the bridge of the *USS Ramser*.

The low-pitched scream of the two shells approaching culminated in two rather large explosions and huge water spouts about 200 yards off to the starboard and slightly forward of the destroyer.

"What the hell was that?" the captain yelled.

"CIC to bridge, we fired at it with Phalanx and launched radar countermeasures, sir, but it had no effect. We picked it up on radar, but didn't have time to launch anything else."

Jeff recovered himself enough to move to the side of the captain, which took some doing because the captain was now a moving target. "Those were shells, Captain. 14-inch ones." he whispered in the captain's ear. The captain stopped dead in his tracks and turned to a nose-to-nose stance with Jeff. "How in the hell do you know how big those shells were, by just the sound of them?" he hissed.

Jeff, being many years a chief, enjoyed mentally putting that hat back on as he replied, "Well sir, they sounded a little smaller than those we used to fire off the *New Jersey*, and ... they could come from only one ship capable of throwing anything that size, and it has 14-inch guns, 10 of them."

"And what source might that be...?" the captain screeched between clinched teeth, wagging his head back and forth like a signal flag as he focused all his fear and anger on this obstinate Texan standing before him.

"The battleship *Texas*, Captain."

The Captain's face went from fury to puzzlement to the pale white of comprehension in just a few short seconds. He had heard about the demonstration celebrating San Jacinto Day, but he had not been fully briefed on what activities might take place at such a demonstration. Word of the firing of 14" naval guns had not "filtered down" all the way to him, but he was a quick study.

"How did a commissioned battleship slip up here without our knowing it?"

"I couldn't tell you that, sir. All I can tell you is that you have been effectively bracketed by rounds from a dreadnaught class battleship, and I would suggest that since you have no defense for 14 inch naval guns, you move down the channel until you are out of range."

"Where the hell is this battleship anyway, parked up on I 45 somewhere…?"

"It is moored at the San Jacinto monument, which commemorates the final battle in the war between Texas and Mexico, when Texas won her independence on the 21st of April, 1836. Oh, I believe that is today's date too, sir. I guess they are just throwing a little San Jacinto day party up there to celebrate. Still, just for fun, sir, I recommend that you move south a few miles…"

"Get the fuck off my ship!" the captain exploded. "Marine, escort this man to the rail and see that he leaves the ship immediately."

Jeff grinned slightly as he hustled out the port side flying bridge access hatch.

"Bobby," Jeff said, speaking into the pilot's handy walky-talky, "bring the pilot boat up alongside port, I've been tossed…!"

"On the way." replied Bobby, who had already shoved the throttles forward when the fireworks started. Bobby had given the word that the range was clear to start this whole process. He had feared for his friend Jeff, but knew that hitting the destroyer at 19 miles would be a low probability event. He had assumed that his little pilot boat could just as easily have been hit, so he had hung back a mile or so. After the first shells exploded in the water, he shoved the throttles all the way forward on the twin Merc 300s and the light aluminum boat that was about 3 times the size of a good bass pro shop special leapt toward the ladder hanging from the side of the destroyer. As he pulled alongside, he could see the bow thruster of the destroyer throwing ripples as it tried to pivot the ship around in the narrow channel. He sent the boat banging into the side of the destroyer just under the ladder about the time the Jeff was half way down. Jeff let his feet fall free of the ladder and descended the remaining 20 feet like a tree climber doing a controlled fall at a woodsman's competition.

He touched a few of the rungs on the way down with his hands as they passed with ever increasing speed until he landed in a heap on the foredeck of the Percy. Bobby eased the throttles forward and gained a little distance from the huge ship hanging

131

over him before slamming the throttles forward again and spinning the wheel to the left, taking them out of the channel and onto the flat. By then the boat was traveling about 40 knots and was virtually flying over the six inches of water it needed to stay afloat. Once Bobby finished his quick turn back to the South headed for Galveston, the deck became stable enough for Jeff to pick himself up. Slowly at first, he moved arms, legs, back and head to make sure they were still attached. Rolling to his knees and grasping the safety rail, rolled to his feet and carefully made his way back to nearly vertical and then along the rail to the pilot house.

"Kicked you off eh?" yelled Bobby over the gnarling scream of the dual 300 horsepower outboards trying to launch his boat skyward.

"Yea, he was pretty pissed. Guess he didn't expect to have to do anything but sit there and look impressive and we would all shit in our pants and go home."

The radio on the console broke into the conversation..."*Texas* Ready"

Bobby grabbed the mike..."First shot good, fire again when ready, all clear."

He hung the microphone back in the hook under the radio and smiled at Jeff.

"We got their attention last time; this one should make them really concerned that it might go on all day..."

"No, I think he got the point...they were trying to turn around and leave as I left. He wasn't happy about it, but short of launching missiles, he doesn't have anything that can touch the *Texas*."

Once again, the sound of a 14" shell traveling nearby attracted their attention. Bobby and Jeff both looked out of the open back of the shelter of the wheelhouse to watch for the large water spout of another near miss that they expected to appear somewhere near the destroyer. What they saw wasn't a waterspout. It was a direct hit on the bridge of the destroyer...the explosion started at about the bottom of the nicely tilted stealth aluminum superstructure of the destroyer, launching the mast upward like a rocket. The bottom of the superstructure expanded to reveal the fireball erupting from inside, shedding the phased array radar like shingles off a mobile home in a tornado.

"Good God, we hit her…"

"Cease fire, cease fire…the last shot hit the target, I say again it hit the target and she has blown up." Bobby yelled into the microphone he had ripped from its holder.

Greg Brothers, aboard the *Texas* looked in stunned disbelief at the walky-talky in his hand…"Hit what?" He yelled.

"The damned destroyer that was parked just North of Red Fish Island"

"You mean we actually hit it?."

"Right through the clear window, Greg. She went up on the spot."

There was a long pause as the enormity of what had just happened dawned on all those involved.

"Right, don't shoot any more until we can work this out down here."

The gun captain in turret 2 of the *Texas* pulled his radio to his ear to hear the conversation that was going on. He could only hear one side of it because he was near the water and inside a metal room, but he thought he heard Greg's voice.

"Ready to fire port side gun…in 3, 2, …" he announced.

"Cease Fire…Cease Fire…"Greg screamed into his radio.

"Cease Fire." The gun captain held his hand out toward the man holding the lanyard. The gunner was looking at him, and didn't need to hear what he was yelling…the gun captain's eyes were as large as stop signs, and that was all he needed to know…he relaxed his grip on the lanyard and waited. He was disappointed that he had not been able to fire what was probably going to be the last big shot fired by the *Texas*.

Bobby looked at Jeff as he pulled the throttles back and began to turn the pilot boat back toward the now blazing remnants of the destroyer. He grabbed the radio and began transmitting the most dreaded words any mariner can hear or say…"may-day, may-day, may-day…this is the pilot boat Percy, the Destroyer Ramser has blown up in the Houston ship channel just off Red Fish Island. All ships in the area are needed for search and rescue for her crew…I repeat…"

And so ended the San Jacinto Day celebration of 2012.

133

Chapter 17: I Just Wana Go Home

10:45 PM
April 21, 2012

Beijing China

The ride back in from the airport to the interior ministry in Beijing was about the same as it had been the first time he had made it, Peter Canton thought to himself. He had been here nearly forty five times now, and this is more like the first trip than the 45th. He don't know for sure where he was going. He wasn't sure what he was going to do when he got there, and what he really want to do was just to go home. Go home. Home. Those words had much more meaning to him now that someone had told me that he couldn't go there. When the flight was canceled, he didn't worry too much. When they pulled him out of the lounge and turned him over to the US embassy personnel, he didn't think there would be a problem. But now, in the Limo, with no passport, no help from the embassy, and no way to get home, now he was worried.

The conversation with the embassy counselor was short and sweet. "Where are you headed?"

"Home, to Houston."

"Individuals traveling on US passports are not allowed to travel to Texas destinations." He said, as he looked Peter in the eye.

"I just want to go home." he repeated.

After a long pause, he asked "Do you want to go home to Texas, or do you want to remain a citizen of the United States?"

"Can't I do both?"

"No, you have to choose."

"This is ridiculous, all I want to do is to go home. Don't I have the right to expect you to help me do that?"

"No" he answered, "Not since the state of Texas has attempted to become a separate nation, You are either a citizen of the United States, or of Texas, but not both. If you choose to return to the United States, you will be met at the airport for further processing. If you choose to return to Texas, you will be deemed to be a criminal under US law, but having no authority to enforce that law here, all I can do is to take your passport and inform you that the United States of America does not consider you to be one of its citizens any longer, so what will it be?"

"I just want to go home, can't you let me do that without making a federal case out of it?"

"No, choose now."

Well, he was such a jerk, and Peter was so far from everything he cared about that he figured that being on his own here was better that being "processed at the airport" when he got back to the US.

So, here he sat in the limo, headed for the interior ministry with the magnitude of what he had just done sinking slowly into his tired brain. It was nearly 11PM, but Mr. Li might still be in his office. Peter didn't know what Mr. Li's reaction to Peter's situation would be. This could put all our previous business in jeopardy he thought. The Chinese don't like surprises. Peter had been negotiating contracts with Mr. Li and his office for nearly 8 years now. Oil and gas drilling rights, service contracts, transportation contracts, exploration contracts, terminal construction contracts, and he still couldn't tell how they would react to the next word that he spoke. They were a mystery to Peter. He did know however, that Mr. Li needed to hear about Peter's troubles with the embassy from Peter himself before the embassy people had a chance to call and mess things up any more than they already were.

Peter flipped open his cell phone and got another shock. The display was blank. No display at all. He checked the battery, pulled it out and put it back in. The phone came to life, started to load its software and then went blank again. It was pretty clear what was happening. The long arm of Uncle Sam was reaching out and touching him. Nothing to do but wait till he got to the Ministry and call Mr. Li direct.

The car pulled into the circle drive in front of the building used by the interior ministry. Peter slid out of the back seat through the open door before his driver could come open it for him. He told the driver to wait, as all his luggage was in the trunk and right now, he didn't know where he was going to sleep. He hoped that the next phone call might solve that problem. He entered the glass doors into the foyer of a building that could have been anywhere in the world. It was a modern glass steel concrete affair like you would find in any major city in the world. The reception desk straight ahead, the elevators to the right and left, the directory posted on a pedestal near the reception desk, and guards discretely watching you as you entered the lobby area. The guards weren't actually necessary, as the multiple television systems watching the lobby were enough to alert anyone who cared that they were being watched. And, they certainly weren't enough to resist any serious intrusion. They were ubiquitous symbols. They were everywhere. Discrete, small in number, but everywhere, always everywhere, reminding you who you were actually dealing with.

Fong Li answered his phone on the 5th ring. "Mr. Li, this is Mr. Canton. Please forgive me for calling you at this hour, but I have no one else to ask for help."

After a short pause, Mr. Li said hoarsely, "How can I be of assistance, Mr. Canton."

"The American Embassy has refused to allow me to return home because of some difficulty with Texas and I really don't know who else to ask for assistance."

"Where are you now?" he asked quietly.

"In the reception area of your building at the information desk."

"Please wait there and I will send someone to you."

"Thank you very much, Mr. Li."

Good God, what have I done Peter thought. I'm not a US Citizen any more. I have no passport, I can't get home, my phone doesn't work, I'm on the other side of the earth and now I'm a criminal.

Just this morning Mr. Li had told Peter that the contract they had been working on concerning the LNG loading facility would have to be reviewed again because there had been a

137

problem. This was the 5th time, but that was normal. What was unusual was that this time he told Peter in less than 24 hours from when they had submitted the last changes. That was blazingly fast. More like Hong Kong or Singapore speed than Beijing. Interesting, hadn't thought of that till now. Perhaps he is getting more direct attention that he was before.

Mr. Li himself came down the marble steps and walked toward Peter.

I'm really screwed he thought. He isn't even going to let me in the building; I'm just going to be sent out the front door…then what do I do???

"Good evening Mr. Canton. I'm sorry to hear of your travel difficulties and would like to help in any way that we can."

We, he had said "we". So they have already run this situation up and down their chain and I'm am going to get the official line. Peter thought to himself.

The handshake was the normal greeting one, quick, firm but not graspy. "We think that we may be able to help you make contact with people at your office, and perhaps they can help you find a way to get home. Would that be acceptable to you, Mr. Canton?"

"Thank you very much, that would be most acceptable and appreciated. I am grateful for any assistance that you might be able to provide." He thought he did that right, the 'you' could be plural, so he would know that Peter knew that he was under orders.

Mr. Li led the way upstairs to one of the conference rooms on the 2nd floor where most of their previous meetings had taken place. They entered the floor to ceiling double doors of the conference center as we usually did, but turned to the right down a hallway, which Peter had never seen before. After passing several closed doors, they entered one to find a small room with a coffee table and two comfortable chairs on either side. Mr. Li motioned to the chair farthest from the door and seated himself in the other one. The door was slowly closing when a young man dressed in the uniform black suit and tie, white shirt and lace-up shoes appeared with a tray carrying two coffee cups and two tea cups with a pot of coffee and urn of tea arranged neatly in the center. He placed the tray on the center of the table, and then the other young man, who Peter hadn't seen enter the room, brought in a telephone instrument and plugged it into the receptacle in the floor beside the table. They were facing out of the windows over the street where Peter had just entered. The view was nice, but he couldn't get to enjoy it very much.

"Would you care for something to drink Mr. Canton?"

"I would enjoy some of the tea I believe Mr. Li." The coffee was good here. They imported it from Hawaii, but the tea was like none he had ever had and he never passed up a chance to have some.

Mr. Li also poured a cup of tea for himself and then leaned back in the overstuffed chair. "Mr. Canton, you have placed me in a very difficult situation. I hope that my being frank with you will not offend you." Peter nodded, raising his hands from his lap and extending them to the side making the universal "there is nothing I can do about it now" sign. He continued "this is a very complicated situation with many opportunities to cause serious harm to our ability to work with you in the future. I have received a telephone call from the American Embassy regarding your status. They have made it clear that they would like very much for us to not have anything further to do with you. They made it quite clear that any aid from us to you would jeopardize our future relations with the United States."

"I don't know what to say Mr. Li. I certainly don't mean to be the cause of any difficulty between you and anyone else. I am very confused by the situation and am also concerned about all the potential difficulties that could arise."

"What do you want from us Mr. Canton?" he asked rather formally.

"Well, my original intent this morning when I left you was to return home to Houston and see if I couldn't work out the arrangements we discussed concerning the LNG facility. Our partners are in Texas, the shipping company is based in Qatar and I cannot contact any of them. My phone has stopped working, so I am unable to contact anyone until I get free from this immediate situation." Peter felt sure that the Attaché at the American Embassy had made a call and his counterpart in Chinese Telecom had pulled the plug on his cell service. Peter thought Maybe I'd better just keep this simple. "I would like to return home, Mr. Li. I'm sure that all this treaty dispute between the US and Texas will settle down pretty quickly and until then, I want to be with my family and at the home office where I can still work with you effectively on our continuing projects."

"I see." He paused as though he was considered how to break the bad news to Peter. "The US has stopped the departure of all flights from here to Texas. You will not be allowed to travel there. They told us that they have removed your passport, so you are actually a stateless person at the moment." Another pause, "Perhaps your office in Houston would be able to help you sort out your situation satisfactorily. Would you like to call them?"

"Yes, that would be very helpful."

"Please feel free to use this phone." Mr. Li indicated the instrument that had just been placed on the immaculately polished glass and chrome table in front of them. "Just tell the operator whom you would like to call and they will handle it for you. I will excuse myself if you would prefer." As he put down his tea on the tray and prepared to rise from his chair, Peter knew he would have a transcript of the conversation before he hung up the phone, so there was no need to even consider that any of this would be private. That was just something you assumed about all forms of communications here, so no need to make a big deal of it now.

"No, please stay, if you don't mind."

"Of course." He settled back in his chair, lifted the hand set from the phone and spoke to the operator. It sounded like he instructed the person on the other end of the phone to make the requested call or the prepared call or something like that, but then he handed Peter the phone and said, "Please, tell the operator whom you wish to call." Instead of speaking into the hand set, Peter pressed the speaker phone button and hung up the hand set. He wanted Mr. Li to feel absolutely secure that he had nothing to hide.

"Houston, Texas, Please." Peter gave her the number of his father-in-law, Matt Ralls. Within a few seconds there was a little whirring noise on the line, then a ringing sound followed after a minute by the first Texas voice Peter had heard since the

140

revolution. "Peter, what the hell is going on, we tried to call you but the call went to some screening center. I got interrogated for a while before I hung up on'em. Where are you and are you ok?"

"Actually, I am still in Beijing, with Mr. Li in the ministry at the moment, and I don't know if I'm ok or not. Mr. Li is with me here and has been kind enough to arrange this call. I'm just trying to figure out a way to get home. It's a little complicated over here: They took my passport and won't let me fly to any Texas destination. They even threatened me with being arrested when I arrived back in the states if I was allowed to return at all. This is truly a mess."

"I know, Peter. We have been trying to talk to the people in Austin all day and haven't been able to get through. I talked to the governor. I told them you were over there in China and needed to get home. They sent me an email back with a phone number you're supposed to call. I can conference you up with them on my phone here if you want."

"Go for it, Matt."

"Ok, just give me a second." The line went dead as he set up the conference call. Matt Ralls had a better phone system in his home office than most companies have at their headquarters. "Ready, Peter, here is Cullen Atkins on the Governor's staff at the crisis center."

"Good morning Mr. Canton, I understand you are having a little trouble getting home."

"Yes I am."

"Do I understand correctly that you are an attorney and that you are in Beijing, China at this very moment?"

"That's correct."

"If you have a fax machine near you, I may be able to solve your passport problem and we can start working on the transportation thing in a minute." I looked at Mr. Li and he nodded and leaned over to speak into the phone and gave the fax number from memory.

"Got it, hold on while I send you something. We are very excited here that you called, this is a real opportunity." Opportunity hell, Peter thought, obviously he was dealing with a graduate of some positive thinking seminar, but this was the real world.

Mr. Li quickly motioned to the young man who had plugged in the phone, who then left the room for a minute, returning with several pieces of paper handing it to me. "Ok, I have the fax." As Peter began to scan the several pages of fax paper, the phone spoke again.

"I think that should take care of your citizenship problems and as for a passport, you can write your own, Mr. Ambassador." Peter looked at the piece of paper and knew that he wasn't going to get home any time soon.

The cover page read

From the President of Texas
To Mr. Peter Canton

RE: Your appointment as Ambassador to China

By order of the Governor of the Nation of Texas, you,
Peter Canton, are herewith appointed Ambassador and
Plenipotentiary to the Nation of China
with all the privileges and obligations pertaining thereto.

Please see the appointment declaration attached.
Please see the list of activities that you should undertake immediately.
Please call the attached phone number as soon as possible from a secure phone.

The second page was a black and white rendition of what must have been a rather ornate official-looking document announcing that Peter Canton, a citizen of Texas, was herewith appointed Ambassador to China.

The third page had a short list of things to do, the first of which was to establish a place of business where FedEx could find him.

The fourth page was a list of contact phone numbers and addresses, FedEx account numbers and a bank account number in a Hong Kong bank.

Stunning. Absolutely stunning Peter screamed without making a sound. How in the hell was I going to be able to do any of this. Who did they think I was he yelled to himself. He turned from the paper he had been reading and looked at Mr. Li with a look that was sure to convey complete confusion.

"Mr. Li, I have been appointed the ambassador to China from the Nation of Texas"

Mr. Li was already smiling as he extended his hand and said "Congratulation, Mr. Canton."

Within minutes, Mr. Li had made several phone calls, the last of which resulted in a quick trip by car down the street to another more ornate-looking building that Peter had never visited before. The meeting with the Chinese equivalent of the state department left him confused, excited, concerned and even more frightened than before. After handshakes all around, they had received his credentials, and then returned them. They said that it would be inappropriate for them to receive him as Ambassador from Texas, until Texas had been recognized by China as a nation. Peter had asked how and when that might happen and received a most polite range of gobbledygook answers with lots of handshakes, smiles and good wishes. Mr. Li had remained in the meeting for a few minutes after Peter had been escorted from the room in a crowd of what appeared to be very senior people in whatever state organization inhabited the building. They very carefully distracted him with polite conversation as though that had been the plan all along.

Mr. Li caught up with the group that was meandering with Peter toward the front door smoothly enough that Peter hardly noticed he had been MIA. The group picked up speed and arrived back at the limo rather quickly, again with lots of handshakes and nodding and bowing and smiles all around. Mr. Li sat quietly in the limo as they returned to the ministry building. Without much ceremony, he turned to Peter and said very quietly, with a very deadpan expression, "Your driver will take you where you need to go." He shook Peter's hand, then paused as if he wanted to say something else, but didn't. He did allow a brief but definite smile to emerge across his face. A face that Peter had come to think of as stone.

As Mr. Li departed the limo, he had instructed the driver in Chinese to take Peter somewhere that Peter did not quite understand and then took Peter's hand again, smiled and stepped out of the limo.

The driver drove out of the circular drive of the ministry building, joined the traffic on the divided highway for a moment, moved to the left lane and made a U turn. He accelerated a short distance, then moving to the right he exited into the parking lot of a building that stood directly across the freeway from the interior ministry, and entered its circular drive. The doorman walked to the car and opened the door as the car came to a stop. He bowed slightly and waved his white gloved left hand toward the entrance to the building.

As Peter walked through the doors being held open for him by the doorman, another person who was talking on a cellphone appeared behind the glass doors. He completed his conversation on the phone, folded it and put it in his pocket as Peter cleared the last entry door.

"Mr. Canton, how nice to meet you."

"Thank you, and you as well I'm sure…" he said in his most ambassadorial style.

"Mr. Li has called and suggested that you may need some office space for your 'company'."

"That was very kind of Mr. Li."

"I think we can provide what you need, if you will follow me, please," He said as he bowed slightly and waved Peter past the security desk toward the elevators.

The security guards rose from their seats as Peter approached the desk and his escort nodded to them. They remained standing as the new ambassador passed and stayed that way until he boarded the elevator that his escort had summoned. The escort pressed the button for the 12th floor and they began the ride up in silence. As the doors opened on the 12th floor, the lobby became visible, with another security desk to the right of the elevators and a waiting area to the left. Again, the guards rose from their seats as they passed and Peter sheepishly waved at them, before his escort took him behind the guard station rear wall and into the hallway that extended both left and right from the central receiving area.

Peter followed him down the hallway to the right as they wound around gentle bends and corners until they reached what Peter perceived to be the end of the hallway. In front of him stood two huge wooden doors, dominating the end of the hall. They were ornately inscribed with black lacquered carvings and a pair of beautifully carved wooden handles and flanked by the most beautiful Ming dynasty jars Peter had ever laid eyes on. The doors opened as they approached them and a luxurious waiting room with several secretarial and administrative work stations scattered behind a low wall like you would see in a bank back home in the 50's.

They continued down the hall past the reception area, past the secretarial and administrative area, past the office doors opening off the hall and to a small waiting room at the end of the hall. The escort then went to the wall across the end of the reception room and pressed on a section of wood paneling that looked like the rest of the wall, but became a door which opened outward. They entered this last room decorated on the left with a desk and credenza arrangement and to the right with a very nice representation of a living room with a couch, several chairs, a coffee table in the center, with built-in bookcases along the right hand wall behind the couch. The wall immediately to the right seemed to protrude out into the room a little more than the wall on the left. The escort moved to the center of the room and held out both of his hands, palms forward extended slightly to his sides and said "I hope you find this office acceptable."

"Its beautiful. Did Mr. Li suggest this particular office?"

He looked puzzled at first and then said, "No sir, Mr. Li suggested this floor for your company, but this is the nicest office."

"So you chose this office for me?"

"Well, it is the nicest office on the floor, is it not acceptable with you?"

"Yes, it's very nice, but what about the other offices, won't my coming and going interfere with what is going on in them?"

He looked puzzled again, and then smiled, "I think you misunderstand, Mr. Li suggested the floor, the entire floor for you."

With that he handed me a card with the name and address of the building on it, bowed slightly and turned to leave.

"How about phone service, when can I arrange for that?"

He smiled, "The phones have been installed for a several weeks, but if they are not acceptable, please don't hesitate to let me know." Then he bowed slightly, smiled like a Cheshire cat, and left.

Peter stood there in the middle of the office, at 2 in the morning, trying to get his bearings. He wanted to go home. He wanted sleep. He wanted … He wanted to … call home. There was a phone on the desk. He went over to the desk and pulled the chair out from behind it and sat down. The phone had multiple lines, each of which was labeled simply with 1, 2, 3… Peter pressed the first line and got a dial tone. He pulled the credential sheet out of his briefcase and flipped to the last page with all the contact numbers on it. He picked the first one on the list and typed in the number on the keypad, and almost instantly, "ECOM center, Officer Helms" came the crisp reply.

"Which Comm center is this, Officer Helms?"

"The Texas Emergency Communications Center in Austin, Sir" came the snappy reply.

"Get me the Governor." Peter said in my most official sounding voice.

"Who is this?" came the reply.

"I am Peter Canton, Ambassador from Texas to China, calling the Governor. I'm calling from Beijing, China, I'm not sure how to do all this since I just got this job about 4 hours ago, so help me out will you, son?"

"Yes, sir, I certainly will, sir. Stand by one."

"Peter, boy are we glad to hear from you."

Peter recognized the voice of the David Dalby from their many visits. "David, this is the damndest mess I've ever heard of."

"Tell me about it, where are you Mr. Ambassador?"

"Well, I'm sitting in my new office, but I'm not the Ambassador, they refused to accept my credentials." Peter filled

146

the new Governor in on the last 4 hours knowing that the phone was not secure. Peter even pointed that out several times during the conversation, but nothing he had to say was that confidential anyway, since the Chinese had been present at everything he had done all day.

"So, how did you wind up with an office so quickly?"

"When I left Mr. Li off at his building, he told the driver to take me across the street to this place. They brought me up to the 12th floor, which I think is the top floor, and took me down to one end of the building. They asked me if I liked the office and I said yes, but I was worried about how much I would have to walk through someone else's office to get to the elevators and stuff. He said for me not to worry, that Mr. Li had arranged that I should have the whole floor. The phones were installed over a month ago. There are computers on the desks and I haven't checked, but I bet there is some scotch in the bar, when I find it."

There was a long silence on the other end of the line. I noticed that it was just silence, no pops or clicks or hisses, just silence that can only be produced on all digital fiber links.

"That's incredible" finally came the reply.

"I get the feeling that they have been waiting for all this to come about."

"But, they would not accept you as the Ambassador?"

"No, not until Texas is recognized as a nation, How would that happen?"

"They would make a public statement, give you a formal communication of some sort or have their UN ambassador announce it in response to something happening on the floor at the UN."

I was hoping that whoever was listening was taking good notes, but they had been way ahead of us so far and we were not likely to get too far ahead of them now.

"Ok, anyway, I have an address, and a phone number and I'll get started on that list you sent. Give me a while to staff up the place and I'll get rolling."

"Don't worry about staff, I've got people shoved in hotels and buildings all over China that have the same problem you had this morning. I have military personnel who have been stranded from the embassies. Now that I know where you are, I'll send them to you and you can figure it out."

"Sure, why not. I'll be here."

After a few more rounds of best wishes, the call ended. Peter Canton hung up the phone, leaned back in his chair noticing the beautiful view out the window for the first time. Then he looked around the room for the scotch. It was there, several kinds. He chose the Dalwhinnie 15 year old and poured an ample one in the glass sitting by the sink.

Chapter 18: What a Mess

6:45 AM
Sunday
22 April 2012

Amarillo, Texas

Chuck Hall, a lanky 6' 4" Texan, quietly closed the front door to his sprawling brick home. Normally, he would be headed to church, but today he had to work at the plant. The cool morning air had a bit of a chill in it as he zipped up his windbreaker and trudged across the loose gravel sidewalk toward his SUV. The defroster came on, the seat moved into the correct position, the navigation system and the Sirius radio sprang to life and the engine started as Chuck turned the key in the ignition. Backing out of the drive, he had a chance to look at his rambling home of these many years as the fog cleared from the windshield. The fence he had built, the rock garden near the front door, the new roof…let's see…that was 20 years ago, just about the time he got out of the Air Force.

With the big handle in "D" now, moving off toward the services compound some 20 miles away, he was glad that the city of Amarillo hadn't reached him yet. He enjoyed the solitude of his ranch style life, even though he had never "ranched." "All hat and no cattle" was the way his coffee buddies at the Dairy Queen put it. That was just fine with him. The house was all that remained of his family homestead. Several thousand acres surrounding it were now irrigated by giant creeping pipe arrangements that made the desert bloom. He didn't see any of that…he wasn't into plants much. Nevertheless, it had allowed him to have the antenna farm he had longed for when he was stationed in close quarters during his military years. Out here, there were no building restrictions. His Dad had been a ham, and he had eagerly followed in his footsteps. As early as he could remember, he had heard the chirp of high speed CW coming from the library in that house. His Dad, a retired Navy chief, would read the morning paper, sip his salted black gang coffee and carry on the round table with his buddies over a radio station that would be the envy of many small town broadcasters. Chuck never got the hang of the really high speed CW, he could only master 25 words per minute or so. The dits and dahs were still discernible at that speed, not like the whir of the 50 and 60 word per minute stuff his Dad had run. He hadn't been on the radio much lately. Too busy, too tired, and most of his friends were gone. As this, his second career, was drawing to a close he worried about how long he and Ruth would be able to stay in that house they loved so much. She was getting pretty frail now; she wasn't able to work in the garden much anymore. She went to the farmers market in town more often to get her fresh vegetables. Each of them were taking more pills than any right-minded person would think normal if they were under 50, but Chuck had gone through that age nearly 16 years ago and he had the AARP and NRA seniors cards in his wallet to prove it.

The guard at the front gate waved Chuck on through with an additional good morning salute after the wave. Actually, as a DOE installation, the guards generally didn't salute, but most of the security force people stationed there were ex-military and knew that Chuck was a retired Colonel. They treated him as though he was still on active duty. The retired officer's sticker on the front bumper of his car was a tipoff to the younger guys, but the senior NCO's filled them in pretty quick. While Chuck didn't command the forces at the plant, he was the ranking civilian who decided how the money got spent and what facilities were assigned and how many hoops they had to jump through to get what they needed, so they saluted. It didn't hurt to humor a retired Colonel. So, they "made their obeisance" out of respect for the past, and fear for the future, as enlisted men have always done.

The parking place with the sign marked Director was waiting for the maroon Ford SUV as Chuck wheeled into the lot. The unchecked satnav, quietly talking radio and seat warmer all went off as Chuck stuffed the keys in his pocket and headed for the front door, which was unlocked. He went through the lobby, down the passageway to the right, past the smaller offices, then the conference room and into the break room where he started the coffee maker with his personal recipe. It was getting stronger these days. Energy drinks were for wimps, young people and those who were not about to retire. As the coffee began to drip from under the filter pack into the urn sitting on the heated pad below, Chuck deftly slid his cup under the dripping black cascade in place of the urn to interrupt the stream, filled his cup and returned the urn without letting a single drop hit the heating plate below. This move had been perfected many years ago in the silos buried in North Dakota.

Strolling down the hall to the end, he passed the security officer's area with his secretary's desk, his adjutant's desk, the first assistant's office and his secretary's desk into his area at the end of the hall. Julie wasn't there yet, wouldn't be for about an hour. Chuck opened his office door, walked to the secure safe and twisted the lock. Humm to the right deeeeeee to the left and dddaaaaa to the right and clunk…click the lock opened. Chuck took it out of its hasp so he could remove the bar that dropped down in front of all the file drawers. The bar was stowed on the side of the file cabinet by hanging it on a blank hasp welded to the top of the cabinet just to keep the bar out of the way. The lock was placed on the dummy hasp and snapped shut, preventing it and the bar from "wandering off". The green "CLOSED" sign was lifted out from the bracket on the front of the cabinet, spun around so that the big red "OPEN" on the other side of the sign was pointed outward, and shoved quickly back into its holder. The coffee cup on top of the cabinet sat absolutely still as the 2nd cabinet drawer down from the top was pulled open to reveal a row of folders marked "The Texas Project." The third file was pulled, the drawer shoved closed, the coffee cup retrieved and Chuck headed over to the lime green metal desk with the rubberized top he had called home for low these many years.

Taking a sip of the still steaming coffee, he pulled his chair up to the desk and flipped open the thick, bark-colored file. The contents parted like the Red Sea, half on one side and half on the other. The papers in the folder were pinned in at the top by a two-hole clip that would withstand anything but a direct hit, as many of the things at the plant were designed to do. Chuck ruffled through the stack of paper on the right side of the folder until he reached the phone list at the bottom of the stack. Looking down the list, he noted the one marked "Wingnut." He cradled the receiver of the phone against his left ear with his shoulder as he dialed the number with his left hand, and a few seconds later the ringing began.

"42nd Texas Air Guard, Captain Dale speaking, how can I help you, sir?" came the crisp voice over the phone.

"Are we still on for the run today, Captain?"

"Absolutely, sir. 130 is on the way, crew, fuel, refuel, weather and flight plan all set. Any last minute change in plans, just give me a call and I'll take care of it with an inflight change, sir."

"Thanks, Dale, no changes that I know of yet, but keep your head in the game."

"Will do, sir."

Another sip of coffee while he searched through the phone list again, this time stopping at "Lone Star." Dialing…waiting…sipping…ringing…again.

"Lone Star" came the curt words from the receiver this time.

"This is Pantex."

"Roger That Pantex …what's your status?"

"Ready."

"Very well…wait one…"

Chuck listened to the hum of the fan in the office as it slowly cast its blessing of moving air over the space.

"Pantex…Go…"

"Pantex Go…got it."

Chuck slowly returned the receiver to its home. This was the day. The beginning of something he had hoped he would never see, but it had come at last.

One more sip of coffee as he covered the list of things he had to do in the next few minutes. He had thought this list over many times lately, adding a task here…deleting one there…changing the order…all to arrive at what was to be a

152

relatively simple set of steps that only he could perform…or rather have others perform for him.

He picked up the phone and hit speed dial 6.

"I…T" came the quick reply.

"Has Doug come in yet, Chris?"

"No, sir, but he is usually here by now. He should be here any minute."

"Ok, have him come see me after he gets going would you?"

"Yes, sir…got it."

He hit 99 on the speed dial and instantly got the command post for the Pantex facility.

"Command Post, Sergeant Daily …"

"Sergeant Daily, get the duty officer and have him come to my office, please"

"Yes sir!"

All this moving of weapons was scaring the begezzus out of everyone, including him. The restrictions were unbelievable. All the weapons had to be off the base in 24 hours. The aircraft that would haul them would have to land on the service road and then taxi directly to the bunker locations where they would be loaded. The weapons had to be transport "safed," no matter what stage of modification or testing they were in. The service road was asphalt and wouldn't stand the pounding of the C-130s as they touched down, so the touchdown had to be made in the concrete parking lot just short of the perimeter road with the roll out on the asphalt. Strange people … people Chuck didn't know, would be entering and leaving the facility all day…lots of confusion…or rather … opportunities for confusion…just enough confusion he hoped.

The phone call he had received from his classmate and Air Force veteran buddy yesterday had been a surprise. Overhearing the conversation between Brad and the Lt. Governor had been shocking to say the least. Then later in the afternoon when the ship had blown up near Houston things looked like they might go sideways. He hadn't seen or talked to Brad Elkhart in 10 years before the class reunion at the Turkey Day game last year. Now he had talked on the phone with him 4 times in 1 day. It was a bit surreal. It seems that Brad worked for the CIA these

153

days and one of their concerns was external folks getting hold of a nuclear weapon. At the reunion last thanksgiving, Brad had been particularly interested to hear what Chuck thought about the security at Pantex, given that the place was the single largest storage and maintenance facility for nuclear weapons on the face of the earth. Brad had quietly made Chuck aware that there was something afoot that might involve him and Pantex. It was also clear he couldn't talk about it yet. He assured Chuck that he would call when they all got home and set up some things, but then all the problems had begun between Texas and the Federal Government.

When the call had come, Brad made it clear that the President wanted to make an agreement with the Governor of Texas that the nuclear weapons at Pantex would be moved out of Texas as soon as possible. They were to be moved to two locations. One batch would be moved to Fort Sill, Oklahoma, where there were already some small number of weapons stored. The other batch was to be moved to the old tunnel system above Kirtland Air Force Base on Sandia Mountain in Albuquerque, New Mexico. That plan had been transmitted down through the chain to Chuck directly from the facility commander within 15 minutes after Chuck had overheard the conversation with the governor yesterday. What Brad wanted done during the move was unbelievable, though. Brad had explained that two of the weapons were to be "diverted." That was the word he used..."diverted." Chuck would have to go to the Governor, get permission for a Texas Air Guard C-130 to carry 2 nuclear weapons to Galveston and put them in the hands of a contact that Brad would set up there. This was to be explained to the Governor as a "special favor" for the President of the United States, which under the circumstances might become important. The Governor would be able to confirm this by calling the White House and speaking directly to the president. To Chuck's surprise, everything had been arranged pretty much without a hitch. The TAG C-130 would be made available and its movement would be dictated by Chuck. All he had to do was call the state Emergency Communications Center in Austin and let them know what needed to happen. The folks there had handled getting the plane ready, crewed up and fueled for the flight to Amarillo, and then on to Galveston, no questions asked. The center personnel would not know what was going on except that it was a direct order from the Governor.

The first two aircraft to land at the local airport carried computer experts who would be working on the devices. They were all from Livermore National Laboratory, and had apparently had to work up some special software to use in making that many devices ready to travel that quickly. Normally, Chuck's people would have done the work, but for some reason, the feds had decided that anyone who worked on the devices now had to come from federal installations outside Texas. The two special people, who identified themselves as "CIA Brad's friends," had arrived the night before. All Brad had told him was that they would be overseeing some special work done on the two weapons that were to be "diverted."

The computer geeks were to be picked up by the bus sent from the facility to the airport and dropped off in pairs, at their designated bunkers where they would be working on the devices, all except one person. The one person who was going to work by himself would be accompanied by one of "Brad's friends"…the geeky one that walked into Chuck's office as he hung up the phone from making the call to the Command Post.

"Good morning, Colonel."

"Good morning… you guys all set?"

"Yes, sir, we have everything we need. When the bus gets here I will get on while my partner remains here with you." Chuck noticed the local ID badge hanging around the neck of the geek, and wondered for a split second where it had come from…but then he remembered who he was dealing with.

"That's fine, I'm sure we can find some place for him to hang out…"

"No, … I mean WITH YOU … for as long as I am on site. He won't get in the way, but we need to make sure that if anything comes up, it gets handled correctly. I'm sure you understand."

Chuck had worked around nuclear devices long enough to know how things were done, but this was way out of the ballpark for him. If it hadn't been for the assurance of Brad and the Governor that this was the right thing to do, he wouldn't have

155

gotten within a hundred miles of it on a bet. With the problems between Texas and the federal government, he knew that the safest thing for the weapons was to get them out of harm's way. This diversion had been a wrinkle that made him extremely uncomfortable. Still, it was clearly authorized by every authority that could possibly object, so who was he to be troubled by it? Nevertheless, he was.

The geek turned around and headed out the door of Chuck's office as the bus full of the Livermore techs pulled up outside. His partner, who had been standing just outside Chuck's office door, watched him walk by and then turned his attention to Chuck. He didn't say anything, but what was most disturbing was that Chuck could not detect whether this guy viewed him as a threat or a friend…or both…it was unnerving. Chuck watched through the conference room windows across the hall as the geek boarded the bus in the front parking lot. He noted that the parking lot was clear of cars and that the concrete bumper strips had been picked up and moved into a stack on the side of the parking lot near the building. The guys had been busy last night turning the parking lot into a touchdown area for the planes that were coming in a minute. The bus pulled away from the front door and headed down the perimeter road toward the bunkers. It held the teams, the driver and the geek.

The "partner" spoke for the first time. "When they finish working on the two specials, we are going to have to change the serial numbers on them. You can do that can't you?"

Good grief. "Well, that is going to be difficult…each of the weapons has its serial number engraved in its actual case by a laser, so that it can't be changed without replacing the case."

"I'm aware of that. You have two devices here, with serial numbers ending in 13-10 and the other 13-11." It was a statement of fact. Chuck would have had to look up the inventory in one of the secure folders locked in the CO's safe to know that, but somehow he knew that he had just heard a fact. "Ok, so let's say there are two with those serial numbers … what about it?"

"Those are going to be the two specials. Once my partner and the man assigned to work with him have completed their work, you and I will take the two devices they have worked on

156

and inscribe different serial numbers on them. As it happens, the laser printer used to do that is in the bunker where they are assigned. We will go down there in about an hour, after they have completed their work and left the building. Then you and I will change the numbers..." Another statement of fact:

The drone of a C-130 could be heard overhead as former Captain William Morgan USMC, now the deputy head of DOE security for the site, walked into Chuck's office. "You wanted to see me, sir?"

"Yes, Captain. I just wanted to make sure that you had been briefed on what was about to happen. I visited with Colonel Stovall last night, but I just wanted to check with you."

"Yes, sir. Colonel Stovall briefed the entire detachment last night and we are fully manned today."

"Good...I didn't want to get in your way, but this is so unusual .... Well, I didn't want to drop the ball anywhere."

"No problem, sir. We have teams at each of the bunkers, around the perimeter road, the gates are closed and the comm center is manned. Colonel Stovall is in the comm center and is in direct command today. Now that the experts are headed to the bunkers, we will close the parking lot and the perimeter road and get ready to receive the 6 aircraft ...The loading crews are standing by with the equipment at each bunker ready to load the pallets on the aircraft."

"Good, thank you for the update. I think you will find that there are going to be 7 aircraft though...there was one added at the last minute."

"I hadn't heard about that sir. I'll check with Colonel Stovall and make sure they get the word."

"It will be a Texas Air Guard C-130, not a US Air Force C-130."

"Yes, sir."

"Good...thank you Captain...sounds like you have it all tied up in a package. Just a few tense hours and this will all be done with. This gentleman from Washington and I will be touring the bunkers as work progresses ... if you would let everyone know, I would appreciate not getting shot..."

"Will do, sir...Which vehicle will you be using, sir...?"

"The black Ford parked by the front door," piped up the "partner" before Chuck could answer.

"Yes, sir…I'll see to it."

"Thanks Captain…I'll check in with the comm center and Colonel Stovall in a bit."

The captain did an "in the presence of civilians" about face and headed down the hall. When he was out of earshot, Chuck turned to his newly assigned sidekick and asked, "why are we changing the serial numbers on the two specials?"

"You don't need to know" came the terse reply. He wished there was a lot of other stuff he had not needed to know, but he was in the thick of it now.

The first Herkey Bird hit the parking lot like a ton of bricks, but then it eased down the perimeter road as if they did it every day. It was a long road so they didn't have to get too violent with the props in reverse mode kicking up dust and bits of gravel that could have damaged the props and engines. One after another the six Air Force birds landed. All of them headed to the bunkers at the far end of the site, where they pulled into the large parking area in front of each bunker. One by one they cut engines, opened rear cargo doors, lowered ramps.

The devices were being programmed one after another and then loaded onto pallets, secured by experienced loadmasters and then hauled out to the aircraft where the pallets were slid onto the roller rail systems built into the floor of the aircraft. The rollers made it hard to walk for the uninitiated, but allowed the loading and unloading of cargo to proceed very rapidly. Some pallets were even designed to be air dropped out the back by throwing a parachute out the open cargo door in flight and then letting the parachute pull the pallet out the back of the aircraft. That was not the plan today. Fast loading, not unloading was the order of the day.

The seventh C-130 landed on the parking lot and drifted on down the road to the nearest bunker, made the corner and set up for loading like the others…It was parked a little further from the road, though, and was turned at an unusual angle.

"Partner" motioned for Chuck to head outside…Chuck nodded, went to the desk, flipped the file closed and walked to the safe. Dropped the file in the drawer where it came from, shut the drawer and then grabbed the locking bar. He lifted the bar to the front of the safe, just off the side of the handles and dropped the bottom in the loop of steel welded into the bottom of the file cabinet. As the bar dropped into the hole in the bottom the top slid over a hasp that received the lock. With a click that was done and Chuck headed to the door, flipping the sign from OPEN to CLOSED on the front of the cabinet as he turned to go.

Chuck passed Jane on the way out. Things had been so busy this morning he hadn't even seen her come in. "Good morning, Sir..." she smiled. "What a mess this is making with the parking lot...I had to park on the grass around the back of the building and the sprinklers were on last night..." she said, pulling off her damp and muddy shoes while seated at her desk. The motion was one that placed her in a rather awkward position both men noticed as they passed. "We're headed down to the bunkers, I'll be back in a bit...." Chuck caught "partner" grinning at him as they turned down the hallway. Sneering was more like it. He didn't deserve that. Jane was a perky 32 year old English major with a husband and two kids, but... then again, I'm not dead yet either... he thought to himself.

The black rent car headed down the perimeter road. Chuck noticed the touchdown marks the tires had made on the parking lot. They could have been covered with about 4 good size RV's. Not bad spot landing technique for a bunch of AF zoomies. They turned into the first bunker where the last plane had landed. As they pulled closer to the plane Chuck noticed the tail number was a TAG that stood for Texas Air Guard, rather than the USAF numbers on the other planes.

Partner pulled them around to the back of the bunker, out of sight of the front entrance and switched off the ignition, but made no move to get out. "We'll wait here till I get the call, then we will go in and do the serial number thing..." It was all rather matter of fact...like there was nothing to it...staying out of sight of the other workers...changing the serial number on a nuclear weapon. What the hell difference would that make...wherever it was headed, surely they wouldn't care what serial number they were getting. How could that possibly matter? Chuck just couldn't see going to all that trouble. In fact, he wasn't sure they would be able to do it. The machine that engraved the serial numbers on the casings wasn't portable, and they would have to move the device into the laser. On a new casing it didn't matter much how you did it, there was plenty of space on the casing to engrave the number. But altering one number...how ... without messing up the original engraving...that was going to be a chore. And it was a chore that Chuck didn't know how to do, but so far Brad's friends had gotten it all correct so maybe they knew how to work this one out.

The cell phone beeped and "partner" pulled it out, glanced at the screen and said, "They are done with the programming. We just have to wait another minute or two while they leave the building and get on the bus. It seemed like forever, but it was only about 30 seconds when the sound of the bus driving in the parking lot on the other side of the bunker could be heard clearly as it bounced off the concrete walls surrounding them. You could almost hear the door opening and closing, but the sound of the bus leaving was very distinct. Chuck looked across the front seat at his "sidekick" and got a nod, so they both opened the doors and stepped out. The back door to the bunker was through a maze of concrete and dirt-filled blast diversion channels, and it was open. This should never happen, but it was ajar. Chuck grabbed the door handle and jerked it the rest of the way open, leading the way down the corridor toward the loading door at the other end.

"The laser printer is in here, but where did they leave the special...?"

"Damned if I know, but it should be on a pallet ready to go out the door at the other end. We just need to touch up the serial number a bit and wipe it down real well, then we're done."

The fork lift was still tied to the rubber tired cart that held the pallet. Sitting on top of the pallet, strapped down ready for loading and flight were two 25 Megaton thermonuclear bombs. The hair on the back of Chuck's head, what was left of it, stood straight up in a lifelong ritual salute to being in the presence of devices that were capable of killing millions of people in a split second.

"Shall I drive?" Chuck asked and received an "away we go" motion in response.

The rising whine of the electric motor powering the forklift and the squeak of rubber on spotless gray painted floors were the only sounds in the building. Chuck drove the forklift, pulling the trailer down the hallway to a point directly in front of the doors to the utility room where the laser was located. The doors opened from the inside and there stood the geek. "Back it up in here" he said, turning to his partner. "Swimmingly...just swimmingly...I told him I had to go take a crap...and he did the deed. When Chuck got back he was wrapping it up and was happy to leave. I told him I would lock up and catch the bus back later since I worked down the hall and had a bunch of paper work to fill out anyway. I'm pretty sure he bought it."

"Now all we have to do is change the ID so he won't detect that these are the same ones on the other end."

The laser was mounted to a 6-axis CNC robotic arm so that it could pretty much work on anything at any angle. Chuck backed the cart with the pallet of bombs up to the base of the robot arm while the geek waved him into place. When he stopped and started to get off the forklift... "partner" was standing there and held up his hand indicating that Chuck should stay seated on the forklift. It was clear that Chuck was not supposed to know what was about to be done.

Geek took a memory stick out of his pocket and plugged it into the CNC machine...a flash or two from the stick showing that the data was being read was the only indication that anything was going on. Geek then pressed a button on the robot and grabbed the joy-stick on the control console. He maneuvered the laser cutting head over the first bomb and stopped it just above its surface... "partner" jumped up on the cart, pulled a metallic looking piece of paper out of his pocket and placed it on the first weapon.

Chuck couldn't see exactly where, but guessed that it was near where the serial number was. The geek turned a dial and pressed another button, and the robot quickly jumped to a position just over the piece of metal that had been placed on the device. A dim light came out of the laser, Chuck guessing this was the secret to matching the old serial number to the new one...some sort of alignment mask...so they could see where the laser was going to hit. Partner pulled a cell phone looking thing

161

from his pocket, pointed its camera toward where the light from the laser was hitting the top of the bomb and said "OK, try it."

Geek pushed a button and the robot swung into motion and the light traced an outline on the metal but not nearly powerful enough to score the metal or even heat it up. When the motion finished…Partner held the cell phone up, hit a couple of keys and read 9 numbers to the geek. The geek pressed the numbers into the robot keyboard; partner stripped off the metal and jumped to the other side of the cart to get ready to work on the other weapon. Geek hit the go button and the laser, now at a considerably high setting, began moving smoothly over the surface of the weapon. When it finished, Geek touched a couple of more buttons, grabbed the joystick again and the process was repeated on the second weapon. It had taken about 30 seconds for each bomb…start to finish…amazing.

Geek shut down the robot, Partner jumped off the cart and waved Chuck to take the whole assembly back out the door and down toward the loading area. At the front, where the forklift, trailer and bombs had originally been, Chuck stopped the forklift, pulled up the handbrake and got off. Geek waved for Chuck to follow as he went by and handed Chuck the 2 ID badges he and "Partner" had been using. They walked out the front door and headed for the plane…Chuck and the forklift with Geek at the wheel began to move, taking the cargo to the plane waiting out front.

The pallet slid off the forks and onto the back ramp of the airplane. The loadmaster and the copilot pulled it inside. They moved it to the center of the plane over the wheels and under the center of the wing. The weight of the bombs wouldn't matter much at takeoff since the plane was equipped with external fuel tanks and was full to the brim with JP-5, just like Brad had specified. With that load of fuel, it was capable of flying a long way, much farther than to Galveston.

As Geek jumped down off the forklift, he waved for Chuck to follow him around the left side of the plane. They walked close to the bulbous wheel well and avoided the propeller of the inboard engine that was resting with its shark like blades sitting quietly, belying the violence with which they would claw through the air in a few minutes to force the small aluminum cloud down the runway and into the air. They climbed up the sandpaper-covered steps and into the darkness as the whine of the APU starting up filled the air. Geek and Partner met at the bottom of the cockpit stairs and then motioned for Chuck to take a seat next to the door they had just come in.

The ramp came up and the external doors closed and the inside of the aircraft got a lot darker, illuminated now only by the ceiling lights only half on and the windows only partially covered.

The other aircraft were still being loaded at their bunkers further down the road because they had many more devices to handle. In fact, they would have to make several trips, so the last LLNL worker that had worked with the Geek had been moved down to help out finishing up the rest of the conversions. It would end about sundown.

The sound of compressed air escaping coincided with the slow rotation of the propeller blades on the outboard port engine of the C-130. Chuck jumped up from his seat intending to get off before the other engines started, but Partner stood too close for him to get up. With a "Talk to the hand" motion, Partner persuaded Chuck that he would be remaining onboard. Geek closed the door as the loadmaster came to sit by Chuck. The Copilot bounded up the cockpit stairs and headed for his right-hand seat a few feet forward of the engineers panel. Geek followed him up the stairs leading to the cockpit.

"I thought I was supposed to stay here!" Chuck yelled at Partner above the building noise of the Allison Turbo props, their 4,300 horsepower being equivalent to a top fuel dragster engine with really big blender attached up front. The blades cut through the air with a high-pitched hissing sound, as they effortlessly prepared themselves for the violence to come. Partner just shook his head, looking Chuck squarely in the eyes.

The nose of the plane rose with a quick bounce as the pilot let off the brakes and eased the propellers into a little forward thrust and the 150,000 pounds of aircraft, people, fuel and bombs began to roll. The TAG C-130 pulled onto the perimeter road, and the engines sped up to their normal high-speed whine…then quite suddenly the sound of the engines changed from the high-pitched hiss and whine/hum to a sound of a tornadic wind of much lower tone and dust began to rise behind the plane as the props dug in and started kicking huge amounts of air behind them. Dust and rock were spraying up but the plane was already out of the way … moving ever faster…until as it hit the parking lot, the nose came sharply off the ground and the body lifted skyward and started a hard bank to the left…which was north.

Silence fell over the parking lot as the plane receded. Chuck glanced out the window at the traffic that was stopped on the road outside of the fence while people were watching the spectacle standing outside their cars. They are going to get an eye full today… he thought to himself. But by the end of the day, there will be no nukes in Texas. At least that he knew of.

As the aircraft climbed out of sight of the base, it began a slow right turn that brought it to a heading of roughly 130 degrees. Looking out the window Chuck could only make out that they were headed generally southeast, but the pilot had been given specific instructions to head for Galveston by Geek. When the Autopilot was set and the course stored in the Nav system, and the aircraft stable at 30,000 feet, Geek shot the flight engineer in the back of the head, being careful to point down so the blood wouldn't spatter on the engineers control panel. The shot sounded like a little pop and was hardly audible to the pilot and copilot through their headsets. The pilot looked to his right, thinking he might have heard something. The bullet from Geek's silenced pistol entered his right eye, shattered his sinus and scrambled his brain all the way back to the helmet that had failed to protect him from the frontal assault.

The copilot only saw the pilot turn and then slump out of the corner of his eye, but by the time he had turned, the navigator was dead, and he was looking down the silencer of Geek's gun. Geek motioned with the barrel of the gun for the copilot to get out of his seat and come with him down the stairs to the cargo bay. He unplugged his headset from the intercom console and pulled the earmuffs down from his ears. He carefully worked his way past Geek to the ladder, passing the engineers chair with the now dead occupant strapped in it, facing Geek all the way. As he reached the stairs, he grabbed the handrail outside the cockpit wall and lowered his left foot to the first step. Geek shot him in the same spot he had shot the pilot with pretty much the same result, except that the copilot did the beginnings of a very nice back dive off the top step of the ladder and landed at Chuck's feet on the cargo deck below.

Partner put a round in the loadmaster sitting next to Chuck and then moved the muzzle of the gun slowly to the right until it was lined up with a point directly between Chuck's eyes. He leaned forward and yelled into Chuck's face … "Brad says hi." He clicked the de-cocker on the side of the Walther P99 and lowered the barrel to point at the floor. Then he yelled again… "Any questions?"….

Chuck could only shake his head.

Partner went up the ladder to the cockpit. Soon, he yelled from the door to Chuck and motioned for Chuck to clear the body of the copilot out of the way. Chuck noticed that his crotch was wet as he stood up and he was sure he knew what the cause was. It wasn't every day you got that kind of a hello message. He looked at the expressionless face of the copilot, and grabbed him from under the shoulders and dragged him to the right side of the aircraft back toward the pallet. When he returned to his seat, Partner was holding another body at the door. He shoved it out face forward this time. Chuck, now a part of the "team," dragged this body and ultimately 3 more back onto the cargo deck. Only the loadmaster remained strapped in his seat next to where Chuck had been sitting. Chuck unsnapped his seat belt and pulled him toward the others. He laid them out in a row, face up, about halfway between the wall of the cockpit and the pallet. He looked for something to cover them with, but finding nothing immediately visible, he headed toward his seat, but Partner motioned him to the cockpit. As he climbed up the ladder, Partner motioned him into the engineer's chair, Geek was already sitting in the pilot's seat.

Partner glanced at the fuel valves and gauges and moved on to the copilot's seat. Chuck moved in and sat in the engineer's seat right behind him. He couldn't think of anything else to do, so he strapped in and waited for his pants to dry and his nerves to settle down. The urge to vomit was passing and suddenly he was very sleepy.

Chuck woke up at about sunset with the roar of rushing air and thrashing propellers thundering in his ears, even though he was wearing headphones. He looked outside through the cockpit windows and saw only water below. Clearly, they had not landed in Galveston as planned. Geek was still sitting in the pilot's seat, and Partner was missing. Chuck looked around to find out where this cold-blooded bastard might have gotten off to without a word. Over his right shoulder, he noticed the lower of the two crew bunks was occupied. Partner was taking a nap. Chuck needed to know where he was, so he glanced forward to the cockpit front panel in hopes of spotting something that looked like a map or position display. By looking over the right armrest on the copilot's seat, he could see the digital navigational display and could just make out the shape of the nearest landmasses in their vicinity. The little plane symbol in the center of the display at the bottom was over the little yellow line drawn on the display from the center of the bottom to the center of the top. Off to the left of the course line on the display was a series of what looked like islands, while at the end of the little yellow line was a coastline he did not immediately recognize. Just then, Partner reached in front of his face and turned a knob on the engineer's panel and flipped a couple of switches, almost bumping Chuck's nose with his fist as he did so.

The sting to the back of his neck was followed by a warm flushed feeling and then everything went dark as Chuck slumped over onto the engineer's small desk in front of him. The next thing he remembered was the bang associated with the landing gear being lowered. He almost fell out of the seat as the aircraft landed and the engines reversed, filling the sky around the plane with a cloud of dust. He held himself upright by pushing on the back of the copilot's seat. As the plane slowed and the cloud of dust parted, he could see out the front of the cockpit window that they were headed for a parking area near the end of the runway. They turned off the main runway onto a slightly larger pad as the geek cranked on the nose wheel steering wheel near his left knee. They made a quick 180 degree turn, came to a stop and the Geek tripped off the fuel buttons to all four engines with a flick of his right hand to the overhead panel above his right shoulder. They stopped wing tip to wing tip to a FedEx MD11, the freighter version of the Lockheed L 1011. The freighter had its cargo door open and a lift ramp in place. Partner pushed back the copilot's seat and headed for the rear of the cockpit, down the ladder and out of sight in the back. In a second or two, Chuck heard the whine of the rear ramp being opened. He was still groggy, but was recovering quickly now. The Geek got up out of the Pilot's seat and turned directly to Chuck.

"You will remain seated in that seat. You will not touch anything. I will come get you when we need to leave. It will be about 20 minutes."

Chuck nodded the nod of someone who had seen five perfectly innocent people shot in the head and who had pissed in his pants when the prospect of his own death had come to him. He sat in the chair. The plane rocked a few times as noises of the palettes being removed from the rear of the aircraft sifted through the open cockpit door.

The sound of the engines on the FedEx MD-11 starting was unmistakable. It was the only other aircraft near them. Chuck could tell that the freighter turned around on the tarmac because the blast of the hot air that smelled of jet fuel filled the little C-130. The freighterquickly picked up speed and in 12 seconds it was airborne.

After a brief period of quiet, footsteps could be heard coming forward in the cargo area and Geek stuck his head in and yelled above the whine of the apu, "Get up and come with me...!"

Chuck flipped the handle on the seatbelt and got up, moved to the cockpit door half expecting to see a gun, but only saw Geek waiting for him at the bottom of the steps. The hatch out the port side was open and the stairs had been lowered to the ground. Geek pointed for Chuck to head out that way. As he turned to head for the exit, Chuck glanced at the cargo deck and saw the bodies of the five Texas Guardsmen still lying there. The blood from their wounds had formed a mat under them and probably seeped through the floor plates. They will never be able to get all that clean Chuck thought to himself...which is exactly why he knew this aircraft would never be seen again. There was a green Jeep Cherokee parked a few steps from the door and Chuck headed for it. The driver's side door opened and out stepped CIA Brad, grinning from ear to ear. Chuck smiled back until he got within range and then planted a good right cross to the cheek of this asshole former friend who had gotten him into the murderous mess. He saw that Brad was unconscious as he fell, face forward onto the tarmac. Chuck was pleased with the results of this punch, as he had never really gotten any experience with fighting before and was surprised with how little his hand hurt. Chuck felt another prick on the back of his neck as he finished his swing and was getting his feet under him again. It had been administered with a little extra force, sending him to the ground on top of CIA Brad.

This time when Chuck woke up, he was sitting in the seat of a small business-jet type aircraft, across the table from CIA Brad, who was not smiling at him. Brad had a bandage over his right eye, and his left eye was purple.

"You asshole…why would you do that?, I saved your life and this is what I get."

"Saved my life, bullshit…you killed five men, men who I was responsible for."

"They were going to die anyway…and you were going to go with them if the President had gotten his way."

"Bullshit…! What the hell was so important that anybody had to get hurt? I thought we had this all worked out. I deliver the plane, you fix the nukes, you get what you want, we get what we want (oops…had he really said "we") and then we all go home, what happened to that plan?"

"It wouldn't work. Too many people were left who knew what happened. The President ordered a clean slate."

"Clean slate, what does that mean?"

"No one who was involved in the direct handling of the nukes as they were diverted was to survive. That meant you, the crew, everybody!"

"Well what about your guys?"

Chuck glanced around and didn't see Geek or Partner; they were alone in the 8 passenger cabin. They might be up front, though…there was a door to the cockpit and it was closed.

"They are mine, and I will take care of them as I need to, and by the way, SO ARE YOU."

"What do you mean, I'm YOURS!"

168

"Well, the plant is closed. You talked the governor into loaning you a plane. The plane is missing. The crew is missing. And, now it turns out you have given two nuclear weapons to the Iranians."

"That's bullshit and you know it."

"I know it, but nobody else knows it, so you are going to have to tell them."

"How am I going to tell anybody anything if I'm arrested the moment I set foot back on US soil? How could you do this to me, Brad? Hell, how could you do this at all, five dead men, a plane stolen, bombs stolen, this is beyond the … it doesn't make … how can I ?" Finally, Chuck fell silent with CIA Brad smiling at him across the table.

"It's not what it seems, Chuck. I have been doing my job, and you have been a great help. When we get to Texas, which is where we are going, by the way, you are going to go to the new Governor and tell him what I am about to tell you. At the end of that meeting, he is going to be happy with you, and thrilled with me, in fact, he is going to be so thrilled that he is going to appoint you as head of the Intelligence Service for Texas."

Chuck sat flabbergasted as the plane tilted slightly forward toward its destination about 200 miles away.

"So, tell me how I am going to convince the Governor not to have me shot?"

"Everything I am about to tell you is absolutely classified. I mean beyond what you might think of as classified, but like between you and me and the governor and if it ever comes back to me you guys will wind up like the crew of that C-130, got it?" Brad had leaned across the little fold down table and stopped smiling.

"Got it."

"I am a technical officer for the CIA"

"I knew that, so what?"

"Shut up and listen. One of the people I had been working with had a son that …" and he told Chuck the story of Haliel L. Jamallie. All the cultivation, the alienation, and the final loss of contact by the FBI. "When I found out that the FBI had lost contact with him, I began to track back his network from the other end. What I found was that Haliel had begun to assemble a team of people to acquire a nuclear device from your facility. They were going to transport it using a Texas Air Guard C-130, just like it was done. They were going to fly it to Venezuela and turn it over to a FedEx crew who would transport it to Iran. They had been working on the plot for over a year without the FBI catching on to it because they were communicating through intermediaries in the states and overseas. I found the trail only because one of the people they were talking through in Turkey was a friend of Haliel's father, and Haliel's father is my friend of many years."

"How were they going to get the weapon?"

"They had been surveying your facility for some method to get one of the weapons, and found that the trucks that haul the devices in are the same type as the Texas Guard trucks, so they started enlisting people in the Guard. They had foreign airline pilots, truck drivers, lots of folks. They still hadn't figured out how to do it when the problems between the US and Texas brought things to a head. I thought I would help them along a little by giving them access to a couple of devices."

"So, you knew this was going to happen, then. You knew that they would take the weapons and take them out of the country?"

"Of course, I knew. I knew the names of the people he had recruited in Texas to help him. I know the name of the pilot of the FedEx plane. I know the names of the crew that he put together to crew the C-130 they used to fly the equipment out of the country. And, I had my guys shoot all of them, except the FedEx pilot, because we wanted him to take the weapons to Iran."

Just then, the cockpit door opened and Geek stepped out and eased his way between the seats to where CIA Brad and Chuck were seated over the port wing of the aircraft. Chuck was facing the rear of the plane, so he didn't see Geek until he patted him on the shoulder. The smile that met Chuck as he turned instinctively to face the new presence in the plane was one that you might see in the locker room after winning a tough game. But it didn't sit well with Chuck.

170

"About 20 minutes out skipper." Geek said to CIA Brad, still leaning on Chuck's shoulder. Brad nodded, and Geek returned to the cockpit after hitting the head.

"Why did you put me through all that if you knew they were all conspirators?"

"If I had told you, we would probably have gotten you killed, either as they left with the equipment, or on the way there. There was no guarantee that we would be able to pull this off with only two people and you, and quite frankly, this all happened so fast I didn't know how you would react. Don and Jimmy here could handle the crew, but you had to be present and functioning in your normal capacity at the facility for everything to look on the up and up. You see, Chuck, one of the people they recruited to help with the theft of the bombs was a member of your staff."

"Who?!"

"You don't need to know. It's being taken care of as we speak. What you need to know is that I was doing my job for the CIA protecting the nation against terrorists who wanted to do us and our friends harm; and, I want you to tell the Governor that I will continue to do that job at the CIA, while beginning to set up the intelligence service for Texas. Tell him to think of it as my becoming his part time consultant on the subject, actually, your part time consultant, since you are going to sit in the head of intelligence chair, so I can stay in touch with you without suspicion. Washington thinks you are a hero because of your participation in this high priority mission. In fact, we in Washington are going to represent you as being a double agent, controlled by me, that we have gotten placed very highly in the political structure of this new state/country/enemy or whatever it is."

"This is all too fantastic. It will never work!"

"Yes, it will. I have sent a short message to the Governor through my channels, invisible to any US authorities, that you are coming to brief him. He knows the message is from me, and he knows that the last time I talked to him I was talking from the White House switchboard. He knows that you were instrumental in preventing a shooting war from breaking out and that you are a trusted federal employee who is coming to see him with

171

sanction from me. He will receive you with open arms, skeptical perhaps, but at least he will receive you. It's up to you to sell this deal. The Governor, to you, to me, to the CIA, and back: That's the path. And it has to work!" Then, after a short pause to let all that sink in, "Besides, the facility is going to fire you anyway, so you need a new job, right?"

The engines on the plane quieted down considerably as it leveled off and slowed to the 250-knot speed limit for jets below 10,000 feet. A few minutes later after the wheels and flaps were lowered and the tires had chirped on the runway, the small jet taxied back from the end of the runway toward the hanger that had a big "Welcome to Texarkana Arkansas/Texas Airport". And there, right below the sign was a small twin engine turboprop plane with a Texas Ranger standing next to the ladder with two rather large Texas Department of Public Safety Troopers with their Smokey the bear hats on right behind.

"I sure hope this works."

"Me too, but mainly for your sake, Chuck, you see, I still have a job, and in this economy..." The joke fell a little flat.

Chapter 19: Open Says Me

7:00 AM
Sunday
22 April, 2012

Beijing, China

The crowd extended beyond the lobby out into the circular drive in front of the building, preventing Peter's driver from letting him off at the front door. He got out and began pushing his way through the buzzing clumps of non-Asians toward the door and finally reached the elevator lobby. The Chinese guards at the reception desk were stopping the crowd from going further. Getting up to the desk took over 10 minutes. When he finally made it, the guards nodded for him to come through the metal detectors that had been set up overnight. He dropped his briefcase on the conveyor and emptied his pockets into the cup and proceeded through the trellis-like sensor. Nothing beeped, and his briefcase and pocket change were returned to him. He saw the fellow who had given him the tour the previous day standing behind the reception desk and waved him over.

"What the hell is all this?"

"They began showing up last night. Apparently the word is out that your embassy is here and open for business."

"Well, we may be here, but we are certainly not ready for business..."

"What would you like for me to do about all these people?" he asked as he waved his hand around the lobby.

"Give me a minute, do you mind if I stand up here?" Peter said as he motioned to the reception desk.

"Of course, please, let me help you."

Peter got up on the counter of the reception desk and was half again taller than most of the crowd. The buzz of voices subsided a little as some people near the desk saw what was happening and stopped talking. He gazed out over the crowd and then realized that he had to do a little impromptu organization or he would never get this thing going. He put his hand to his mouth, curling his thumb and ring finger to form a gap, rolled his tongue and produced a shrill whistle that would have made any New York construction worker, Yankees fan proud. All heads snapped toward him and the noise stopped immediately. He had their attention; now what was he going to do with it?

"Are there any military people here?" he asked.

Several shouts of "here, sir" and "yo" rang out.

"You people move up here and stand behind me in this little area, and I'll brief you in a minute."

He turned to the guards at the scanners and indicated with a wave of his hand to let the people through without checking them.

"Are there any computer people here…like IT and secretaries that know how to use computers and that kind of thing? Raise your hands." Fully 1/3 of the crowd raised their hands. Too many; "What I need is people who can work our computers for a couple of days 'till we get all set up with permanent staff. This will be night and day work, and you won't get to leave until I let you go, is that clear?" Some of the hands went down.

He turned to the military group that had assembled behind him. "Get organized. I need a commanding officer, two lead noncoms and two groups, one for down here, the other upstairs. Figure it out and send the commanding officer to me as soon as you can."

Turning back to the milling crowd,

"How many of you want to go home to Texas?" Almost all of the people inside held up their hands.

"How many of you have real emergencies? I mean real emergencies at home, life and death, not money, but life and death that you have to get back for?" The hands began to lower one by one, then in larger groups as he stared coldly across the crowd making eye contact with individual people. Only a few remained in the air.

"You emergency people come through now. The rest of you will be coming up next. Send someone outside to tell the crowd out there the following. We are just getting organized.

We should be able to get enough documents to get everyone who wants to go home to Texas together by the end of the day, tomorrow at the latest. Each of you may be required to work here for a few days to help make this embassy work. If you all cooperate, we will get through this in a hurry. If you don't, you will be thrown out and have to go to the back of the line. This thing is too big and too important for anyone's personal desires to get in the way. We are all stepping over the line here. It's just us. We are the only ones here who can work this out. There is no help coming; in fact, there are people who wish us harm already here. So, we have to get our shit together immediately. I'll do the best I can, and it will all happen very quickly if you do your best to help. I'll see all of you upstairs as soon as we can." The royal we, I guess it's about time to start using that he thought to himself.

As he turned to step down off the table, a young man grabbed his arm to steady him. The dress was casual, but the haircut could only sit on top of a marine.

"I'm the ranking military person here, sir."

"Well, what have we got?"

"We have five officers, seven noncoms and forty enlisted personnel four branches of the military. We have divided into two outfits as you directed, each with a commanding officer and staff. I am Lt. Col. Ferguson, sir, and will act as force commander and liaison to you for all forces in China under your command."

"Do you have any weapons?"

"Not here sir, but I know where we can get some if it comes to that."

"Ok. For now, you come with me and bring any staff that you need; bring one unit up to the top floor with us, leave the other one down here to help sort out this mess. Tell them to get in contact with us up there and figure out how to keep people moving without running over each other. We will let them know when to send folks up. Have them plan to keep the process running 24 hours a day for at least a few days. Find a place to sleep and feed everybody, not just the military, but the folks who came here too. This is going to be a mess for a while and we have to take care of our people, all of them."

175

"What about the people that the US is sure to send over?"

"Let's figure out about that after we get going. Get your crew upstairs now and have one of your men down here get connected with that Chinese gentleman over there. He runs the building and is very well connected." Peter walked over to the building manager and introduced his military commander. "Mister, I'm sorry, I don't even know your name, please forgive me..."

"Not at all, I am Mr. Chow. How can I help you Mr. Ambassador?" he asked with a beaming smile.

"This is Lt. Col. ah what the hell is your name?"

"Ferguson, sir:"

"Lt. Col. Ferguson: He will act as my military attaché. I have asked him to organize our personnel so that we can manage this crowd. Please assist him in getting what we need for our people."

"I would be honored to help you and the Colonel; just let me know what you need and I will try to get it for you." He said turning to Col. Ferguson. Obviously, this Chinese understood military protocol. That in itself was interesting.

"Colonel, When you get set up down here come upstairs and let's get started."

"Yes sir!" There was almost a salute, but there were no uniforms, and they were indoors. Peter felt comfortable that the marine had received instructions he understood to be a lawful order and would carry them out. Good grief; how I pity people who have never seen 50,000 people march off at the sound of a single voice. Only in the military was that possible. Thank goodness, for that Naval reserve duty all those years ago. Then it crossed his mind that Mr. Chow may have seen nearly a million men step off at the signal of a single person. Humbling.

Peter squeezed through the mash at the elevators and stepped on board the first available one headed up. About 20 others boarded the same one, filling it to capacity.

"Where are we going?" someone near the floor buttons asked.

"Home, with any luck," came the reply from a back corner, which produced a bit of a chuckle.

"Top floor," Peter said. "That's where the embassy is being set up."

Peter headed back toward his office as soon as he got off the elevator, but was immediately stopped by questions from the people who had ridden up with him. There was a chorus of "Where do we go…What do we do? … How do we get home?" He turned to the group and asked, "Have any of you been an executive assistant to anybody before?"

One older woman stepped forward: "I used to be the executive assistant to the head of a department store in New York."

Another young man said quietly, "I'm the executive assistant to the Ambassador to China from the United States."

Peter smiled and quietly said, "You two come with me. The rest of you make yourselves comfortable; find the bathrooms so that you can tell the others where they are when they come up." This was going to be fun.

Chapter 20: Colonel Ferguson's Promotion

8:14 AM
Monday
April 23, 2012

Beijing, China

Lt. Col. Ferguson entered the room about the time that Mrs. Caruthers and Morris Abbot were getting comfortable at the conference table. He moved to one of the unoccupied seats near where Peter was sitting.

"Col. Ferguson, I'm sure I can't make you a general in the Texas Military, that honor is probably reserved for the Governor…or somebody, but I can damn sure make you a Colonel. So, you are now Colonel Ferguson of the Military forces of Texas, whenever that gets established."

"Thank you, sir." He had the same look on his face that Peter had when he figured out that he wasn't going home any time soon either.

"I'm almost sure that will rate you a bigger bullet when they shoot us." Peter said with a grin, and was pleased to see his humor appreciated by the ramrod straight marine standing in front of him who was now grinning from ear to ear.

"Mrs. Caruthers, if you are able to dedicate the time to help us for a few days, I would appreciate it if you would act as my executive assistant."

"I would be happy to. What would you like for me to do?"

"This is going to have to work like Mary Kaye. You will sit outside my door, take all my calls and such. Go to the front up there and get 5 other people to help you by sitting out front with you. Here is a list of phone numbers that are in Texas where people have promised to help us. Start calling them and asking them how we are going to get all these people identified and transported. Can you do that?"

"Yes, I think so." As she took the paper with the phone numbers Peter handed her from his briefcase.

"Let me know how things are going and if you need for me to talk to anyone, otherwise, you handle it, ok?"

"Ok." She said quizzically as she headed for the door with he stack of papers.

Chuck turned to the meek little man seated across the table from him.

"Mr. Abbot, tell me again what your position is at the US Embassy. "

"I am the executive assistant to the Ambassador to China."

"What do you do for him?"

"I handle all his scheduling, send and receive all his communications that don't require his personal security clearances; I organize his staff and assign their specific duties as he directs. We have an extensive communications network so that we can deal with the problems of US citizens abroad and provide documents to those applying for visas and passports. He has a social secretary who deals with his appearance calendar and I coordinate that with our security and transportation people."

"Were you kicked out of the Embassy for being a Texan or what?"

"No sir, actually, I've lived in Washington D. C. ever since I went to school there at GWU."

"Then why are you here?"

"Well, I just thought I might be able to help. My folks are all from Texas and that's where I want to wind up after all this is settled, so I thought I would get over here and get started. I saw what they are doing to people from there who are just trying to get home, and I didn't want to be a part of that kind of thing."

"That's bullshit and you know it!" Peter shouted. "They either sent you over here or you want something over here that you can't get over there, what kind of trouble are you in?"

179

The look on Abbot's face immediately told Peter that he had missed the mark with that outburst. Abbot looked like he was about to throw up and he could barely speak.

"Sir, I'm sorry if I have somehow offended you, and that you might think I came here to somehow do harm to you and this group you are assembling. Thank you for your time." His hands were trembling as he pushed himself up from the table, faced Peter for a moment as if about to click his heels and bow, but didn't, and turned to head out the door.

"Hold it. I want to ask you a few questions…"

He continued to walk to the door.

"Stop, damn it. I'm sorry, but I need to ask you some questions before you leave. Please at least stay for that." Peter's voice was not pleading, but it was headed in that direction. Colonel Ferguson was beginning to get to his feet to prevent the exit of this quiet little dignified man.

Abbot slowed as he reached the door, grabbed the big vertical brass bar on the door and stood still, not opening the door or turning around for what seemed like a long time. Then his body seemed to collapse, as he let his hand slide down the handle and turned slowly to look at the group still seated at the conference table. It was clear he had hoped to become a hero and had instead been treated again as part of a servant class. He didn't like it, but he seemed resigned to it now.

Peter stood up and walked over to Morris. "What do you want to do?"

"I don't know; I just thought I could help by doing the things I know how to do over here."

"And you say they don't know you have come over here?"

"I don't think so; I pretty much come and go as I please."

"Do they know that you are interested in helping us, I mean did you say anything to anyone about how you felt about the situation before you came over here?"

"No, certainly not: I have been busy working on stuff for the ambassador this morning and I don't visit with anyone in the embassy about anything other than business."

"I think I have a job for you."

"Good, thank you, that's all I wanted was to help out."

"I want you to go back to the American Embassy."

There was a long pause as Abbot's eyes first locked on Peter's and then they got bigger as he realized what he was going to be asked to do next.

Then he said; "I could do that," he said quietly.

"That would be the most valuable thing you could possibly do, and probably the most dangerous."

"I don't know if they will suspect me immediately, but later it may not be possible to be of much use."

"I know, but NOW is when we are in the most danger and need the most help. Your instincts about that were right on target."

"How would we communicate, I mean if I need to send you a message or something, how would we do that?"

"I don't know anything about spy craft stuff except what I've seen on TV. In fact, you may have been followed as you came over here, or they might be observing the front of our building and doing facial recognition on everyone who shows up here."

"No, they aren't doing that. They wanted to, but the Chinese told them not to."

"Good grief, how do you know that?"

"Well, the ambassador had a conference call with the head of the local Chinese intelligence service, who is our liaison with the overall Chinese government for intelligence matters. I set up the call and made sure the CIA local representative was present at the ambassador's desk while it took place."

"When did this happen?"

"At 05:22 this morning."

"And what happened after the call?"

"Our CIA guy, Colonel Andrews, told the Ambassador that he wanted to set up a full coverage environment on you and the building here. He had come over early this morning and found out that the building was shielded for electronic surveillance and that it was not possible to use lasers on the windows because of the double pane windows with noise injected between the panes. He said he tried to park an RV type surveillance truck across the road to do visual surveillance of the entrance, but they were told to move by the Chinese police, and besides, they were too far to get good facial images this time of year with the heat shimmers coming off the parking lot and driveway that were freshly paved with black asphalt. The smoke in the city was also a problem."

Peter leaned back in his chair and looked at Col. Ferguson, who was beaming form ear to ear. "Morris, you are already a hero. This is the best news I could have hoped for. I hope you understand that I will have to be somewhat skeptical for a while, though, because I don't know you, and there are just too many people out there who want us to fail."

"I completely understand. I would be myself. I don't mind, just as long as you let me help somehow; that's all I want."

"I can do that. I'm sure that going back to the embassy would be the best possible way for you to help. We can work out details later on communication. I will let Col. Ferguson and his men figure out how. I think some of them have that kind of expertise. Just let them find you and we will work it out from there."

"Ok."

"Here are the phone numbers and data addresses for our servers email. I don't know how secure they are, but assume that the Chinese are watching and listening to everything."

"That is pretty much the way we have been playing it over there. The only secure system is the one-time pad data and voice environment and we try not to use that too much."

"Right."

"So, I'll go back and wait to hear from you."

"Yes."

"Thank you."

"You're very welcome, Morris."

Peter extended his hand to the meek little man and they shook as they rose from the conference chairs. Abbot turned toward the door, this time looking quite confident and happy about his role in life, for however long it lasted.

"How much do you know about intelligence work?" Peter asked Ferguson, who was still seated stunned at the conference table.

"Some, I worked for an intelligence unit as part of my training, but not for long."

"Did you do any of that spy craft stuff?"

"No, we were mainly analysts and report writers. We had agents who did the fieldwork, but they came in a couple of layers. There were the techies who did the listening and correlating, and the walk-around spooks who actually went into the field and found people and things and brought back information. We didn't usually run 'agents' per se, just gathered enough information to know who the players were and where they liked to play."

"I have sent Mr. Abbot back to the US Embassy."

The Colonel smiled a little sheepishly and said sarcastically, "Yea, that's too bad sir; I actually kind of thought he might be able to help."

Peter smiled at the thought that at least there were two of them now who felt the same way about Abbot. He wouldn't be alone at the hanging when Abbot turned out to be a plant.

"Actually, he is going to be the first intelligence asset of the Nation of Texas."

"I guess that's right, isn't it."

"You bet, and that is absolutely the highest level of security secret that we have, you and I are to be the only ones who know."

"Got it."

"We need to figure out how to communicate with him. Do you have any field experienced people in your outfit?"

"I don't' know. I haven't had time to get with everybody one on one."

"How soon will you know?"

"I won't go home until I do."

"Good, let me know how many folks you have. If it's only one, pick about 5 other guys, or gals, and give them a crash course in the tradecraft of following conspicuously."

"Conspicuously, you mean you want us to be seen?"

"Right, I figure we don't have time to get good enough not to be seen, and if we look like we can always be detected, maybe they won't worry about us too much. We will follow several of the key staff from the embassy, so that when we follow Morris, Mr. Abbot, it will look like part of our normal bumbling around, except we will find a way for him to drop us notes and for us to do the same. The rest, we just follow as we can, anything we find out about where they go and who they see will be a bonus. Got it?"

"Got it!" Ferguson smiled. He wasn't sure, but he though this lawyer might be just devious enough to pull this off. Strangely enough, that is exactly what Peter was thinking.

Chapter 21: She was Beautiful Lying There

5:00 AM
Tuesday
April 24, 2012

Beijing,

She was truly beautiful, especially lying there half-naked and half-asleep as Peter Canton rolled out of bed and headed for the bathroom. What a joy it was to have her here. What a pleasure it was for an older man like Peter to somehow revisit, at least for as long as it lasted, that part of his life that was focused primarily on sex. And, what a disaster it would be if anyone back home found out about it.

He had met Ming Lo about 2 years after he began coming to China for the company. His work in locating, contracting and providing development consortium services had been small at first. After a while, his firm had done some deals on oil and gas reservoirs that were big enough to get the attention of the higher-ranking members of the Chinese ministry of interior. He had been invited to meetings about once a quarter where the interior minister and his staff had outlined the continuing interests of the government in developing international relationships that could aid their country in not only developing their own oil and gas properties, but in gaining access to the energy produced in the rest of the world. Following one of those meetings, Peter had been invited to a social gathering at a resort near the East Coast of China.

The Chinese began doing business at these high dollar resorts some years ago, and this was one of the hundreds that were springing up all over the country. A mix of Chinese stoic gardens and grounds, Old Hong Kong mahogany interiors and

Arnold Palmer, Jack Nicolas built international class golf courses, and the special introduction of female ministry representatives. These were not the Japanese Geisha, but professional women who were employed in the ministry doing high level work.

Ming Lo, for example was a researcher in the oil and gas reserve valuation section. She had worked for several different financial houses in Hong Kong and had taken on the air of the driven, frenetic professional that all successful Chinese in Asia assume. Entrepreneurs, hard driving, focused, experienced, connected, intelligent and in her case quite beautiful. She was less than half Peter's age.

There was no getting over the fact that she should never have taken an interest in him without the intervention of external factors. But she did, and Peter realized that she was "connected", and had been "assigned" to make sure that he didn't find out anything about China and its people that the interior ministry didn't want him to know. She had become his primary contact within the ministry. When he needed access to some part of the country, she could make it happen. When he needed to submit documents to the ministry for their consideration, he always gave them to her first, just to get her reaction to what he was going to submit through formal channels later. Her communications with him had become more frequent over the years, and had developed into a social relationship.

There was no getting around it, she had been sent to him. He was old enough to know, and certainly old enough not to care. He assumed that they knew everything he did there anyway, so Ming was just an unnecessary bonus that he was prepared to accept. He didn't care about what it might mean to him in the future. It simply made his trips to China more frequent, pleasant and productive. As the son-in-law of the owner of the company, obviously he had to be careful at home, but not here; not on the far side of the earth.

The owner had come to China with him only three times over the years; two times pre-Ming, and once post-Ming. He had no problem in keeping the situation under wraps. In fact, he had just told Ming that his father-in-law was coming and that she would have to stay clear of him for a few days. He had an apartment, which he hardly visited, one that he used when anyone from the US came, but the rest of the time, he stayed with Ming at her place. That seemed to be the best way to handle it.

Now that he was becoming a political figure, being the ambassador and all, he didn't see any reason to change the arrangement since he would obviously be spending more time here than ever. Besides, Joyce, his wife, seemed perfectly happy for him to be out of her bed and life so that she could pursue her duties as a leading socialite in Houston. After 43 years of marriage and three children, they had no secrets from each other, except for Ming.

As he finished tying his tie, he glanced into the bedroom to take one more look at Ming's lovely compact body. He didn't give a crap whether she loved him or not, just as long as she was with him. Over the years, he had sensed that she had come to care for him, even though he had been awful to her at first. As much as he tried not to, he had developed feelings for her as well, whether it was fear that his relationship with her would somehow surface at home and cause problems, or whether he actually cared for her beyond the company, and the inspirational sex, he couldn't decide. Nothing was forcing him to make that decision, so he just wanted to keep on, undisturbed. He wondered how the mess he had gotten into would affect their relationship.

It occurred to him that since she was connected and had most probably keeping the interior ministry up to date on his activities that she would probably be contacted to provide a broader range of information now, not just related to oil and gas. Who was he kidding, they had a building selected. They knew about the two of them all along. She had probably already been briefed on what was going on and told what to look for. She might even be connected directly to the political branch of the intelligence services now rather than the technical.

He grabbed his coat from the dressing room closet and headed for the door. "Coming by to see the new office today?" he said casually as she stirred from the bed. "Uh Huh." came the sleepy answer, as she put on her robe and headed for the bathroom. "I could be there around 9 or so, would that be ok?"

187

"That would be great. I want to show you how Mr. Li fixed me up. You won't believe it."

He knew she would believe it, she had probably helped plan it.

As he exited the building and headed to the waiting car, dawn was just breaking over one of the largest cities in the world, in the most populated country in the world. The lawyer in him relished the organization challenges facing him as he put together a foreign embassy here during what amounted to a revolution at home. The man in him was tired, old, and fearful. As the car pulled away from the curb, his new cell phone beeped and he pulled it out of his inside coat pocket. That was the first he knew about the nuclear weapon being missing.

The message read, "Call secure...NOW, Tex.". He told the driver to step on it. There wasn't far to go, as both he and Ming, working for the interior ministry lived nearby. They were close to the building now being used for his "company headquarters" until he could figure out some way to get China to recognize Texas, then he would be able to make it the Embassy.

He made it up to the office in record time, noting that there was a rather clean cut American looking guard, in civilian clothes, posted both downstairs and in the upstairs elevator lobby. Col. Ferguson was apparently getting things organized. He dialed the number on the SMS message and the voice of the new Governor of Texas answered the phone.

"Hello, Governor, this is Peter Canton, I got your message." he said in his best before coffee voice.

"We have a serious problem, Peter. The Chinese..."

"Sir this phone is not secure, and I don't know when we will be able to get one."

"I know that, but this is too important. During the transfer of nuclear weapons from the Pantex facility to other US facilities outside of the state, two weapons disappeared. We want you to let the Chinese know about this and ask if they can help us find out what may have happened to these weapons."

"I can do that sir, but I am probably not going to get much of a response from them, as they don't think of me as a real 'Ambassador' yet. I don't have any real political relationship that they care anything about. And, why are we asking the Chinese, do we have any idea that they are involved or what?"

"We don't know yet. I got a call from someone in Washington indicating that China might know something about this and that I should check into it."

"Do I know the person who called? Should I mention who it was to the Chinese?"

"I don't know who it was, but I got the call the same way I got the call when they asked me to help them transport the weapons out of the state, and it was definitely from an official in Washington."

"That's not much to go on, sir, but I'll see who I can find to ask and get back to you."

"Hurry if you can, I get the sense that something is going to happen quickly and that we are going to be in the middle of it. Get back to me as quickly as possible, will you please, Peter. I can't think of anything more important than this, except maybe getting China to recognize us."

"How did all this happen in the first place, Governor, if you don't mind my asking?"

"Well, after the shooting at Washington-On-The-Brazos, the President demanded that we cooperate with them to get the nukes out of Texas. I agreed because it seemed like there was no real way to keep them from taking them out anyway and because I didn't want to get blamed for anything stupid that might happen if the weapons became an issue because some yahoos decided to steal some to help out the cause."

"Sounds about right."

"The only problem is, the feds asked me to provide a plane, which I did, a Texas Air Guard C-130 transport. They provided all the others, but now the Air Guard plane is missing. It was supposed to go to some location near Galveston where two weapons were to be transferred to a federal agent for special handling. The plane never showed. The agent never showed, and I don't have any answers. The director at Pantex that coordinated the whole thing is missing and now I've got the press asking me what happened to the plane. This morning, I got a call from a reporter and he asked about the plane. No one was to know about all this, but someone obviously leaked it. He asked if the plane we were missing was involved in the transportation of nuclear devices out of the Pantex facility. It was a pretty public event up there, and seeing that many C-130s in one spot attracts some attention. The reporter said that Washington is denying they ever asked us for help with air transport for the weapons and all the people involved have disappeared."

"That's not good, sir. Let me see what I can find out from here."

"Get back to me as quickly as you can. Nothing good can come of our not knowing."

"Will do."

What the hell do I do now Peter thought. He got up from his desk and walked down to the elevator lobby.

"Get Col. Ferguson to my office, now." He said to the civilian guard who immediately pulled a walky-talky from his coat pocket and spoke quietly into it.

"He will be here in about 8 minutes, sir. He is on his way in right now."

"Good, send him down when he gets here."

"Will do, sir."

Peter headed back to his office, pleased that he had people working with him who appeared to know what they were doing, because he was sure he didn't. He had not even had a chance to revel in the previous evening's activities with Ming Lo before going to work. What a pleasure she was. He wondered for a moment how much she knew about what the ministry was doing that she would be willing to share with him. She did seem to be honestly fond of him, perhaps enough to at least pass on trivial information from the ministry.

Damn, he thought, he was turning into a spy/diplomat/tycoon/philanderer, but then again, he thought, … after all, I am a lawyer, what difference does all that other stuff make?

Col. Ferguson entered through the big doors as he was finishing his thoughts about Ming Lo.

"Ferguson, good, I need you to get hold of our friend at the American Embassy, Morris Abbot. His first assignment is to find out if there has been any talk about a missing nuclear weapon that disappeared from Pantex on a Texas Air Guard plane."

Ferguson looked like he had just found out that his roommate had flunked the don't ask, don't tell test. "We have five men that have been following the top five personnel in the American Embassy since last night after our meeting. We could bounce some of them this morning on the way to work."

"Bounce?"

"Yes, sir, bump into them on the sidewalk, cause a couple of accidents and the like. "

"I like it, make several of them late for work. We may as well start up the dirty tricks now, it's only a matter of time before they stick it to us anyway."

"Right, so tell Morris we need this right away. I can't imagine anything more serious than a nuclear weapon running around loose, unless there are two of them."

"I'm on it."

As Ferguson left the office, Peter thought about Ming again. She was going to come see him this morning, "to see your new office" she had said. He figured she would not be bringing extra listening devices. Peter felt sure the office and building were loaded with them already. Nevertheless, he wouldn't be able to ask her anything about the ministry activities in the office, so they would have to go somewhere unexpected for a few minutes of secure conversation.

Ming arrived at the office at about 9:30. He was delighted to see her, for many reasons. She was introduced to Mrs. Caruthers, the lady seated outside his door acting as his executive assistant, as the liaison with the interior ministry. He showed her the view, the bar, and then took her down the hall to the elevators. She looked a little puzzled as he walked her out of the back door of the building into the nicely landscaped garden out back. He knew that they could be monitored there, but by covering his mouth while he puffed on a cigarette he might be able to get away with mumbling to her, and she to him, without the details being discovered. He asked her for one of her cigarettes and she looked at him sheepishly, and produced a package from her purse.

"I thought you gave these up years ago."

191

"I did, but I need to have one today."

"Ok" she said politely as he took the cigarette from her and lit it with the lighter from her purse.

"You have one too."

"Why?"

"Because I need to ask you something that you will not be able to answer if anyone hears you or sees you but me." He said into his hand as he released a cloud of smoke.

She stopped walking and looked at him, as if for the first time she realized that he was more aware of her real role than she thought. After an appropriate pause, she lit a cigarette and returned the pack and lighter to her purse and snapped the clasp shut. He could feel the ties between them change, like the first cool rush of winter.

"Well?" she said without attempting to block the view of her mouth.

"I know that you are working of the ministry of the interior."

She just looked at him. Clearly, this was no shock.

"I know that you report to them what I say and do."

She kept looking at him, without saying or needing to say anything.

"What I need to know is, do you care enough for me to tell me anything at all about what the ministry is saying and doing about me?"

She lowered her eyes, and puffed on her cigarette while walking again down the path through the garden that neither of them saw.

"Peter, I care for you. I think you know that. This is not a job for me. I ... I ..."

It was clear that she had never considered the possibility of having this conversation, and now that she was, it was uncomfortable for her.

"What do you want to know?" she said into a cloud of smoke imitating the hand over mouth speech he had demonstrated a minute ago.

"I want to know what the deal is with a nuclear weapon that is missing. I know that your country is involved and I need to know what they are trying to do."

192

She kept walking but turned her head to the side to look at him directly. She spoke with a voice that was as cold as ice. "If I tell you, and they know that I have told you, I will be … removed."

"I understand." Peter didn't really understand, he suspected that something might happen to her, but quite frankly he didn't care as long as he got what he needed, and he could keep on seeing her.

"No, I mean I will be completely REMOVED."

The meaning of the term dawned on him. She would be removed from his company, his life, probably from her life. This was getting to be a way too high stakes game for him in a hurry.

"I understand." He repeated, knowing a little more about what he was really asking of her this time.

"You are wrong about my working for the interior ministry." She slurred into a cloud of cigarette smoke.

"so, who do you work for?"

"Another ministry."

"Which one?"

"You don't need to know, but they know about us and are ok with it."

"Are they going to be ok with us if you tell me what you know about the bomb?"

"Actually, they have asked me to find out from you about it. That's why I was late getting here this morning."

His mind was racing like he had gotten an unexpected answer to a question at trial and now he had to put his whole case back together again or lose, and he didn't like to lose. He didn't want to lose. This was his chance to do something significant and here he was on the second day about to screw it up.

"We think the Americans here at the Embassy know something." She finally said.

"Really?"

"Yes, we believe that they were involved somehow."

"Can you find out and tell me."

"No, we have lost our capability to gain further information on the subject and have been very concerned."

He had almost decided to tell her the whole story when he noticed Col. Ferguson trotting across the garden entrance toward him.

"Please excuse me for a moment. I need to visit with this man."

"Of course." she said as she halted her stroll and turned her back toward Col. Ferguson as he approached. Peter moved at a quick walking pace to meet the Col.

"We nearly lost Abbot, sir."

"How?"

"As we approached him to give him the message our car was T Boned by a car from the American Embassy. We bumped two of their agents before we went after Morris to give ourselves cover when we approached him. I guess they read that as us interfering with all their high-level folks and put their security forces on alert…sorry, sir. I didn't get a chance to communicate anything to him. And now, I think he probably has a really secure ring around him. I doubt that we can get to him."

"Shit!" That seemed the only appropriate summation of the situation. He had probably exposed the meek little man to a higher level of scrutiny, and was not going to be able to use him again without risking completely exposing him. Americans stand out in China. Then he thought… BUT CHINESE DON'T.

"Come with me." He said as he turned from Col. Ferguson back toward Ming Lo, who had drifted further out of earshot along the path they had been walking.

"Ming, this is Colonel Ferguson. Colonel Ferguson, this is Ming Lo."

They smiled and shook hands without any inkling of what was to come.

"Ming is connected to one of the Chinese intelligence ministries, and Colonel Ferguson is my head of security and intelligence here." Their hands froze in mid shake. They had both been outed in a rather public way by a man they thought they could trust.

"Ming, we have a man on the inside of the American Embassy who can get information for us about the nuclear device." Ferguson almost visibly wretched. "We can't get close to him because the security detail around him as been alerted that we are harassing other members of the embassy staff and they have tightened things up."

"Ferguson, Ming wants to know about the nuclear device. She told me so this morning." This time it was Ming who nearly wretched. "Her ministry doesn't know, but they believe that the American Embassy people may have been involved." None of us apparently was cut out for hard-core intelligence, so what the hell Peter thought to himself.

"Ming, I will supply you with the name of our contact, we will point him out to you. You and your people obviously have some choices. You can partner with us Texans in this thing, or you can manipulate us to get our contact and get him killed. If you help us, I will share everything I know with you about the bomb."

All three of them stood frozen for a minute, in the midmorning haze of Beijing, listening to the sounds of the traffic bouncing off the building that surrounded them.

"I have tried to be as open as I could be with you and Mr. Li ever since I got here. I have assumed that it was important for him to know what I was doing and that you were telling him. I didn't like it, but I would rather have continued cooperation from both of you than to attempt to gain some advantage through secrecy now. Besides, it sounds to me like you have the same problem we do. You don't know what is going on."

"Thank you, Peter." She said quietly. "What do you want me to do?"

"Can you have one of your people get hold of our person at the embassy and ask him what he knows about the device?"

"Yes."

"Ferguson, where is he now?"

The stunned Colonel pulled his walky-talky from his inside coat pocket and asked "Where is Duck 1 now?" The answer must have come back through his earpiece because after getting a faraway look in his eyes for a moment, he answered, "He left his office with his tail about 10 minutes ago and went into a restaurant near the embassy. He has been sitting there for just a minute."

"Good. Ming, this man's name is Morris Abbot. I met him yesterday. He is the administrative aid to the American

Ambassador. Can you have one of your people get to him and get our question?"

"Yes, but how will he react when he is approached by someone other than one of you?"

"Give him my phone number to have him call and verify that it is coming from me."

Ming took a final puff on her cigarette, glanced up at the building behind Canton.

"Ok, will you excuse me for a minute, please?" she said quietly, once again turning her back on Peter and Col. Ferguson. He didn't see her reach for her phone, or her purse, or anything. She simply strolled down the trail into the garden for a few moments, paused and then returned to the group.

"Well, are you going to help us?" Peter asked a little agitated at the hold up. The answer to his question came in the form of a buzzing noise from his cell phone in his pocket. He pulled the phone out of his pocket and answered with "Hello."

The voice on the other end of the line was that of Morris Abbot, who said; "Good morning, have you got the order for the flowers for the ambassador's office straight for this afternoon's reception?"

Peter was stunned, but quickly played along. "Yes, Mr. Abbot, you can handle anything further to do with the order with the gentleman there on the spot with you now."

"Thank you."

Good grief. That was easy.

"How did you do that, Ming?"

"Mr. Abbot is a senior member of the American Embassy. He is ... well ... known to us ... ."

Mike Ferguson chuckled "Babes in the woods, Peter. We are not playing the same game that everyone else is playing."

"I think that's right, Mike. Maybe we shouldn't even try at this point."

Ming smiled a bit and said, "I think we are all out of our depth a bit here."

Ming glanced up at the building again for a moment and then turned back to Peter and Mike Ferguson with the news.

"Anyway, he says it's not a problem working with us. Apparently, Mr. Abbot went into the Ambassador's office and

196

offered to help so that they would help him get his parents out of 'occupied' territory, and they agreed." The American Embassy security chief will pass him things he needs to find out about us and he will let us know.

"Cool!"

"Our first double agent, how cool is that?" Ferguson smiled.

"I don't know."

"He said he had already been told about the missing device and needed to meet with us to fill us in completely."

"Amazing." Peter sighed.

"He said they had already given him some questions about us they wanted answered so he would be calling to set up lunch with a 'contact' over here." Ming said. She was apparently simultaneously listening to whatever communication device she was using, translating and putting her own spin on the information.

"Have him call me." Ferguson injected.

"Right" she said.

12:42 PM

After lunch, Ferguson burst in the door to Peter's office.

"Iran, they are giving the devices to Iran…"

"Who is giving what devices?"

"The Chinese Army, is giving the nuclear devices to Iran."

"Why the hell would they do that?"

"It seems that it is a face saving thing between them and the North Koreans, but there is more to it than that. They have worked with the CIA to get the weapons."

"Why would the CIA want to help the Chinese?"

"Morris said that the CIA was doing it to please the Chinese Army so they would layoff of their pressure on Taiwan a little. And, the CIA sees a chance to blame the Chinese politicians or Texas or both for anything that happens in the Middle East because of the bombs. That would increase the power of the Army, and they like that. The CIA wants to get rid of Israel because they keep complicating things in the Arab

197

world. Without them, well, let's just say, 'the spice must flow'"
Ferguson said.

"Let me get Ming."

Ming had left that morning after they had their
conversations. She had said that she would need to spend some
time with her people to talk over the new situation between her,
Texas, China and the Americans. That seemed like a good idea
to Peter, so he had tried to kiss her on the cheek as she left, but
she had been seemingly distant and cold about it. Things had
already changed between them. This was no longer a pleasant
diversion for him or her either. They had moved into the big
leagues, and it was clear that they both wanted to play the game
more than play with each other. Peter was sad about that,
because he knew it meant the end of their playful and exciting
sex. He wouldn't be using nearly as many, or any, of the little
blue pills for a while.

Chapter 22: Armit

10:23 Pm
Tuesday
April 24, 2012

Iranian Nuclear Test Laboratory

Haliel climbed the stairs to the FedEx MD11 and entered the boarding hatch just behind the cockpit. The pilot stood in the cockpit door and smiled at him as the physicist removed the sunglasses he used to block the extreme brightness of the desert surrounding the remote airstrip and nearby research facility. As his eyes adjusted to the darkness inside the air freighter, he saw the box strapped to the center of the floor about 20 feet to the right. The other box had been pulled out of the cargo bay hours before on a roller pallet to the waiting transporter that took it to the bunkers deep within the laboratory. The cart he had asked for was sitting next to the plane's entrance door, so he pulled it over to the crate and flipped his backpack onto it and moved the cart over next to the bomb.

After removing the straps holding the crate to the aircraft floor, he took the battery-powered drill from the toolbox on the lower shelf of the cart and began to loosen the screws holding the top of the crate. The pilot joined him and they lifted the wooden top off the crate and sat it on the floor against the starboard side of the aircraft's cargo bay. They pulled the sides off the crate the same way, putting them into a stack of wooden crate pieces out of the way so that they could work around the device.

He looked a little surprised at the type of device sitting on the cradle before him. He had seen a bunch of these just two days ago in Texas and was surprised to see this one of the same type again so soon. Then he realized that it had to be one of the ones his crew had just configured for travel. Chaos! In chaos there is confusion. In confusion there is the opportunity for mistakes. This was clearly one of those times when confusion had allowed the two weapons to be brought here. Until this very moment he had doubted that there was even a remote chance of getting one of these devices or anything like it out of the very secure system in the West, and into his hands, and yet, here it sat, praise be to Allah. The confusion of the move from Texas to New Mexico and Oklahoma had been enough for these two weapons, the one in the bunker below and this one on the plane, to be placed in his hands, praise be to Allah.

What had happened to the two weapons he had programmed to explode? Why hadn't they gone off? Surely, he would have heard about it, they couldn't keep a nuclear explosion secret, even if it happened underground. He checked the serial number on the weapon sitting on the cradle again just to be sure. "*BEV0.*" That was not even one of the ones he had worked on. He was sure.

He unzipped the backpack and pulled out the laptop inside. He pulled out the USB cable, connected it to the laptop, and let the other end dangle off the edge of the cart. He took a small toolkit from the backpack and opened it next to the computer. He reached for the little Torx screwdriver that fit the screws holding the maintenance cover on the nuclear device. He carefully removed the 26 screws that kept the cover in place. He placed the small suction cup like device from the tool kit on the maintenance cover, pumped up the vacuum and pulled the cover loose. Since the unit was sealed, and the nitrogen gas pressure inside the electronics unit was less than the air pressure outside, he had to pull a bit harder than usual. Once the seal on the corner of the cover was broken, air rushed in and neutralized the pressure between the outside and the small connector bay under the cover and the outside air with a satisfying hiss.

He put the cover on the cart next to the computer, picked up the dangling USB cable end, and plugged it into the matching connector in the device he had just exposed by removing the cover. Once he finished downloading the targeting simulation information into the device, he would be able to replace the cover and the plane could be on its way. The missing nitrogen wouldn't cause a problem because it was meant to prevent corrosion of the electronics over the years of storage and movement of the devices. This time, there would be only about an hour from the time he closed the maintenance cover again and when the bomb and Israel no longer existed. So the nitrogen wouldn't matter.

He turned on the laptop, plugged in the USB cable and then pressed the on/off switch in the test port of the bomb to the on position. There was a bleeping sound as the computer recognized the new USB device that had just been attached, and the screen on the laptop turned a vivid red, with the big number 5 in the center. Then he saw the number change to a 4. A chilling realization hit Haliel, how was it possible this bomb was rigged like the ones he had rigged to explode when the maintenance port was accessed? That couldn't be, why would anyone else have written an auto detonation sequence like he had,

3

This must be one of mine, how did they do that? He had seen the serial numbers, he saw this one and it is not the same serial number. I can stop it anyway, he thought to himself. All he had to do was hit the control alt F8 key combination …

2

… so he hit the combination…control alt and as he hit the F8 key the laptop screen went blank…THAT'S NOT RIGHT…IT SHOULD STOP THE PROGRAM…in a flash he realized that instead of stopping the detonation program, he had missed the control key so the laptop had transferred the screen to the graphics output port on the back of the computer. All I have to do is hit F8 again a couple of times to get the screen back and hit num lock and then do it all again and it should be ok, he thought in a flash. His fingers flew across the keys.

The plane, and a good portion of the valley where it had been sitting, turned instantly into loosely associated batch of raw ionized molecules just as he hit the F8 key again. The blast was detected by all the nations of the world who had nuclear detonation detection systems operating. The signature would be unmistakable. A US made thermonuclear device had just exploded at the Iranian nuclear testing and manufacturing facility.

Chapter 23: Epilogue(s)

Epilogue One

3 Months after the blast

Peter Canton took his briefcase out of the overhead bin above his spacious 1st class seat on the Air China 747. He was tired from the flight. He was beginning to recover from the frantic action of the last 3 months. Texas was now a nation, although that status was disputed by the now fractured United States; it was a fact nonetheless. Peter had been able to cobble together a diplomatic mission in Beijing and rescue the 10,000 some-odd Texans who had been stranded there when the United States had temporarily canceled all their passports. By the time the US had rescinded the passport directive, Texas had already installed a modern, web-based and "secure identity and citizenship" process that was the envy of the world. Peter was proud of the fact that during the first days he and his pick-up team of diplomats and soldiers had forced the Chinese to recognize Texas as a sovereign nation in the UN and to sign an interim trade and diplomatic agreement with them. He knew that for the most part, China had used him to set up the US for future discussions about Taiwan, but he didn't care.

The nuclear device explosion was certainly a devastating event, and it very nearly derailed the entire Texas independence movement when the US tried to blame the blast on Texas. Instead, he and the Chinese had been able to prove that somehow, unknown to them, the US had lost control of a nuclear device and it had fallen into the hands of Hugo Chavez, the ruler of Venezuela, who had given it to the Iranians. That was the story anyway, and everyone was sticking to it.

What a reception. The press pushed around behind the felt-covered security chains that bordered the walkway from the plane into the terminal. There, with the new President of Texas, stood Peter Canton's father-in-law, Matt Ralls, an imposing man whom he still feared. There was quite a crowd. The welcoming group moved across the walkway to the VIP lounge, where the President...of Texas... put his arm around Peter's shoulder as they stepped to the microphones.

"We finally have with us the first Ambassador to China from Texas. The name of Peter Canton is now as important to the history of Texas as the name of those who fought at the Alamo, as important as Houston, Austin, Crockett and Bowie. He is a Texan who did what his country needed for him to do without a thought for himself. He has done our new country proud. Thank you Peter, and welcome home."

"Thank you Mr. President. It's good to be home. I look forward to a short visit before resuming my duties as your Ambassador to China. It is an honor and a privilege to serve and I thank you for the opportunity." It doesn't hurt the oil business either, he thought to himself.

As the proceedings drew to a close, his father-in-law, smiling from ear to ear, led him and his wife along with the president's party out to the roadway where the cars were parked. There, just behind the two limos waiting at the curb for them, stood a very attractive oriental woman with a roller suitcase getting into a yellow cab. She was looking straight into his eyes across the 50 feet that separated them. Good God, it was Ming Lo!

Epilogue Two

Newly minted Texas Ranger Dan Whitaker hated flying, and yet he had been on the plane for nearly a full day now and hadn't minded it a bit. He had never flown first class before and wasn't used to being able to lie back in a seat and actually sleep comfortably, or as comfortably as his slowly healing neck and shoulder would let him. It really hurts to get shot in the back, even when you have on a bullet proof vest. His Stetson was tucked carefully in the overhead, and his Colt was still holstered snuggly under his arm.

As the plane descended into Istanbul International Airport, he filled out his visitation card as the rest of the passengers did. Who are you? Why are you here? Where are you going to stay? His diplomatic passport would be tested for the first time. No one knew whether the Turkish authorities would accept his status as a diplomat, but he needn't have feared. He was met at the exit to the plane by two gentlemen who waved his visitation card aside and smilingly took him in tow, walking directly through the customs check in. Obviously, they had decided to play nice, and that was a good thing. Dan had learned to speak Turkish while he was stationed there during his years as an Air Police officer. He loved the food, the atmosphere and now he loved being admitted once again under special circumstances.

As soon as he got to the hotel and ditched the company, he called his friend Ender Kaya, who was supposed to be looking for a property suitable for use as a Texas Embassy. That was the first call. Then he called his friend Cezmi Kervan, because he needed a ride. He had to make a pickup. A very important package, and he didn't need any help from the local authorities making it.

Cezmi hadn't asked any questions when he got the call from Dan, because he knew the answer he would get even before he asked the question. It would be the same answer he had gotten the hundreds of times before when he had worked with Dan doing investigations and background checks back in the Air Force Security forces days. So, when they drove up in front of a three story apartment building and Dan told him to stay in the car, Cezmi had done as he was asked, without question.

Dan went to the apartment, took out the key he had gotten personally from Chuck Hall, the new head of Texas Intelligence. He turned it in the lock. The door swung open to reveal Haliel L. Jamallie's apartment, exactly as the diagram had told him it would be, only in much more vivid color, lots of Red and Green. Closing the door behind him, Ranger Whitaker stepped over to the open bedroom door, turned to his left and faced the picture of the sunset that overlooked the room. He slid the picture to the side, and dialed the combination into the safe that was tucked neatly into the wall behind. The locking handle moved easily and pulled open the door revealing the contents. He only wanted one item, and there it was, sitting on top of a stack of paper. He picked up the memory stick, tossed it lightly into the air, caught it and stuffed it safely in his pocket.

Back in his suite at the hotel, he placed the memory stick in his laptop and began transmitting the contents back home using the encryption dongle they had given him at home. As he transmitted the contents of the memory stick, the names of the files flashed momentarily across the screen. He wondered briefly if this was the only time these files had been copied. When the transmission was complete, a list of the last few files transmitted remained on the screen. Some of the file names were incomprehensible, but a couple stuck out, particularly the one that read

"Remote_Detonate.exe".

Biographies

Dr. Tom Talley is an experienced and highly educated engineer, corporate director, and space systems researcher. He holds multiple engineering degrees and is now a gentleman rancher with time to think about the world situation. His broad perspective makes this fictional adventure story an exciting and intriguing tale.

Dr. Louis Buck is an experienced corporate executive and Dean of a College of Business and Distinguished Professor of Business Innovation. He holds degrees Naval Science, Business and Finance. He retired from the Navy Reserve at the rank of Captain. His insights make this story live.

Made in the USA
Charleston, SC
01 May 2012